AN OFFER OF MARRIAGE

"Will you marry me, Verity?" he asked, his voice low. "I have waited for twenty-five years to be able to ask you that."

He asked, but she could tell by his manner that he was certain of her response.

"Have you indeed?" she asked. "It would have been helpful had you asked me that question twenty-five years ago."

"I knew that you held that against me," he responded quietly. "I cannot pretend that what I did was well-advised, but I hope that you will not hold that against me. We could be very happy together now."

"I suppose we could, Lord Mayfield."

"And I would, naturally, help your sons. I understand that they both have problems that could be solved with an adequate amount of money."

She shook her head. "I appreciate your kind offer, sir," she said dryly, "but I do not wish to marry—even for the sake of my sons."

With a single step, he enveloped her in his arms and kissed her—a lingering kiss that took her breath away.

"I don't wish you to marry me for the sake of your sons," he responded. "I want you to marry me because you wish to do so." And he kissed her again as Verity felt herself giving way to him, her body yielding to his . . .

—From "A Match for Lady Verity" by Mona Gedney

BOOK YOUR PLACE ON OUR WEBSITE AND MAKE THE READING CONNECTION!

We've created a customized website just for our very special readers, where you can get the inside scoop on everything that's going on with Zebra, Pinnacle and Kensington books.

When you come online, you'll have the exciting opportunity to:

- View covers of upcoming books

- Read sample chapters

- Learn about our future publishing schedule (listed by publication month *and author*)

- Find out when your favorite authors will be visiting a city near you

- Search for and order backlist books from our online catalog

- Check out author bios and background information

- Send e-mail to your favorite authors

- Meet the Kensington staff online

- Join us in weekly chats with authors, readers and other guests

- Get writing guidelines

- AND MUCH MORE!

**Visit our website at
http://www.kensingtonbooks.com**

FLOWERS FOR MAMA

Mona Gedney
Cindy Holbrook
Mary Kingsley

ZEBRA BOOKS
Kensington Publishing Corp.

http://www.kensingtonbooks.com

ZEBRA BOOKS are published by

Kensington Publishing Corp.
850 Third Avenue
New York, NY 10022

All Kensington titles, imprints, and distributed lines are
available at special quantity discounts for bulk purchases
for sales promotion, premiums, fund-raising, educational or
institutional use.

Special book excerpts or customized printings can also be created to fit specific needs. For details, write or phone the office
of the Kensington Special Sales Manager: Kensington Publishing Corp., 850 Third Avenue, New York, NY 10022. Attn.
Special Sales Department. Phone: 1-800-221-2647.

Zebra and the Z logo Reg. U.S. Pat. & TM Off.

First Printing: April 2002
10 9 8 7 6 5 4 3 2 1

Printed in the United States of America

CONTENTS

A Match for Lady Verity

Mona Gedney

Verity Devlin stood perfectly still beside her carriage, unaware that her footman had opened the door and was waiting to help her in. For a moment she was transported to a long ago spring that she had almost managed to forget. The fragrance of lilac and the freshness of newly cut grass in the garden square across from her home had blended into a perfume that pierced her to the heart. It was curious, she thought, that the scent could move her through time in an instant.

The footman cleared his throat unobtrusively, and she returned reluctantly to the present, allowing him to help her into the carriage. Her son Julian was waiting for her at his club; the two of them were to attend a ball together. She had no time to linger there in the fresh spring evening, and her footman and driver would think she had run mad if she said that she wished to stroll through the dusky garden in her ballgown. Julian would be waiting impatiently for her, too, so she put the thought by and sighed as the carriage bowled over the cobbles through the soft spring night.

After all, she thought wryly, what was spring to her? She was a widow with two grown sons, and springtime belonged, as it always had, to the young. She was pleased enough, she told herself, to be out in company again, able once more to dance and to enjoy the pleasures of cardroom and conversation at a ball. She had hopes of seeing at least a few familiar faces tonight, and after two years spent in the seclusion of Devlin Hall, this would be dissipation indeed. She had been back in London long enough to attend the theater, drive in the park, and have an ice at Gunter's after shopping. This, however, was her first ball, and she reveled in the color and commotion after the long, dreary months in the country.

She danced first with her son, enjoying the music and the movement and the variety of faces. When a friend beckoned to Julian from across the room, she smiled and assured him that she was in no need of his constant companionship. After shooing him away, she turned back to survey the scene once more, drinking it in as a traveler stumbling in from the desert would swallow water.

Then, finding herself swept once more into the dance by partners ranging from an elderly general to a dapper young dandy no older than Julian, Verity began to think that perhaps she had not put her youth by completely after all. She was a widow, to be sure, but she would not as yet begin to wear a cap and think of herself as a grandmother-in-waiting. She stood chatting with Caro Spencer, a friend she hadn't seen for several seasons, when she realized that someone had joined them.

"May I have the pleasure of this waltz, Lady Devlin?" asked a dark-eyed, smiling man, bowing low over her hand.

Startled, she stared at him for a frozen moment. Her expression made clear how little she wished to accept but, not wishing to make a scene, she forced a smile and allowed him to lead her onto the floor.

She had practiced the waltz back at Devlin Hall, even before she was out of mourning, determined not to be thought a dowd when she returned to town. This most daring of dances had only recently been countenanced at Almack's and other formal gatherings, and normally Verity Devlin would have been delighted to be partnered for it with a dancer as graceful as Vincent Carrington. It was simply unfortunate, she reflected, that the man was Carrington.

"As always, you dance charmingly, ma'am," he observed,

looking down into her dark eyes, his own bright with amusement.

"You are too kind," she replied stiffly, looking away at the other dancers to avoid his gaze.

"Those are words that I don't believe I've ever heard from your lips, Lady Devlin," he returned, hoping to provoke a response.

He was unsuccessful. Lady Devlin continued to follow his lead smoothly, still staring into the distance as though her mind were a thousand miles away.

Undeterred, he tried again. "In fact, I may say that in twenty-five years you have seldom offered me any compliment at all."

This time she did look directly at him, her eyes snapping. "You are mistaken, sir," she replied.

"Indeed?" he asked, startled. This was not the response he had expected, and he searched his memory swiftly.

Lady Devlin nodded once, sharply, as though she wished to waste not even the slightest movement for his sake. "I have never offered you a compliment, sir. Using the word seldom' would imply that I had."

His disarming smile was a sudden flash of white against his dark skin. "I am reassured, Lady Devlin. For a moment I feared that you were losing a little of your tartness. I should not wish you to become cloyingly sweet."

When there was no response, he continued. "I know that we agree upon that, if upon nothing else—and perhaps upon the fact that it is more than time that you put away your widow's weeds." After a brief pause, he added softly, "Perhaps I could persuade you to take an early morning ride with me, dear lady."

She did not respond nor meet his eyes, but he felt her stiffen in his arms. "I could meet you tomorrow morning at whatever time you say," he whispered, drawing her closer. "You need not bring a groom this time."

Without a word, she pulled away from him and walked from the ballroom, ignoring the curious expressions of some of the bystanders. He stood and watched her leave, his eyebrows arched thoughtfully.

Lady Devlin called for her carriage and went directly home, determined to put that part of the evening out of her mind. The driver could go back to wait for Julian, but she could not stay longer and risk another meeting. She had been back in London only a week, happy to be there and to be free of her long period of mourning, but he had spoiled it all by seeking her out. She had hoped that he would be miles away from London.

She went quietly to bed that night, hoping that sleep would drive all thought of him from her mind. She had banished him from her memories long ago, but the nearness of him had brought them all rushing back. When her maid opened the casement before leaving Lady Verity's chamber that night, the lingering scent of lilac and cut grass floated in on the cool air, once again making her feel that she had stepped back in time. Determined to shut it out, she got up and closed the casement, then pulled the bedclothes up over her nose so that there would be no chance of the fragrance betraying her once more.

Staying busy helped her to put the unhappy episode behind her, and for the next few days she was able to give herself entirely to the pleasure of being once more in London. She encountered Carrington on more than one occasion, but she was able to continue about her business after acknowledging him with a cool bow. His presence, she told herself, she could tolerate with little difficulty. Had it not been for that cursed fragrance reminding her so poignantly of him on the same night that she once again had to come face-to-face with him, she would have had no problem at all. She had not the slightest intention of allowing him into even a corner of her life, and in the meantime, she enjoyed a daily round of social pleasures that she had missed for the past two years.

"How charming of you to arrange a birthday dinner for me, my dear," said Lady Verity several days later, smiling warmly at Julian. "I am looking forward to this evening more than I can say."

He really was an extraordinarily handsome and graceful young man, polished to perfection, she thought wistfully. She had feared that such attributes might prove to be his undoing, and he was, she admitted to herself, usually quite self-absorbed. Even her birthday dinner, although he had planned it for her, was being prepared by her cook and served by her butler with wines from her own cellar. Still, it was gratifying that he would think of doing something special for her without any prompting from his older brother. Julian was normally so immersed in his own affairs that he had scarcely a thought to spare for her or for Alex.

The dapper young man bent over her and kissed her lightly on the cheek. "It is my pleasure, Mama," he murmured, "though I must say that no one would suspect that you are old enough to be my mother."

Her smile melted and her voice grew stiff. She had always detested flummery merchants, and all too often he behaved like one of that detestable species. "Yes, well, you must save such flattery for your flirts, Julian. They will believe you, but I'm afraid that it only annoys me." Much as she loved town life, she could abide neither empty compliments nor empty flirtations. She enjoyed banter, but not flattery.

"But you know it's true, Mama!" he protested. He pushed his hair back with one hand as though he were upset, but Verity noticed that he was careful not to disarrange it. "You have only to look in the glass to know that it's so."

And it was true, he thought gratefully; there was no need for him to stretch the truth. He would be hard pressed to solve his problem if she looked wrinkled and gray like some of the mothers he knew. Her dark hair had not a thread of gray, her complexion was fresh and smooth, her slender figure still lithe. If he could only convince her to dress more daringly, she could be all the rage, just as she had been as a young woman.

"Alex would tell you the same thing," he insisted. "You know that I wouldn't give you false coin."

Verity, who knew no such thing, was momentarily sidetracked by the mention of her older son. "I do wish that Alex had been able to come to town for the dinner you've planned," she sighed. "He needs to get away from Devlin Hall, just as I have. The flowers he sent this morning are lovely, but I would so much rather see him."

Julian shrugged. "What can you expect, Mama? He spends all of his time and every shilling he possesses on that moldering estate where everything is going to seed. We're lucky if he even recalls that he has a family. You were wise to return to town."

Verity's smooth brow creased. "I do worry about him, Julian. He spends too much time and energy trying to correct the forty years of damage caused by your father. Albert milked Devlin Hall and its lands dry, just as he did everything. Then he gambled the income away and left Alex to pick up the pieces after his death. I fear that he will never be able to do so."

"You know that I've heard that a thousand times, Mama! Why must you always talk about how all of that hurt Alex?" demanded Julian impatiently, his pleasant façade once again slipping. "What about me? Don't you ever worry about me?"

She looked at him gravely. "You know that I do, Julian. We talked about it only yesterday."

He waved a hand to dismiss her remark. "That was a different matter, as you very well know! All gentlemen gamble. You simply wanted to call me to order like a child, just as Alex always does! Why not talk about *my* future?"

"I am," she replied. "And that's what I was speaking of yesterday, Julian. You know all too well what happened to your father—you *must* stay away from gambling."

"That's a pretty thing to say to me, Mama," he returned petulantly, "when you know that what Alex is doing is just another form of gambling—and you never preach to him!"

Verity sighed. There was never any reasoning with Julian.

When she did make a point that he knew was justified, he deftly changed the focus of the conversation—and everything always centered on what was best for Julian.

"Well, at any rate, you must use some caution, Julian. You know that I have scarcely enough to keep this house and manage from quarter to quarter. I cannot do more for you than I already am doing."

It pained her to speak so frankly, but he had left her little choice. Julian still behaved as though he were a young man with great expectations. That had not been true since her husband's last great loss two years ago at a small but exclusive gambling hell in elegant Mayfair, where he had lost the last of their land that was not entailed, the last remaining silver and artwork of value in the Devlin estate, the remnant of her own inheritance that he had not yet squandered, and a set of sapphires that she had inherited from her grandmother.

Unable to face what he had done, Albert had chosen to put a period to his existence by insulting a man known to be a devil with a dueling pistol. It was, she reflected with annoyance, precisely what she might have expected of her husband: to land them in an impossible situation and then leave them to sort out the mess he had left. The only thing that he had spared them was the act of outright suicide and the shame of a burial at the crossroads rather than in hallowed ground.

She had been fortunate indeed that her own brother, who had died shortly after her husband, had left her this house in town. Even though she had scarcely enough money for its upkeep, with care she could manage it.

Verity surveyed the young dandy before her. From the tassels of his mirror-bright Hessians to the crown of his shining blond hair, artfully arranged to look elegantly careless, he was a valet's dream, for he displayed his clothes to perfection. On Julian's twenty-fifth birthday, he would receive a modest inheritance from her late father and an even more modest amount that his father had not been able to gamble away. It would certainly not be enough to support him in the style of life that he wished, but Julian did not appear to have realized that. In the months since he had finished at Oxford, he had been living on funds gained by selling some of her own jewelry. Her one hope—although she had not yet shared it with him—was that he would make a good marriage, one that would bring him a substantial dowry and provide him with a comfortable life. He was certainly handsome enough—and charming enough, when he wished—to make such a connection.

"Yes, I understand, Mama," he agreed eagerly, leaning toward her, "and you must not continue to live in such a manner. I cannot allow it."

Verity looked at him in surprise. She had never seen him so concerned about her before. Perhaps, she thought, she should take advantage of this moment and mention marriage. Thus far she had avoided referring to the matter, but she knew that he had encountered any number of marriageable, wealthy young women during his time in London. It could be that he had found one that at least interested him.

She cleared her throat slightly. "Are you referring to marriage, Julian?" She kept her tone light. She didn't want to put him off by appearing too pleased by his concern, and if he was indeed thinking of marriage, he was being unexpectedly practical.

He stared at her. "How did you guess?" he asked, sitting down a little more suddenly than he had planned.

Verity shrugged delicately. She knew that she must tread very lightly here. "It seems the most sensible route, after all," she replied, watching him carefully.

His expression grew noticeably brighter. "But of course it is the sensible route, Mama! I am delighted that we find ourselves in agreement!"

She glanced at him anxiously, hoping that he had no illusions about what he could bring to a marriage. "Since we have no fortune, however, I fear that marriage might be difficult—"

He shook his head quickly and took her hand. "Don't

trouble your head about that, Mama. Our lack of fortune will be no problem in making this match."

Verity blinked. This was such an unexpected stroke of luck that she could scarcely take it in. "But, Julian, who is it that—"

"Never mind the particulars just now, Mama," he interrupted hastily. "You must go upstairs to dress for dinner. You know how you dislike having to rush."

"Yes, of course I do," she responded, "but I *would* like to know . . ."

He countered her again. "Will you wear that delectable gold gown that you wore to the theater, Mama? It is quite my favorite, you know."

She gave up the struggle with a smile. She would know soon enough whom he had chosen to marry. "Naturally I will, Julian, if you wish it. Will you tell me now who the dinner guests will be?"

He lifted one eyebrow and gave her a knowing look. "I told you that it's to be a surprise, Mama. You must wait and see."

Verity was still smiling as she went upstairs to dress for dinner. She was certain that he was bringing his young lady and her parents to dinner. No doubt that was why he had wanted to plan the dinner. She had been mentally reviewing the last few evening parties that they had both attended to see if she could determine the identity of his choice. He had not seemed to pay marked attention to any one young woman, but obviously she had not been as observant as she should have been. As her maid helped her array herself, her mind remained busy with the possibilities.

Only once did she allow her mind to wander back to Vincent Carrington and their dance together. She had early learned to control her thoughts and to avoid thinking about matters that could only distress her. She remembered all too clearly what being with him years ago had been like. Firmly, she closed that door to memory, concentrating on the present moment.

Dressed in the golden gown Julian favored, her dark hair

carefully dressed, she started down to the drawing room, her heart lighter than it had been in months. If Julian were to make a good marriage, one of the greatest weights she carried would be removed from her shoulders. Surely, she thought, if Julian could be taken care of in such a wondrous way, the same might happen for Alex, who was the more deserving and conscientious of her sons. She grieved that his struggle to restore Devlin Hall and its land was such an impossible one—or at least it would be unless he also made an advantageous marriage. Alex was aware that it was his duty to provide an heir for the family name and property, but, as he had pointed out to her when she tried to persuade him to spend more time in London, he would like for his heir to have something to inherit. With great determination he was attempting to make the land productive once again and to restore the once famous stable of Devlin Hall, noted for its fine hunters.

When she entered the drawing room, she saw that Julian had already welcomed one of their guests. She was both startled and displeased to see that Julian was deep in conversation with Vincent Carrington, Earl of Mayfield. She drew a sharp breath, then steeled herself. She had carefully avoided him for years, but now he seemed to be cropping up in her life with painful regularity.

Still, since he was here, he must in some way be connected with Julian's young lady. As she walked slowly toward them, she quickly considered his close relations and thought suddenly of his niece Caroline. She had become aware of the girl only recently. With the unexpected death of Mayfield's younger brother a year ago, Caroline had become both his ward and heiress to a fortune. Doubtless Caroline was his reason for being here, she told herself. For the first time in years, she smiled at Lord Mayfield, suddenly genuinely pleased to see the man in her home.

"Lady Devlin," he said with alacrity, bending over her hand. "As always, you are a vision of delight."

At this fulsome compliment, Julian glanced at her apprehensively, knowing full well what her reaction was likely to be. To his amazement, although she stiffened slightly, she did not even blink at Mayfield's greeting, and when she spoke, her tone was not the acidic one he expected.

"As I have said before, you are too kind, Lord Mayfield," she murmured, forcing herself to be winsome, "but then, you have always been gracious."

Unaccustomed to a pleasant greeting from the lady, who was always very short with him, Mayfield looked up in surprise. Since he knew that she considered him anything but gracious, he was startled by the absence of sarcasm in her tone. Before he could comment, however, she surprised him further by adding, "And how is your lovely niece Caroline?"

At this unexpected inquiry, both of the gentlemen stared at her. Blushing, she recalled that she must be discreet, and hurried into speech once more.

"I noticed her at the Hartley ball the other evening, Lord Mayfield, and I must say that I was greatly struck by her face and her manner."

Julian watched her, his mouth slightly ajar. His mother was never "greatly struck" by anyone. The same thought appeared to occur to Lord Mayfield, who smiled and said, "And I, dear lady, am greatly struck, as always, by *your* face and your manner."

"Nonsense!" retorted Verity indignantly, forgetting her resolve to be gracious and snatching back her hand when he attempted to take it once more. She had thought that she could force herself to enact this charade, but she really could not do it. Listening to such twaddle always made her angry. One would have to be hen-witted to believe the compliments that so many gentlemen felt obliged to make, and she prided herself upon being anything except hen-witted.

"I wish that it *were* nonsense," he responded, his eyes twinkling in amusement. This was the Verity Devlin that he knew. "Yet you know quite well, ma'am, that I am most sincere."

"Doubtless you believe yourself to be sincere," she snapped, "but . . ."

"But since I have so little experience with sincerity, I have no way of knowing whether I am or not," he interjected smoothly, finishing her sentence for her. "I do remember your opinion of me very clearly. Your momentary lapse into graciousness when you inquired about Caroline made me wonder for a moment if you had changed your mind."

"I'm certain that my mother intended to say no such thing, Lord Mayfield!" protested Julian, hurrying into the breach.

By this time Verity had herself in hand again. No matter what her personal feelings, she must not alienate the man and spoil Julian's chances. She needed to put by her personal history with this man. Embarrassed by her own lack of delicacy, she nonetheless did a quick mental review of the fortune of Vincent Carrington, Earl of Mayfield. Caroline Carrington was his ward and would doubtless be the recipient of at least a portion of his fortune, as well as the bulk of her own father's estate. If Julian won her hand, he would be a fortunate young man, indeed—and she would simply have to learn to accept such a regrettably close connection to Mayfield.

Before she could decide how to reply to him, the butler appeared at the door. "Dinner is served, Lady Devlin," he announced solemnly.

"Oh, surely it is too early, Danby," she protested, glancing around the empty room. "We must wait for the other guests."

The butler paused for a moment, looking at Julian, who colored and tried to avoid his mother's eyes. "No, Mama, Danby is correct. There will be just the three of us for dinner."

A stunned silence followed as Verity stared at her son. When he finally met her gaze, he had the grace to look uncomfortable.

"Is there not at least one more guest coming, Julian?" she asked blankly. Certainly Caroline must have been invited, too, she thought, her mind whirling. Why had she not accompanied her guardian?

"One more?" Julian asked, puzzled. "No, Mama, we are not expecting anyone else."

By a supreme act of will, she did not allow herself to show dismay. Distasteful though it was for her to spend the evening with Lord Mayfield, she could not endanger Julian's prospects by her demeanor.

"Well, then Danby is correct," she said briskly. "We must go in to dinner." Here she accepted Lord Mayfield's arm, and Julian followed in their wake to the dining room.

Over the loin of veal in béchamel sauce, Verity smiled at her guest with gritty determination. "And how *is* Caroline, Lord Mayfield?" she inquired, bringing the conversation back to her focus of interest. "As I told you before, she appears to be a charming girl."

"Caroline is very well, Lady Devlin. Thank you for your interest—and for your good opinion." He paused a moment, his dark eyes studying her carefully. "I wish that you might spare a portion of that for me."

The tart rejoinder rising in her throat made it almost impossible for her to swallow, but she forced herself to look unperturbed and to focus upon Julian's future.

"Naturally, Lord Mayfield, I hold you in the highest—" Here she broke off in some confusion, unable to force herself to say the word. Duplicity had never been a part of her nature.

"Yes, Lady Devlin?" he prompted, leaning toward her with interest. "I must confess that I would be startled—delighted, of course, but startled nonetheless—to hear that you hold me in esteem. I believe, however, that the name Verity suits you all too well and you will not be able to tell me that."

Before she was forced to reply, Julian unwittingly granted her a reprieve. A footman had brought him a letter on a silver salver, and he had been reading it silently.

"Mama, Lord Mayfield," he said, rising suddenly and

bowing to them, "I hope that you can forgive me, but I must leave. I do apologize."

"Leave?" she demanded, horrified. If he left, she and Lord Mayfield would be left completely to themselves. "Where are you going, Julian? Why must you leave?"

"It is an emergency, Mama. It's Freddie Quince—he needs me." Julian was already halfway to the door at this point.

"Freddie Quince! What emergency could Freddie have that you could rescue him from?" she demanded in disbelief, her voice rising. "He has never had a more pressing problem than deciding which waistcoat to wear! You must remember that you have a guest, Julian!"

"No, no," demurred Mayfield, rising from his chair. "If you have an emergency, my boy, you must by all means attend to it."

"My profound apologies, Lord Mayfield," replied Julian, bowing, "and my thanks for being so understanding."

He turned toward his mother, still without actually meeting her eyes, and said quickly, "I am sorry, Mother—my best wishes for a happy birthday. I shall see you later tonight."

She watched in disbelief as the door of the dining room closed behind her son. He knew how she felt about Lord Mayfield, and now he had just abandoned her to an evening in his company. Freddie Quince, she thought bitterly, had best be lying on his deathbed.

Lord Mayfield leaned toward her, lowering his voice confidentially. "You must remember, ma'am, that it is scarcely flattering to me if you persist in looking like a hare caught in a trap."

She glared at him, furious to see that his eyes were dancing. "I cannot imagine what possessed Julian to behave in such a scatterbrained fashion," she said, attempting to control her anger and determined not to respond to his charm.

"What can we do, my lady?" he asked, shrugging lightly. "When the young think that they have emergencies, they are impulsive."

"And since we are no longer young," she replied dryly, "we know that they seldom have any real emergencies."

"Just so," he agreed comfortably, settling back into his chair and taking a deep sip of his wine.

Verity forced herself to marshal her thoughts. Even though Julian had behaved abominably—and of course this was precisely the sort of behavior that she had come to expect of him—she must do her best to be civil if they were to keep Mayfield interested in the connection. And, she told herself—like it or not—she knew that Mayfield was still interested in her, even after all these years. She had no illusions about her own attractions; she was no Circe. She knew that she had the charm of the unattainable for Mayfield. If she expected to help her son, she would have to force herself to take advantage of his weakness.

She sighed and, in the next breath, mustered a smile.

"You keep me humble, ma'am," said Mayfield, studying her with a brief laugh. "I am not accustomed to ladies finding it so difficult to smile at me."

"I'm certain that is the truth," she responded crisply. "A healthy dose of humility would mean that you would be only twice as high in the instep as most gentlemen."

He bowed his head in acknowledgement of the hit. "Touché, Lady Devlin. You have, as I recall, always done your best to keep me humble—even upon the occasion of our first meeting."

His dark eyes searched hers, and she was annoyed to see both tenderness and amusement there. She was more annoyed to feel herself warm to him as she had once long ago. She had carefully avoided being caught in such a situation again. Mayfield, as she had good reason to know, was a dangerous man.

"I'm surprised that you recall it still," she returned coolly. "Twenty-five years is a very long time to remember one evening."

"Somehow I find it very easy to remember," he said, leaning toward her. She noticed with irritation that the creases in his face merely served to emphasize his smiling eyes instead of making him look older. Trust Mayfield to make even age an asset, she thought.

"As I recall," he continued, "we met at a ball given by Sally Rutgers. I discovered to my great indignation that a young lady was imitating me. One of my own friends told me about it, and he was scarcely able to tell me for laughing."

She looked meditative, conjuring up the evening once more in her mind. "You did deserve it, you know," she observed. "You were disgustingly arrogant. You held up that odious quizzing glass and looked at all of the young ladies as though we were specimens to be studied."

"And so you were," he replied, waiting to enjoy her reaction. "After all, I was a wealthy young peer with the world at my feet. Why should I not have been selective?"

Verity forced herself not to rise to the bait; she knew that would disappoint him.

"To be certain," she responded lightly, "why should you not have been so? You were, after all, the catch of the season, every mother's dream. You were justified in thinking well of yourself—but not in thinking so poorly of us. After all, we were not cattle."

"If memory does not fail me," he mused, taking her hand absently, as though unaware of his movements, "you pointed that out vividly in the little enactment you were doing in the Rutgers's drawing room. Rockwell could scarcely hold himself together long enough to tell me about it."

She had slipped her hand away as absently as he had taken it, but her face lighted up at his last words. "Dear Rockwell!" she exclaimed. "I have not seen him for years now! How is he?"

"I should have known better than to mention him," Mayfield said dryly. "You were always far more taken with him than with me."

"Well," she prompted, ignoring his comment, "tell me how he fares."

"If you wish it," Mayfield conceded. "He has not yet

come to town from Briarwood, but I will tell him when next I see him that you inquired for him. He will be delighted."

"Well, do tell me about him, sir! Don't be so contrary, even though you are, naturally, old and ill-tempered."

"May I remind you, my girl," he said, arching one dark eyebrow, "that you are a scant seven years younger than I. I should not, if I were in your place, cast aspersions upon my age."

Verity laughed in spite of herself. "And you are still as graceless as you ever were! It is hardly well-bred to mention a lady's age to her."

"Well-bred!" he remarked, as though the matter were suddenly illuminated for him. "Ah yes, I should certainly not have done so were I well-bred—but then I believe you have never considered me to be so. At the Rutgers's ball, you were pointing that out to anyone who would listen. I could only be grateful that your audience was quite a small one."

"No," she said, thinking deeply, "I believe the group was quite large, actually. I remember seeing dear Rockwell and Sefton and Merry Colton and—"

"Yes, yes, never mind! You have conveyed your point nicely, my dear," he interrupted, taking her hand again and smiling down into her eyes. " There is no need to identify each person that was a witness to my abject humiliation."

Verity appeared lost in memory, and she smiled as she recalled Lord Mayfield's outraged expression on that long ago evening when he had entered the drawing room and seen her performing.

Merry Colton, whose disposition suited her name and who had become Verity's fast friend in the agonizing throes of their first Season, had just exclaimed, "Oh, do it again, Verity! Do the part where Mayfield looks through his quizzing glass at me as though I were an odious bit of refuse caught on his boot!"

Verity had lifted the borrowed quizzing-glass to her eye, and looked haughtily toward Merry. Then, dropping the glass and waving her hand as though dismissing Merry, she turned to one side and remarked pompously, "Too tall! Far too tall and pale to suit me! Let me see the next specimen!"

Verity had just lifted the quizzing glass to her eye once more, ready to begin again, when she had seen Lord Mayfield, seemingly frozen in place at the door, with Lord Rockwell's wicked laugh ringing through the sudden silence. The rest of the group had suddenly melted away. When she had turned to walk away, she had heard Mayfield's voice, stiff with anger.

"Well, Rockwell, I had heard that she was a mannerless minx, but I had no notion how accurate a description that was."

Verity could see that his expression was as angry as his tone, and the momentary stab of conscience she had felt upon seeing her victim dissipated in an instant. He was fully as arrogant as she had portrayed him.

She had dropped him a curtsey, saying sweetly, "Having just seen your display of good breeding, sir, I shall take you as my model. I had no notion that there were new depths of mannerlessness to which I might sink. You inspire me."

So saying, she had slipped past him and out the door, Rockwell's laughter ringing out again. "Well, she's got you there, Mayfield!" he had exclaimed joyfully.

It was Lord Mayfield's voice that called her back to the present.

"Come now, Lady Verity, there is surely no need to punish me again and again for the sins of my youth," she heard him saying in amusement, "and I am certain that you are doing just that in your memories."

She found herself smiling warmly at him as she had once so long ago, wondering as she had then how such an engaging spirit remained hidden so completely behind the frozen arrogance of his façade. The fact that her beloved Rockwell held him in such esteem should have made her wonder, but she had been too young—and too insulted by his attitude toward her—to give the matter any thought.

When she had discovered the truth of the matter, it had taken her completely by surprise.

"And how can you be so certain of my thoughts, Lord Mayfield?" she asked, smiling up at him despite her best intentions.

"Your face betrays you, ma'am," he informed her tenderly, leaning toward her. "I wish that I had learned to read it more closely all those years ago."

His eyes were bright with affection, and she knew full well how dangerous he could be.

"Our lives would have been very different, my dear," he said gently, putting out his hand to push back a curl from her face.

Before she could respond, the door flew open and Alexander strode in, his face shining. In three strides, he was at her side and stooping to kiss her, hugging her fiercely. Lady Verity clung to him, the favorite of her sons, for a moment.

"Forgive me for almost missing your birthday, Mama," he said cheerfully. "I would have been here sooner, but we had a problem at the Hall, and I couldn't get away until dawn this morning. I've ridden like one possessed to get here, and I'm afraid that I shan't be able to stay for long. Jersey Lily is about to foal, and I'll need to be there."

She knew that the long expected foal was the product of Alex's prize mare, Jersey Lily, and one of the best hunters in the shire and that Alex expected it to establish a new line of hunters for the Devlin stable.

Always mindful of his manners, he turned to Lord Mayfield without a sign of surprise and bowed. "Forgive me for bursting in, Lord Mayfield. I didn't realize that we would have guests tonight."

Mayfield returned his bow, smiling. He had always liked the young Lord Devlin, little though he had cared for his father.

"Not at all, Devlin," he responded kindly. "In view of the fact that this is your mother's birthday and that you have made such a long journey in her honor, I shall leave you two alone now. You should have at least a little time together before you must return to your estate."

Alex bowed again to their guest and Lady Verity smiled at him—a sincere smile Mayfield noted at once, grimacing inwardly—a smile to reward him for leaving her with the son she adored. If this did not give him a proper sense of his place in the scheme of things, nothing would. He closed the door behind him with a decided snap.

"Alex, my dear!" Verity exclaimed, turning to him and embracing him as the door closed behind Lord Mayfield. "I did not expect to see you at all. You should not have come when you have so much to do."

"You know that I would not have missed your birthday, Mama," he protested, hugging her tightly. "I had told Jules that I didn't think I would be able to make it to London, but then I had a slight break in my business and I saw that I would be able to come for today—or at least for the last moments of today!"

Lady Verity patted his cheek gently, looking carefully at his face. "You did not need to ride all this way for my dinner, Alex," she responded tenderly. "You know that I didn't expect it."

Her son looked once more about the room, a little puzzled. "Where is Julian, Mama?" he asked. "Surely he came to see you on your birthday."

"Yes, of course," she returned brightly. "He planned this birthday dinner, just as he told you, but he was called away at the last moment. Freddie Quince had an emergency."

Alexander was puzzled by her reference to the birthday dinner that Julian had told him about—for Julian had told him nothing—but he was completely floored by the news about Freddie Quince.

"What emergency could Freddie Quince possibly have?" he demanded in disbelief.

Lady Verity laughed. "Poor Freddie! No one seems to feel that he is capable of having an emergency. It might be enough to drive him to having one."

"And what is this about a birthday dinner?" Alex asked.

"And why in heaven's name did you invite Lord Mayfield to your dinner? I know that you can't endure the sight of him."

"Why, Julian planned this dinner for me, Alex," she reminded him, a little hurt. "He wrote to you about it."

Alex shook his head slowly. "I didn't know anything about this," he said. "Jules hasn't written to me in weeks."

"How strange," she replied, puzzled. "I wonder how his letter could have gone astray." She mused for a moment, then smiled and patted her son's cheek. "Well, never mind. You are here and that is enough."

She had enjoyed the next two hours in Alex's company, after which she had made her way happily to bed. Her bright ray of hope was Julian's marriage. She would talk to him tomorrow and see what she could do to help matters along. At least, she thought, Mayfield did not seem to pose a threat to the marriage. He was a threat to her own peace of mind, perhaps, but not to Julian's future.

While she was preparing for bed, Julian came strolling into the drawing room and saw his brother sitting comfortably before the fire.

"Alex, what the devil are you doing here? And where are Mama and Mayfield?" he demanded.

"And I'm very glad to see you, too, Jules," responded Alex, grinning at him. "Did you take care of Freddie's emergency?"

"Freddie's emergency?" replied Julian blankly. "Oh, I'd forgotten—Freddie didn't have an emergency. That was just my excuse so that I could leave Mama alone with Mayfield."

Alex looked at him with some concern. "Have you lost your wits, Jules?" he inquired. "Why in heaven's name would you do such a thing? You know that Mama has always held Mayfield in disdain. Why would you leave her alone with him—and on her birthday at that?"

"It was for the good of the family, Alex," said Julian. "I had no other choice."

"Now I know that your wits are addled, Jules. You're making no sense at all."

Julian sighed and sank down into the chair opposite Alex's. "I had a small problem," he responded. "I had a gambling debt that I didn't have the funds to pay."

"Gambling! After Papa lost everything that wasn't bolted to the floor and left us with no money at all? Haven't you a grain of sense, Jules? A debt to whom?" demanded Alex.

"To Mayfield," responded his brother, looking put upon. "And you don't understand at all, Alex. The debt offered me a golden opportunity."

Alex stared at Julian as though he were a candidate for Bedlam. "And so I am to believe that being in debt to a man like Mayfield for an amount that you have no ability to pay is a *good* thing?"

Julian nodded complacently. "You know that he has always appeared drawn to our mother," he observed.

"And we know that she has always appeared to dislike him intensely," replied Alex.

"Would it not be a fine thing for us if Mayfield were to marry Mama?" Julian asked. "Wouldn't that solve all of our problems? Mayfield is an immensely wealthy man."

Alex, who had been sitting forward to study his brother, fell back in his chair as though he had been pushed. "Now I know that your wits have gone begging, Jules," he said finally. "Mama would no more marry Mayfield than she would ride in one of the races at Ascot."

"If she were in company with him for a little while, she might change her mind about him," responded Julian. "Mama can be quite unreasonable, you know. We don't know why she dislikes Mayfield—it is very likely that she simply hasn't given herself the opportunity to get to know him."

"And you were giving her that opportunity this evening—on her birthday?" inquired Alex.

Julian looked slightly abashed, but only for a moment. "It simply worked out well that I try it on her birthday because she allowed me to arrange the evening for her."

"Very thoughtful of you," said Alex dryly. He thought for a moment, then added, "You haven't told me about your debt to Mayfield. How do you plan to pay it?"

"I've already done so," said Julian smugly. "That's why he was here this evening. I agreed to arrange an evening with Mama for him—so you see that he is still interested in her. That's also why I had to pretend that Freddie had a problem."

"So now you are free of your debt because Mama paid it for you," replied Alex, shaking his head. "You are incredible, Julian—and you are also extremely fortunate that Mama knows nothing about it."

Julian frowned thoughtfully. "No, she knows nothing of it, of course—or at least I don't think she does. She behaved a little oddly, though."

"I am astounded that she remained in the room when she realized that Mayfield was the dinner guest—the one and only dinner guest," continued Alex. "And she did so, for they were still together in the dining room when I arrived."

"It was strange," admitted his brother, "but she mentioned the matter of marriage herself—and said that it was the only solution to our difficulty."

Alex stared at him in disbelief. "She said that, Jules? You're not just making it up?"

Julian shook his head vehemently. "I was as startled as you are, but it's a godsend that she sees the situation clearly. Of course," he added a little reluctantly, "she didn't know that Mayfield was the one I had in mind, but she didn't run from the room when she saw who I had invited. She was even quite civil."

Alex nodded slowly. "Yes, I would have to say that much is true. She was still seated at dinner with him when I arrived, and they were talking. We both know that Mama would have felt no qualms about simply leaving the room if she wished to be rid of him."

He stared into the crackling fire and frowned. "I wish that I knew what she is thinking."

"Well, she has spent at least part of an evening with him," observed Julian briskly, ready to get down to business. "That much, at least, has been accomplished. Now we need to work on the matter of her marriage. We know that Mayfield is still interested in her. I'm certain that he would marry her in an instant."

He paused and looked at Alex. "And you, my dear brother, are the one that must convince her to do so."

Alex shook his head vehemently, rising from the chair to stride up and down in front of the fire. "No, Julian. I'll do no such thing! You can't ask me to do it!"

"You must, Alex!" insisted Julian. "She is more likely to listen to you than to anyone else. You must convince her for her own good!"

"For her own good?" demanded Alex. "Why is it for her own good?"

"You know that she has scarcely enough money to live on, Alex. This house came with little more than pocket money and she continually tries to help each of us with what she does have. She could very well soon find herself in dire straits!"

"She certainly will if you continue gambling," remarked Alex grimly. "The chances are excellent that she will have to sell this house."

"And are you saying that she hasn't sent you any funds to help you with the restoration of the estate?" asked Julian, watching his brother closely. "It seems to me that I recall her doing that recently."

Alex flushed. "Just once, Jules. I won't allow it to happen again."

Julian walked to his brother and put his hands on Alex's shoulders. "You have to do it, Alex. It's the only answer to our problem. This is Mama's problem, too, and if you don't have a solution of your own, you must help me with this."

Reluctantly, Alex nodded. Little though he liked it, what Julian said was all too true. "I'll talk to her," he said slowly.

* * *

The next morning Lady Verity awakened in a more cheerful mood than she had in months. The impossible situation in which they had been living for the past two years would be resolved with Julian's marriage to Caroline Carrington. He would be provided for, she was already taken care of, and between them they could help Alex. When she entered the drawing room, she was humming cheerfully, and she embraced both of her sons.

"How simple it all seems now!" she exclaimed.

Alex and Julian looked at one another uneasily. "What seems simple, Mama?" asked Alex.

"Why, our financial difficulties, of course," she replied in surprise. "Julian is quite right—marriage is the only solution. Hasn't he explained to you what is happening?"

Alex nodded slowly, saying, "Yes, he has, but it doesn't seem so simple a matter to me."

"Well, of course marriage isn't quite so simple as all that," she temporized, smiling a little at her own words. "And certainly the young lady would not feel that way."

They both looked at her blankly, and Julian asked, "What young lady?"

"Why, the young lady you wish to marry, of course," she responded. "No matter how charming you are, my dear, the young lady will expect to be courted—although it is clear that you have her guardian's approval. You must remember that even though we have no fortune, our name is an old one."

She patted Julian's cheek and smiled. "I must begin making plans."

A sudden silence descended upon them as she hurried to her desk, and it was a moment or two before Julian was able to gather his wits and reply.

"Mama, what are you talking about?"

She looked up happily from her writing. "Why, about your marriage, of course, Julian," she answered.

When she saw his expression, she put down her pen.

"I'm not getting married, Mama—you are!" he blurted. Then, glancing at Alex, he said, "You talk to her." And he hurried from the room, closing the door carefully behind him.

Julian waited anxiously in the tiny library across the passageway. All too soon he heard the door open, and then his mother's footsteps as she hurried up the stairs. When he was certain she had had the opportunity to reach her chamber, he let himself cautiously into the drawing room.

"Well, what did she say, Alex? Will she do it?" he demanded.

His brother stared at him without replying while Julian paced the room nervously, rumpling his normally carefully arranged hair.

"Well, Alex, don't be dramatic! Were you able to make her see reason?" Julian asked impatiently. "After all, she *is* our mother! If she won't act in our best interests, who will?"

"An excellent question," returned Alexander, collapsing into a chair, "for it certainly won't be Mama."

"What does that mean?" Julian inquired, pausing a moment. He stared at his brother when there was no immediate reply, his eyes widening in disbelief. "She refused?" he whispered. "But, Alex, she's our mother! How could she refuse?"

"It appeared quite simple," was the reflective reply. "In fact, I should say that she told me with comparative ease that there was not the least chance of her making a marriage simply to accommodate us. She did not appear to be moved by my suggestion that the marriage would benefit her as well."

He sat up suddenly and grinned at his brother. "She told me, Jules, that Prinny would be crowned king three times over before she gave a passing thought even to nodding on the street to Vincent Carrington again, let alone becoming his wife."

He chuckled, leaning back a little farther in the chair and stretching his long legs out before him. "Then she asked me if both of us had gone mad at the same time and assured me that if we were committed to Bedlam, she would send

Benders to come and see to our needs—though she herself would not, naturally, enter such a place."

Here he eyed Julian with bright amusement. "She said that she knew we would not expect it of her because hers is such a sensitive nature."

When Julian showed no sign of sharing his amusement, Alex sighed. "It is fortunate for us, then, that Benders is made of tougher fabric," he added dryly.

Benders was the long-suffering butler of their boyhood, who had patiently extricated them from more difficult situations than either of them cared to recall. Loyal to Lady Devlin and her two sons with the devotion of a man who had no other family, he had—so to speak—brought them up, from the time they were in leading strings. Their father had been often away, so it had been Benders who had first placed them on ponies when they had been large enough to straddle them, and Benders who had taught them how to shoot. Just before their father's death, he had gratefully retired to a small spa town to live in the comfort he had worked for so patiently.

Julian gasped. "She said that to you?" he asked. "How completely unfeeling! How callous! How, how—" Here he broke off, lost for words.

"How lacking in maternal affection?" offered Alexander helpfully. "She said that you would say that. And she said that it was very typical of you to send me to ask the things that you did not wish to ask yourself," he added, watching his brother's face carefully.

As he expected, Julian flushed scarlet and he stood up abruptly, marching about the room and declaiming to no one in particular, "And this from my own mother! From the woman that gave me life!"

When the chairs did not react with any particular compassion, he wheeled upon his brother. "And you!" he exclaimed. "You allowed her to say these things without taking exception to them?"

Again Alexander grinned. "Mama said that you were

born for the stage, Jules. She told me almost word for word precisely what your reaction would be."

Julian sank down onto the sofa. He was, as always, the picture of dapper elegance, but at the moment staring at the glossy blackness of his top boots did not bring him the usual satisfaction.

"How can you make light of so serious a matter, Alex?" he asked in disbelief. "I know that you're in need of the fortune that Mayfield would bring to the family, just as I am."

Alex nodded. "Of course I am, Jules. But she does have a point, you know," he added reasonably.

"And what would that be?" inquired Julian pugnaciously. "I can think of no conceivable point that would offset our obvious need!"

"She said that she was sold in marriage once, and that she would never allow the same thing to happen again," responded Alexander.

"Sold?" demanded Julian, his chin dropping. "Sold? How can she say that *I* am dramatic? She was obviously intended to become another Mrs. Siddons!" His voice rose an octave. "Is she saying that she was sold to our father?"

Alexander nodded once more. "I believe that is precisely what she is saying."

"And she is saying that we would be selling her to May-field?" Julian persisted.

"That is what she said," agreed Alex. "And it appeared to me that she had not the least notion of allowing that to happen."

There was a long pause as his brother considered his words. Julian was a loving son, but he was also a second son, and a second son very much in debt.

"She must be made to see reason," he told Alex firmly.

"Then you, dear Jules, will have to be the one to show her," he responded. "I have done all that I can, and—short of kidnapping her and literally selling her to Mayfield—I cannot see how you can win the day."

They stared at each other for a moment, and then Alex

grinned. "As we both noticed this morning, she was not speaking of her own marriage when she talked with you yesterday. She thought that you were about to announce your marriage to Caroline Carrington, Jules."

Julian's eyes widened with horror. "I? Marry? I don't even know the girl!"

"Mama suggested that you give serious consideration to finding yourself a suitable partner, Jules—a young lady of family who is also wealthy."

"She expects me to do that?" Julian demanded. "I have no desire to step into the parson's trap—even for money!"

Alex laughed. "Mama said that would be your reply— and she said to remind you that she, like you, has no desire to make a marriage of convenience."

"Well, she must," said Julian firmly, rising and going to the door. "I don't know just yet how we will convince her, but we will. We must, if we are to survive—and Mayfield is too promising a prospect to lose."

"Then you do your best," Alex replied, shrugging, "but I don't think you will be able to pull it off, Jules. And I am returning home to my own very pressing concerns, so it will be entirely up to you."

He turned at the door and looked back at Julian, his expression serious. "And I must say, Jules, that even though we need the money badly, I don't think that you should press Mama to marry Mayfield. Why don't you think about what she said? Perhaps Caroline Carrington *would* have you."

And he closed the door swiftly behind him before Julian could respond. After a moment of reflection, he decided that Alex was wise to be leaving the house so quickly. Encountering their mother again at the moment would undoubtedly be unwise, so he hurriedly retired to the safety of his own modest lodging.

Verity, in the meantime, was sitting at her dressing table, staring into the mirror. Both of her sons were willing to have her marry Mayfield—although she could see that Alex at least was very uncomfortable with the notion. And there was to be no marriage to Caroline Carrington for Julian so that bright hope had disappeared.

She wasn't certain just how long she sat there, but finally a plan occurred to her. Turning to her maid, who had just entered the chamber, she said, "Have my trunk brought up, Kate, and order the carriage. I'm going to Devlin Hall."

Julian felt that it would be best to allow a day or so to elapse before he approached his mother again. He told himself that he wanted to be certain that he would not be short-tempered himself, but in truth he was uncomfortably aware that Lady Verity, although her nature was usually sunny, was fully capable of making life most unpleasant for him. He also had a nagging suspicion that his own behavior had not been above reproach, although Julian had made it a principle never to admit guilt for any of his actions.

Therefore, it was two days before he called upon her. To his indignation, Danby greeted him with the news that she had departed for a visit to Devlin Hall.

"To Devlin Hall?" he exclaimed. "Without letting me know?"

Danby, recognizing the irritation in his voice, bowed. "I believe it was a very sudden decision, sir," he murmured. "She left soon after Lord Devlin's departure, and she did not even take her maid with her."

Julian stared at him. "No maid?" he said blankly. He was certain that his mother had left town because she was still angry, but he could not think why she would not have taken her maid. It was clear, though, that she must hold him responsible for the Mayfield affair rather than Alex, since she was willing to go to stay with him.

Danby nodded. "Lord Mayfield also seemed surprised to find Lady Devlin gone," he observed quietly.

"Lord Mayfield?" said Julian. Realizing that he seemed to be incapable of doing anything more than repeating what the butler said, Julian attempted to marshal his thoughts.

Danby nodded once more. "Lord Mayfield called very

early yesterday morning, but Lady Devlin had already set forth on her journey, as I told him when he inquired."

The butler paused and coughed discreetly before continuing. "And I was just about to send a message to you, sir, although I feared I might offend both you and Lady Devlin by overstepping my place as butler."

"Well, now you have told me, Danby, and quite rightly, too," replied Julian. "I certainly need to be informed when my mother goes on a journey."

Danby coughed again. "Actually, sir, there is a little more that I planned to include in the message."

"Well, what is it?" Julian asked, impatient to be gone. Now he would have to go to Devlin Hall and convince her to return. Or perhaps he would see if Lord Mayfield wished to visit the Hall. That would serve her right, he thought bitterly. She clearly felt no interest in the well-being of her sons, so he would feel no remorse about once again forcing her into the company of Lord Mayfield. His momentary feeling of guilt had fled.

"Lady Devlin's maid informs me that she took a substantial amount of her wardrobe with her, quite as though she anticipated a stay of some length."

"Did she indeed?" said Julian, more affronted than ever. This, he thought, decided matters. Not only had she left without so much as a note to him, but she obviously planned to be gone for a very long time! No doubt this was to be his punishment. Well, he thought, straightening his shoulders, he would not be outmaneuvered in such a manner. She had underestimated him.

Before returning home to pack his own valise and prepare for a journey, he made a stop at Mayfield's home, and was startled to discover that Mayfield too had left town unexpectedly. Julian was a little disappointed by this, for he had almost convinced himself that he could persuade that gentleman to go with him to Devlin Hall. The best he could hope for now was to return to London with his mother as quickly as possible in order to give her relationship with Mayfield an opportunity to prosper. If he did not manage to do so, he was uncomfortably aware that several of his creditors were likely to grow impatient with him. He had staved them off with promises after his father's death, but by now they were all aware that his inheritance amounted to little. Julian could not afford for his mother to be difficult.

As her carriage rolled on its way toward Devlin Hall, Verity allowed herself the luxury of letting her mind wander where it would. All too soon she would be obliged to make some important decisions, but for the moment she could pretend that she was a girl again, before she had made the fateful marriage to Devlin.

Her first meeting with Mayfield had been a fruitful one, for she had also met Lord Rockwell, a cheerful young man with a devil-may-care attitude and the wickedest laugh in Christendom. It was Rockwell who had brought his good friend Mayfield to see her imitation of him, and Rockwell who had followed her when she left the room after crossing swords with Mayfield.

"Why are you being so charming to me when I insulted your friend?" she had demanded of him when he had asked her to dance after pursuing her to the ballroom.

"A little shaking up is good for him," Rockwell had observed, grinning down at her. "I've seldom seen him lose his composure like this. He is too accustomed to having ladies fling themselves at him. Perhaps he will loosen up a trifle."

"And what good would that do?" she had inquired. "I cannot see that that would improve him at all."

"Oh, he's not as bad as you might think," he had assured her. "In fact, he is a great gun once you get to know him— but he doesn't allow many to do that."

She had sniffed, dismissing his comment as that of a man blinded by friendship, and had concentrated on getting to know Rockwell instead. She had eventually discovered, though, that Rockwell was correct in his estimate of his friend. Mayfield had pointedly ignored her for several weeks, excusing himself when he and Rockwell encountered her at a rout or a breakfast or a ball.

One morning, however, that had changed—and quite by accident. She had decided to go riding with only her groom, ignoring her father's careful instructions. He had told her that although she might ride out with only a groom in the country, here in town she would be expected also to have the company of at least one other lady—preferably an older one. However, when her cousin had flatly refused to ride out with her shortly after dawn one morning of that first season in London, she had gone herself. She knew that there would be the devil to pay when her father discovered what she had done, but the loveliness of the morning had overcome her. It seemed to her unlikely that many would be out so early in the day.

Ordering her groom to ride well behind her, Verity had given herself over to the pretense that she was riding once more in the countryside, enjoying the leafy bower of greenery, the lingering scent of new-mown grass, and the haunting fragrance of lilac. She was just congratulating herself on her decision to ignore her father's edict when another rider suddenly fell in beside her, seeming to come from nowhere.

"Riding alone, Miss Darrowby?" inquired a genial voice. "That's not a very wise thing to do here in London."

"I have my groom," she had returned briskly, resentful that her lovely ride was being overset by the arrival of Mayfield. Of all the people to be out at dawn, why must it be one who never failed to look down his nose at her?

"And I'm certain that he is probably the only one of your household who knows what you are doing just now," he observed smoothly, irritating her further by the accuracy of his comment. "I daresay your father would not be pleased to hear of it."

"And I suppose you shall make it your business to tell him," she said tartly, trying to pull ahead of him.

"Come now, Miss Darrowby," he replied. "Don't spoil

a morning such as this. Let's walk for a while. There's a path going back through this copse where dog-tooth violets grow in the spring. Perhaps we can still find some."

The charm of the walk he described overrode her first impulse to refuse. After all, this was the man who had been unspeakably rude to her, and who had been ignoring her for weeks. Dismounting, they walked deeper into the grove, leaving the groom patiently holding the reins of both mounts, Verity had continued to puzzle over this. Finally, she had stopped abruptly.

"Why are you talking to me now, Lord Mayfield? Why spend your time walking with a mannerless minx?"

He had grinned down at her, and she had discovered for the first time a sudden disarming warmth in his eyes.

"I could reply, Miss Darrowby, that my taste in ladies has declined." Before she could reply indignantly, he had pressed his finger against her lips and continued quickly, "But I would not, of course, say that, no matter how mannerless you consider me."

"But of course you would say that—and you just did!" she responded fiercely, pushing his finger away. "I wish that Rockwell were here! He wouldn't allow you to treat me this way!"

"Rockwell!" exclaimed Mayfield in a voice of dismissal. "He won't awaken for another five hours! He was already half-asleep when he told me that you were determined to ride out here this morning. He was going home to change into his riding gear because he said you shouldn't ride alone."

"How kind he is!" she exclaimed warmly. "Although, of course, it is completely unnecessary." She thought about his words for a moment, then looked at him with considerable interest. "Then you came here in place of Rockwell?" she asked. "You came here deliberately to meet me?"

"Naturally," he responded, bowing. "I do everything deliberately."

"And you deliberately came here to see me?" she repeated in disbelief.

He bowed again, still grinning. "I grant you that it sounds far-fetched," he conceded, "but I must admit it."

"Why?" she demanded, her hands on her hips. "So that you can humiliate me again?"

He had shaken his head and smoothed a dark curl back from her face, his hand as light against her skin as a drifting blossom.

"Forgive me," he said in a low voice, his expression serious now. "I have been unspeakably rude, and I swear that I never meant to hurt you."

"That's what Rockwell told me," she replied, measuring his words carefully.

"Rockwell!" Mayfield had responded, an edge in his voice. "You seem very attached to that gentleman!"

Verity nodded. "I am—and I thought that you were, too. Rockwell is a man of great good humor."

Mayfield had grinned again. "He would like that description. It is very apt. And you are correct—I am indeed very fond of the gentleman."

So absorbed had she become in what they were saying that she scarcely noticed as he drew her close and kissed her. He seemed a part of the greenness, the fresh scent of the earth and the morning, the heart-piercing fragrance of lilac that engulfed her. So natural did it seem that not even a second and a third kiss brought her to her senses. She had been kissed before, but only by awkward boys at country balls. This was something else again, and she felt that there was nothing she would rather do than stay with him among the clouds of leaves and lilac blossoms. Eventually, though, he had drawn back and looked down at her, cupping her face in his hands and smiling.

He had left her as suddenly as he had come, leading her back to the groom waiting on the path and helping her onto her horse. Thinking about it now, all these many years later, she thought perhaps he had known just how she had felt. At least he had not taken advantage of her innocence and the privacy of their situation. He had been, to an extent at least, a gentleman, even following in their wake until she was safely at home once more.

When she arrived at Devlin Hall after a rather lengthy pause at an inn along the way, Alex was out riding. The butler, however, welcomed her, telling her that her chamber had been prepared and that they were pleased to have her home again.

"You were expecting me?" she asked, startled.

He bowed and smiled. "Lord Devlin told me that you would arrive this afternoon, ma'am."

Mulling over this unexpected reception, she allowed herself to be shown to her chamber and proceeded to make herself comfortable before seeing him. The maid appeared almost immediately with a can of hot water so that Verity could wash and change her travel-stained garments.

Before she could make her way downstairs, Alex surprised her by coming into her chamber, still in his riding dress.

"Mama, whatever is going on?" he demanded, his voice low and urgent as he shut the door behind her.

She stared at him in surprise. "Why, I've simply come to spend a little time in the country, Alex. Is my being here creating trouble for you?"

"No, of course not," he returned, his voice still low. "You know that this is your home and that you are welcome here at any time. And you must forgive me for indulging Jules in his idiotic attempt to interest you in Mayfield." He put his arms around his mother and hugged her closely. "You know that I would not wish you to be unhappy—nor would Julian, despite what he says."

Verity smiled and patted his cheek. "We both know that Julian is inclined to think only of his own welfare, Alex, so I cannot say that I was completely surprised by his behavior."

He kissed her lightly on the forehead. "Thank you for forgiving me so readily, Mama." Then, holding her at arm's length, he looked at her and said, "But I don't understand why Mayfield is here."

Verity's eyes did not leave his. "Lord Mayfield is here?" she asked, startled by the news.

Alex nodded. "He and his niece, Miss Caroline Carrington, arrived earlier today. He appeared surprised that you hadn't arrived yet, and told me that you would be here soon."

"We had a problem with a wheel and had to stop for it to be repaired," she replied automatically, her mind still on the news that Lord Mayfield was at Devlin Hall."

"He apologized to me for intruding, but, Mama, he told me that he had urgent business with you."

He took his mother's hands and said quietly, "What is the urgent business, Mama?"

She shook her head helplessly. "I haven't the least notion, Alex," she said honestly. "I cannot imagine what brings him here—and with his niece at that. Where are they now?"

"Miss Carrington is resting, and Lord Mayfield and I just came in from riding," he replied. "Since I had to play host, I decided to take him out to show them some of the improvements I have made."

He paused, and added almost reluctantly, "Miss Carrington is as lovely as you said she was. Jules was a fool not to take your suggestion."

"Perhaps that is why Lord Mayfield is here," observed his mother slowly. "It may be that he wishes the match, too."

"But Mayfield didn't know anything about a match between his niece and Julian—and Julian isn't even here!" Alex protested, speaking softly so that he could not be overheard by anyone in the passageway outside the chamber.

"Perhaps then he has thought of the possibility himself and has simply come to discuss it with me," she responded. "It may be that he thinks it a good thing for his niece."

"Forgive me, Mama," he replied, still keeping his voice low, and leading her downstairs into the library, "but why

would you think such a thing? I know that you think Julian
is a worthy match, but we really have almost nothing for
him to bring to a marriage. Why in heaven's name would
Mayfield wish the match for his niece?"

"You underestimate our family and your brother," she
replied sharply. "They could do far worse than seek a connection with us."

"But he knows that Jules is a gambler, likely to lose all
that he has," Alex insisted. "How could Mayfield overlook
such a weakness, particularly after he has gambled with
Jules himself and knows how desperate he is?"

Verity stared at him for a moment before replying. "What
do you mean, Alex? When did Julian gamble with Lord
Mayfield, and how would he know that Julian is in desperate straits?"

Alex groaned inwardly. He had thought that Julian had
told his mother the truth about her evening with Mayfield
and about the bet that had brought it about. If he told her
now, he would be setting the cat among the pigeons, for
she would certainly not take the news well. Still, there was
no way he could see to avoid it.

She listened to him with a frozen, unchanging expression, and when he had finished, she turned and walked from
the room without a word. Knowing there was nothing more
he could say, Alex sat down and stared out the window into
the garden. He could have throttled Julian cheerfully for his
role in creating such a briar patch for all of them.

Despite what she had told her son, Verity was having a
difficult time convincing herself that Mayfield had come
here because he was interested in a match between Julian
and his niece. He had indicated no interest in a connection
with anyone in the family other than herself—and that
would never take place. As she prepared for dinner, where
she expected to have to face that gentleman, she congratu-
lated herself for planning ahead. Julian might intend to
marry her to Lord Mayfield, but she had no intention of
being a sacrificial offering on the altar of family duty. Julian
had no notion what he was asking of her. She had spent

twenty-five years married to a self-absorbed man, and she had not the slightest intention of allowing it to happen again.

She surveyed her reflection with satisfaction. She might be a much older woman than she had been when she first met Mayfield, but she knew that she still turned heads when she walked into a room. She did not use the juice of green pineapples to prevent wrinkles, like many ladies of her acquaintance, but as Julian had gratefully noted, her complexion was still fresh and clear. A graceful gown the color of claret, trimmed with Brussels lace, emphasized her pale skin and delicate figure, and a silk shawl fresh from Paris lifted her spirits. She planned to enjoy this evening, not simply suffer through it as a potential victim, and, fond though she was of her sons, she looked forward to the coming separation from them.

"Lady Devlin," said Mayfield, turning from his place by the fire as she entered the drawing room, "I would have journeyed four times as far as I have to see you. You are even lovelier than you were as a girl."

To his surprise, Verity dropped him a brief curtsey and smiled directly at him instead of over his shoulder as she usually did. She avoided direct eye contact with him whenever possible.

"I am pleased to see you again, Lord Mayfield," she said brightly, "and your lovely niece." She walked toward Caroline Carrington, extending her hand and smiling. "I trust, my dear, that you have been made comfortable. I am afraid that we no longer have many overnight visitors."

Miss Carrington returned her smile sincerely. "This is a lovely place, Lady Devlin," she responded. "Just walking in the rose garden this afternoon was a great pleasure to me. I've only been in London a few months, but I do miss the country."

"Then you must feel free to come to us whenever you wish to escape the life in town, my dear," replied Verity, her voice sincere. "We would always be pleased to have you."

"Yes, indeed," agreed Alex with such unusual vigor that Verity glanced at him in surprise. Her son seldom showed such enthusiasm for anything other than his estate, his horses, and his mother. She smiled. This would, she thought, be a most interesting evening.

"I know that you are wondering why we have descended upon you without an invitation," said Mayfield in a low voice at dinner while Caroline and Alex were discussing the fine points of their favorite hunters.

"Not at all," Verity responded coolly, giving her attention to the cucumber salad. "Perhaps you were on your way to Scotland, to fish or to hunt for grouse."

"You know quite well that the grouse season isn't until August," Lord Mayfield said sternly, looking at her reprovingly.

"Ah yes, of course," she responded lightly. "What does it matter, however, so long as you are on your way? After all, are you not usually traveling on your way to some faraway place?"

His smile faded, and he leaned toward her. "Will you hold that against me forever, Verity?" he asked, his voice low and hoarse. "I cannot forgive myself, but I had hoped that perhaps you might forgive me someday."

"But of course I have forgiven you," she replied, her voice growing still brighter. "Why should I not have done so?"

Mayfield had the grace to look uncomfortable. "I know that your life has been difficult, but you do have two fine sons," he said pacifically.

"Yes, I do have two fine sons," she replied evenly. "And my life has indeed been difficult, although I am certain that you have no notion just what that means."

"I know that I have no idea what your life has been," he said, his tone serious now, "but you know that I would never have deliberately caused you unhappiness. You do know that, don't you, my dear?" he asked, when she showed no sign of response.

Lady Verity nodded slowly. "I know that you believe

what you're saying," she agreed, "and I do believe that you would have done anything for me that did not cause you any immediate inconvenience."

Lord Mayfield's eyebrows had drawn so close together that they looked like a single dark bird on the wing. "And what does that mean, ma'am?" he demanded, speaking sharply enough that his niece and Alex glanced up at him questioningly.

Lady Verity shrugged lightly. "Precisely what I said, sir," she responded. "I am not trying to be enigmatic."

"Then you must have a very poor notion of me," he replied stiffly, his face flushing.

"Not at all," she said, her voice sincere. "You behaved no differently from any of the men that I have known—save Rockwell, of course." Her tone softened at his name.

"Of course—always Rockwell!" returned Mayfield, a definite edge in his voice. "How could I forget that you consider Rockwell the paragon of masculine virtue!"

"Not at all," she said coolly. "I know that he has his faults, but he always treated me with great kindness—and with honesty. I have regretted that I was not able to maintain our friendship after my marriage."

She paused a moment and then added, "My husband did not approve of Rockwell, you see—nor of Merry Colton, once she had married Rockwell. In fact, Albert did not feel that I should have any close relationships outside of the family—which meant our sons, of course, for he was very busy away from Devlin Hall."

Mayfield's expression had softened and he involuntarily put out his hand to take hers, but she drew it away. "I didn't realize that your life was so restricted," he murmured. "I saw you quite often in London."

Verity nodded absently. "When Albert needed me, I was allowed to go to town. Often he needed a hostess, and he certainly wished to keep up appearances. After all, the gentlemen at White's would have frowned upon the idea of consigning his wife to complete seclusion in the country. He simply forbade me to make any particular friends; I could not, he said, live in anyone's pocket. So long as I never spent time with the same people for any period of time, he permitted me my freedom."

They sat in silence for a few minutes, neither of them meeting the other's eyes. Finally, Mayfield said slowly, "I never guessed by your manner that your life was anything other than the way you wished it to be. You always came to town and attended breakfasts and balls—with quite a variety of gentlemen to squire you."

He paused and looked at her. "I knew that you had little contact with Rockwell, of course—but I supposed that was because he had married Merry—and because your husband was aware of your great affection for him and was a little jealous. I know that Rockwell and Merry had no idea that you were so unhappy."

She shrugged. "Why should I have revealed to anyone else what my life was like?" she inquired lightly. "That was, of course, why Albert did not want me to have any close friends. At any rate, pity would have done me no good—and putting a good face upon things allowed me to keep my pride and to bring up my sons as I wished. If I had made Albert angry, he would have taken them away from me without a second thought."

After dinner, Alex and Caroline strolled down to the stable to inspect Jersey Lily, and Mayfield asked his hostess for a tour of the garden. She was, she discovered to her surprise, pleased to go with him. After all, what was an hour with the gentleman when she had control of the situation? She was no longer anyone's pawn—not her father's, nor Albert's, nor her sons'. She would be leaving early tomorrow morning, and she need accept no invitations that she did not wish to. And, for some curious reason, she wished now to walk in the garden with Lord Mayfield. The fragrance of lilacs floated through the French doors that opened to the terrace and once again beguiled her.

"I told your son that I had urgent business to discuss with you," he told her as they left the terrace and strolled toward the puzzle-garden. "Did he tell you?"

Verity nodded. "Yes, he did." She added nothing else, giving her attention instead to the fading evening sky and the garden.

"And are you not curious?" he finally inquired in amusement, smiling down at her.

"If you wish to tell me, you will do so," she responded. "And if it truly is urgent, I assume that you must tell me, whether you wish to do so or not."

"It is urgent, I assure you," he answered. "Indeed, it cannot wait even another hour."

At this, she looked up at him, smiling. "You have succeeded in piquing my interest, sir," she said. "I cannot imagine what is so important that it cannot wait another hour."

She paused a moment, then added mischievously, "You have not been gambling with Julian, have you? If so, that would explain your presence here."

They had reached the entrance to the garden, and he stopped and put his hands on her shoulders, compelling her to look directly at him. "I'm sorry that your son told you about that wager," he told her, "but I would be lying if I told you that I am sorry that I won it. The only thing that I regret is that I did not get to spend the entire evening with you."

"And is that the urgent business?" she asked, meeting his eyes directly.

Mayfield shook his head and led her farther along the path that wound among the tall hedges.

"This used to be immaculately kept," Verity said sadly, looking regretfully at the overgrown greenery. "Alex has done his best, but one gardener simply cannot take care of such extensive grounds."

"Never mind the hedges," Mayfield responded impatiently, once again turning her toward him. "You know what I have come here for, and now that we have at least a degree of privacy, you must allow me to say it."

She looked at him without speaking, but the corners of

her mouth lifted. She was certain of what he was about to say, and she was pleased that she already knew her answer.

"Will you marry me, Verity?" he asked, his voice low. "I have waited for twenty-five years to be able to ask you that."

He asked, but she could tell by his manner that he was certain of her response.

"Have you indeed?" she asked. "It would have been helpful had you asked me that question twenty-five years ago."

His face clouded. "I knew that you held that against me," he responded quietly. "I cannot pretend that what I did was well-advised, but I hope that you will not hold that against me. We could be very happy together now."

She nodded idly. "I suppose we could, Lord Mayfield."

Pouncing upon this bit of encouragement, he added, "And I would, naturally, help your sons. I understand that they both have problems that could be solved with an adequate amount of money."

Verity flushed, not because speaking of money was vulgar, but because she was keenly aware that she could help Alex and Julian with just one word. But she did not wish to say it.

She shook her head. "I appreciate your kind offer, sir," she said dryly, "but I do not wish to marry—even for the sake of my sons."

With a single step, he enveloped her in his arms and kissed her—a lingering kiss that took her breath away.

"I don't wish you to marry me for the sake of your sons," he responded. "I want you to marry me because you wish to do so." And he kissed her again. Verity felt herself giving way to him, her body yielding to his.

When they were able to draw breath, he said softly into her ear, "And have you changed your mind now, my lady?"

Verity smoothed her gown and smiled, then shook her head. "I am sorry, Lord Mayfield. My answer remains the same."

She turned and started back toward the entrance to the

maze, then paused and looked over her shoulder. "Why did you bring your niece here?" she asked.

"It dawned upon me the night I came to have dinner with you that you were anxious to marry your son to my niece."

She nodded. "That is quite true. I thought that you were there because Julian wished to marry Miss Carrington and because you were interested in the match, too. It seemed to me a godsend."

"I can understand that, given the situation that you and your sons inherited from your husband," he replied. "And I thought that I should bring Caroline with me just to see if she might be interested in such a match. I haven't mentioned it to her, of course."

Verity looked at him, puzzled. "But Julian isn't here, Lord Mayfield. You must have known that."

He smiled. "Yes, I knew that," he said simply.

"I see." Verity returned his smile, understanding in her eyes. "I think perhaps you were wise to bring her here."

"I believe that there might yet be a match with one of your sons," he agreed, offering her his arm, "and I must hope that such a close connection would make you reconsider my own offer, ma'am. I have not given up hope, I warn you."

"I did not think that you would," she replied, smiling to herself. She was grateful once again that she had laid her own plans so carefully.

Well before dawn the next morning, Verity reminded herself that she was doing the wise thing. As she looked around Devlin Hall, which had been both home and prison to her for so long, she felt an unexpected wrench. She had to remind herself that her sons would be fine without her, at least for a time. Certainly Alex might have good news for her when they met again, and Julian would have time to straighten himself out. As for Lord Mayfield—well, she chose not to think about that gentleman. Instead, she would concentrate on having a complete break from her life.

Carrying a bandbox, the only luggage that she had brought with her, she stole quietly down the stairs and out into the courtyard, where Baker, her trusted driver, waited for her in an old-fashioned gig.

He helped her in and together they set out for the inn where they had stopped the day before.

"Begging your pardon, Lady Devlin," Baker said as they jogged along the hedgerows, "but are you certain this is what you wish to do?"

Verity patted him on the shoulder. "It is exactly what I wish to do, Baker, and you must remember not to say a word to anyone about what I've done."

He nodded reluctantly. "Of course I'll do what you wish, ma'am, but I hope I'm not doing anything that will place you in danger."

"Of course you're not, Baker. You have arranged for a coach for me, and I shall be traveling post. Nothing will happen to me."

Baker shook his head reluctantly. "I would be easier in my mind if you had one of your own people with you, Lady Devlin. You won't have Kate nor me to see after you. What if something should go awry and you with no one to turn to?"

"I'll be well taken care of, Baker. I give you my word," she said consolingly. "I'm not telling you precisely where I'm going because I want you to be able to tell my sons honestly that you have not the least notion of my where-abouts, but I can give you my word that I will soon be with someone who will look after me as faithfully as you would yourself."

With that Baker had to be satisfied as he left her having breakfast in a private room at the inn. His orders were to be back at Devlin Hall and to have the gig put safely away before the household was stirring, so he could not linger.

Oddly enough, when the door closed behind the faithful Baker, Verity felt freer that she ever had in her life. She had expected to feel uneasy to see this last link with her secure life leave, but instead her spirits lightened noticeably and she ate with a healthier appetite than she had felt for years.

She was accustomed to her own coach, a luxury that she had not had to relinquish as yet, so traveling post was a different experience. Still, she was treated with deference, and she sat back and watched the familiar scenes slip past her. Soon, a new road took her from her normal path of travel, and the view from her window offered the charm of the unknown. She settled comfortably into place, for she knew that a journey of several hours lay before her.

At Devlin Hall, things were not so peaceful. Julian arrived late in the afternoon and was shocked to discover that his mother was missing. She had left a note for Alex, telling him not to worry about her.

"Not worry about her!" exclaimed Julian. "How could we not worry about her when we don't know where she's gone or what she's doing?"

He looked accusingly at Alex. "How could you let this happen?" he demanded. "How could she just disappear with no one knowing a thing? How did she steal out of here in the middle of the night with a trunk and a mound of other luggage?"

"She had scarcely any luggage at all," returned Alex. "The footman took up only a bandbox for her."

"A bandbox!" exclaimed Julian, running his fingers through his hair in earnest now, so that it stood up in tufts all over his head. "Her maid said that she took almost everything she owned with her—that it looked to her as though our mother meant to move back to Devlin Hall to stay!"

The brothers looked at each other for a moment, then turned to Lord Mayfield and his niece who were with them in the drawing room.

"Lord Mayfield," said Alex, "I must ask you. When you

arrived, you said that you had urgent business with my mother. What was the nature of your business?"

Mayfield hesitated a moment before replying. "A part of it you do not need to know, Devlin—but I will tell you that I asked your mother to marry me."

Julian's face lit up. "How splendid!" he exclaimed. Then, remembering that the bride-to-be had run away, his face fell.

"She refused me," replied Mayfield shortly. "And she had no reason to believe that I would try to force her to accept, so I cannot believe that my proposal was her reason for running away."

"It was not," returned Alex, his tone just as crisp and his glance at his brother filled with meaning. "The pressure on her would have come from someone else." He stopped a moment, thinking about the situation, and held up his hand to silence Julian when he started to protest.

"You know it's perfectly true, Jules," he said, "so don't fly up into the boughs with me."

Julian dropped into a chair and stared at his boots, as though studying them might reveal the answer to their questions. Caroline, her eyes fixed on Alex, sat silently listening to everything that was happening.

"The thing is," Alex said, turning to Lord Mayfield, "that she apparently planned to leave this morning, even before you had proposed to her, sir."

Mayfield nodded in agreement. He was pleased to see that the young man was sensible, remaining calm in the face of trouble. "Where could she have left her luggage?" he inquired of Alex.

"Wherever they stopped to have the wheel fixed," responded Alex, suddenly smiling. "I'll send for Baker and ask him where that was. Undoubtedly Mama left her luggage there."

He soon discovered that asking Baker would not be a simple matter, however. Baker had returned to London with the carriage and the footman who had accompanied them, telling the men in the stable that he had been ordered to do so by Lady Devlin.

"I will interview Baker and get to the bottom of this!" announced Julian, rising abruptly and starting for the door.

"No, Jules. I will do it myself," replied Alex. Then he turned to Miss Carrington and Lord Mayfield. "Forgive me for being so thoughtless a host, but I must leave you to go to London. I would like for you to stay and enjoy yourselves until my return."

"That's quite all right, Devlin," Lord Mayfield assured him. "We will also return to town. I hope to be of some service myself in finding Lady Devlin. I cannot help but feel some responsibility for her disappearance."

Alex shook his head. "It is our fault, Jules's and mine," he said. "You must not blame yourself, sir."

And so the house party returned to London, Julian aggrieved because Alex was blaming him for their mother's departure, Alex distressed by his mother's running away and by the need to say goodbye to Miss Carrington, Lord Mayfield puzzled by Lady Devlin's behavior but determined to find her, and Caroline Carrington, charmed by Alex and Devlin Hall and distressed to be leaving them both.

Lady Devlin, in the meanwhile, quite oblivious to the confusion that she was causing, finally arrived in Lammington, a small but elegant spa town where her former butler, Benders, now had his residence. Her post chaise pulled up at The Golden Lamb just as the sun was setting, and Benders himself, now the proprietor of the inn, came out to welcome her and to usher her to the set of rooms he had set aside for her.

"You should not be traveling alone, my lady," he scolded her, as he supervised the delivery of her luggage and selected the quickest of his maids to serve his guest. "You should never have left London without Kate! And I cannot believe that your sons allowed you to travel post instead of using your own carriage."

"That is because neither Alex nor Julian has the least notion where I am, Benders," she informed him brightly, ignoring the visible start that the old man gave at this unexpected news. "I needed to get away for a while so that I could think."

"But, Lady Devlin," Benders said slowly, studying her face, "just think of how distressed they will be by not knowing."

"Oh, I will let them know where I am eventually, Benders," she said, unperturbed, "and I left a note for Alex telling him not to worry."

If Benders felt that this might not be enough to reassure Lord Devlin, he kept his thoughts to himself. He did not know just what was preying upon Lady Devlin's mind, but it was clear that something was. He was concerned that young Lord Devlin would be deeply distressed by his mother's disappearance, but Benders felt firmly that his first loyalty was to his former mistress. He was acutely aware of what her life with her late husband had been like, and he knew the situation in which she had been left at his death. His sympathies lay entirely with the lady.

He was cheered by the fact that Lady Devlin appeared to be in excellent spirits and by her interest in Lammington. She spent the first two days touring the shops, introducing herself as Mrs. Dalton, a widow. At least a portion of her identity was truthful, she reflected, as she decided what she would do next. She had very little money left after paying for the post chaise, nor would she have any more until the next quarter. Benders had insisted upon giving her his best set of rooms and refused any mention of payment for them, so she would have a roof over her head and her meals—along with Benders's stalwart support. After her survey of the shops, she decided that she had a solution for her immediate financial problems, for she would not accept the money that Benders had offered her.

She had visited the establishment of a mantua-maker and had found herself and her gown much admired by that lady. Verity had always been clever with her needle, having trimmed and refurbished a good many of her gowns herself when Albert had forbade her to spend any of her pin money as punishment for spending what he deemed too much time with one of her acquaintances. Since she loved all that was fashionable, she had been quite determined not to allow him to interfere with the manner in which she dressed.

When she announced her intention of becoming gainfully employed to Benders as he was serving her supper that evening, he grew noticeably pale and so far forgot himself as to sit down abruptly at the table with her.

"Lady Devlin, you must not!" he protested, wringing his hands. "Indeed, you really must not do such a thing!"

"Remember that I am Mrs. Dalton, Benders," she remonstrated, settling in to enjoy her supper. "And you must not worry about it! I shall enjoy it tremendously and I shall only be doing this for a few weeks. It will be amusing and it will allow me some time away from my family so that I can think!"

Understanding that there was little he could do to stop her, Benders sat up long that night, struggling with his conscience. If he notified Lord Devlin of his mother's intentions, he would be betraying that lady—who had suffered a history of betrayals. On the other hand, if he did not, she would soon find herself in what he could only consider demeaning circumstances. He could not imagine that she would find such work amusing. As the candle burned low, Benders found that he was no nearer a decision than he had been earlier in the evening.

Her first day in Madame Divina's establishment was an edifying one for Verity. As long as the little mantua-maker thought that Mrs. Dalton was a prospective client, she had been deferential, particularly because of Mrs. Dalton's manner. Now, however, Mrs. Dalton was her employee, and Madame Divina did not feel that employees should give themselves airs.

Accordingly, Verity very soon found that dressmaking was not quite as amusing as she had thought it would be. Her fingers were deft and her taste impeccable, so she swiftly impressed two of Madame Divina's best customers. Since she impressed them at the expense of Madame Divina, however, and since they clearly wished Mrs. Dalton's services rather than those of the owner of the establishment, life for Verity did not improve. Instead, by the time only a few days had passed, tension in the tiny establishment had grown to a very uncomfortable level.

On an afternoon of green and gold, the soft sunlight filtering through the branches of the lime trees outside the bay window of Madame Divina's establishment, Verity was on her knees, trimming a brown silk gown with edging of ecru lace. The client, a matronly woman, stood precariously on a stool as Verity worked her way around the hem of the gown. She heard the bell that announced the entry of a new client, but she remained absorbed in her work. She had a great fear that the lady would suddenly come tumbling off the stool and do damage to them both.

"Verity! My dear, whatever are you doing here? I could not believe my eyes when I read the note from your butler."

"Butler!" exclaimed Madame Divina, who had been following in the newcomer's wake. "Mrs. Dalton doesn't have a butler! You must be mistaken!"

Verity looked up to see the face of Merry Colton, now Lady Rockwell, with whom she had done no more than pass the time of day for twenty-five years. Behind her, to Verity's delight, was Lord Rockwell.

The two of them embraced her and, to Madame Divina's astonishment, Lord Rockwell announced that Lady Devlin's masquerade was over and that she would not be returning to work the following day.

To Benders's intense relief, the Rockwells bore down upon the inn to collect Verity's belongings and move her to Briarwood with them. Lady Verity, slightly bemused but happy, was not angry with him.

"I remembered, Lady Devlin, that long ago your husband forbade Lord Rockwell entry into Devlin Hall simply because he was a friend of yours. I knew that he and his wife lived close by, and I knew that you did not want me to notify your sons of your whereabouts. I do hope I did the proper thing, my lady."

Verity patted his shoulder affectionately. "You have always taken excellent care of my sons and of me, Benders. How could I be distressed with you because you continued to do your best to care for me?"

And she was, she knew, truly relieved to be removed from Madame Divina's sphere of influence. She sighed in relief as she sat back in the comfort of the Rockwell carriage. She had learned in her brief experience with that lady that she was not meant for a world other than her own. She sighed again, and Merry turned to her, examining her friend's face with concern.

"Are you all right, Verity?" she asked, patting her hand. "We will be at home soon, and you can rest. You must have had a dreadful experience in Lammington! I wish that Rock and I had known sooner. We would have had you out of there in an instant!"

Verity smiled. "Nonsense, Merry!" she said gently. "I'm truly glad that I did this—but it was very kind of you and Rock to come to save me."

Lord Rockwell was riding alongside the carriage, leaving the ladies time to talk privately.

"We wanted to come and save you long ago, Verity. You know that," replied Merry, "but we had to give up when your husband turned Rock away. We were afraid that we would make life difficult for you if we persisted in trying to see you."

"I know that, Merry," responded her friend. "I understood—and you were quite right about Albert." She sighed. "It all seems so very long ago now."

"And how different it might have been if Rock had been able to find Mayfield and bring him back in time. He rode like the very devil to the coast, but Mayfield had already sailed. He has always blamed himself for the fact that you two did not marry."

"Nonsense!" replied Verity resolutely. "That was no fault

of his. Lord Mayfield made a choice, and I was not that choice."

"It wasn't as simple as that," protested Merry. "Mayfield didn't think you cared about him at all, Verity."

Verity looked at her friend in disbelief. "How could he have thought that, Merry?"

Suddenly she saw Lord Mayfield looking down at her and remembered his comment that he wished that he could have read her expression accurately long ago. She covered her face with her hands, the realization of what he had meant suddenly sweeping over her.

Worried, Merry put her arm around her friend, but Verity had once again stepped back in time. After their first early morning ride, they had met again on several occasions, and she had been irresistibly drawn to him. Still, he was in public an aloof, haughty man, and when they encountered one another at balls and parties, he was attentive to her, but never as open as he was when they were alone. Rockwell was their common bond, and when he was with them, the mood was light and playful.

She suddenly remembered sharply an evening that the three of them had been together at the theater. The rest of their party had left the box and the three of them had been laughing at something Rockwell had said. Verity had put her hand to his cheek and said, "What a dear man you are, Rock! How fortunate a woman your wife will be."

A sudden sharp movement had drawn her attention to Mayfield. He had turned away from them and was staring intently at a dancer on the stage. The remnant of the evening he had remained coolly distant while she and Rockwell enjoyed themselves. She had thought him a curious blend of pride and warmth, of affection and self-absorption. She knew full well that he was fond of her, and her own response to him in private had, she thought, been unmistakable. In public, she had kept her composure, unwilling to become another of the young women that flung themselves at his head.

At Briarwood, Merry and Rockwell made her comfortable and devoted themselves to amusing her. Both of them were obviously worried about her state of mind, as well as the state of her finances.

"There is no need to worry about your quarterly allowance, my dear," said Rockwell, who been horrified to discover that she was working at a dressmaker's shop. "I have checked with your late husband's man of business," he told her, "and he assures me that you should be receiving more money each quarter than you have been." He grinned at her. "You know how men like that are—very close with the money, as though it's theirs instead of your own."

Verity smiled at him. "That's very kind of you, Rock, but I know that there's no money left. Any extra money that Jeffers would give me now would be from you and Merry, and I couldn't accept it—but I thank you. You are good friends."

"If we were good friends, Verity, you would not have been working at a dressmaker's. We would have been there when you need us—or, at the very least, you would have felt free to call upon us for help," replied Rockwell, no sign of levity in his voice or manner now.

Verity shook her head. "How could you know? And I had been very distant with you for years. You have no reason to reproach yourselves."

It was amazing, Verity found, how easily the years melted away. The easy camaraderie among the three of them returned almost instantaneously. As she walked alone in the gardens one evening, enjoying the thickening twilight and the peace, she reminded herself that she would soon need to return to her sons and to her life. She had been long enough away. She smiled to herself. Perhaps the attachment between Alex and Caroline would have had a chance to develop. As for Julian's problems—well, she would try to deal with those when she returned to London. At least now that she had been away, she felt refreshed and able to face the problems. She had not allowed herself to think about Mayfield, nor about his proposal.

She sat down on a bench and looked out across the view

of green meadows, trying to ignore the fragrance of lilacs that once more lingered in the air. Next year, she decided, she would carry a scented handkerchief with her so that she could press it to her nose whenever lilacs were in bloom. Their fragrance was far too unsettling.

"May I join you?" inquired a deep voice.

Startled, Verity looked up to see a pair of dark eyes, dangerously warm with affection, looking down into her own. Silently she nodded and he placed himself beside her, joining her in looking out across the expanse of green meadows.

"Lovely, is it not?" he asked absently, not looking at her.

She nodded. "Yes, it is," she agreed. "Rock and Merry have a delightful home. I have enjoyed my time here."

"I am sure that you have," he responded dryly. "As I recall, in your eyes, Rockwell could do no wrong."

Verity nodded again. "I suppose that is true. But then, not only did we enjoy one another's company, but he also acted the part of a friend. He always tried to help me." She smiled absently. "He even tried to convince me that my husband's man of business had realized that he had not been giving me the proper allowance each quarter."

Mayfield, still not looking at her, reached out and took her hand, holding it firmly in both of his own. "Yes, Rock is a priceless friend," he agreed. "We could not have done better. I am only sorry that I was such a faulty reader of character all those years ago."

"What does that mean?" she asked, still looking out across the expanse of green.

"It means that I thought you loved Rockwell," he responded, pressing her hand to his lips, his eyes still on the green prospect before them.

"And I do," she responded warmly, "I shall love him until I die."

"As will I," Mayfield said, finally looking down at her, "but I shall always love you, Verity, more than life itself. I have not married for all these years because I could not marry you. Rockwell came after me, to tell me that you loved me, that your father had determined that he would marry you to the highest bidder—but Rock did not reach me in time. The ship had sailed. Your marriage was a year old by the time I came home again."

He put his arms around her, and a tear ran down his cheek. "How can I tell you how I felt when I discovered that your father had married you to Devlin—and that you had been waiting for me?"

Verity tenderly wiped the tear from his cheek. "How could you have known?" she asked. "I thought you a proud man, my dear, but I have only just realized that it was my pride that stood between us. I did not wish to show in public how much I cared for you—and I thought that you knew because of our private time together. I could have changed it all."

Mayfield shook his head and held her more tightly. "You cannot take the responsibility, Verity. I was older, wiser in the ways of the world—and I ran away at the moment you needed me most—all because I was jealous of Rockwell. Imagine my horror when I came home again to find you married to Devlin and Rockwell telling me that he had ridden after me to call me home to you. Whatever unhappiness you have suffered has been because I was too jealous and too proud to be honest with you."

Verity took a deep breath and the lilacs intoxicated her. "If it is any comfort to you, my dear, I was equally at fault. And I have loved you all these years."

His embrace grew tighter and he whispered into her ear, "And I have loved you, Verity. I have stayed with you every step of the way over all these years. I know your sons, I know the problems you have faced, I have wished to face your late husband over a pistol a thousand times. Can you forgive me?"

It was as though a weight of a thousand pounds had been lifted from her shoulders. "Yes," she said softly, running her fingers gently through his hair. "Yes, and yes, and yes."

She pulled herself back from his chest and looked into his eyes. "Do you wish to know why?" she asked softly.

He nodded wordlessly.

"Because I love you. I love you now and I will forevermore." She took a deep breath of the evening air. "Do you know why I cannot escape the memory of you, sir?" she inquired gently.

He folded her close and nodded. "It is the lilacs," he whispered. "I have never faced a spring without knowing that the lilacs will bring those moments back again. You have haunted me for twenty-five springs."

She smiled at him. "That is only fair, sir," she responded. "After all, that has been my lot, too."

"I have a suggestion," he said softly, pulling her more closely still.

"And what would that be?" she asked, smoothing a rough place in his hair.

"I think that when Alex marries Caroline, that you and I should already be wed," he replied.

Her eyes lighted. "Is that about to happen?" she asked joyfully.

He nodded. "Your son and my niece are handling matters more efficiently than you and I did. Therefore, it behooves us to move a little more briskly than we might otherwise do, for I believe that they will wed before the end of the summer."

"And you won't run away?" she inquired. "You will stay to marry me instead of fleeing to a ship that will take you far away?"

"I will stay," he said firmly, pressing her hand again to his lips. "And whenever you awaken in the morning, you will see me there beside you."

She smiled. "I shall expect it, sir," she replied briskly, "and I shall expect lilacs planted underneath our windows."

He nodded and drew her close, kissing her firmly. "I assure you, dear lady, that lilacs will be everywhere."

Verity sighed happily and nestled within his arms. "And I shall be there, my dear, to enjoy them with you. We have missed our first spring together—but this will be our second spring."

As they embraced, they heard Rockwell and Merry laughing in the background.

"There is Rockwell laughing, my dear. Do you wish to talk to him?" inquired Mayfield.

Verity shook her head. "Of course I will laugh with Rockwell—time and time again." She took his chin and turned him toward her. "But it is you that I love, my dear, and you that I wish to spend the rest of my life with."

He smiled. "And you will, dear lady, you will," he promised, lifting her hand to his lips. "We will have lilacs at the wedding, and this will be the first of many springs together."

The Lady Does Not!

Cindy Holbrook

One

"That one's just too bloomin' desperate to be a mother!"

A pungent smell assaulted Brandon's nostrils. Pain ripped through him. Nevertheless, those unusual words invaded the void and ruthlessly forced him into a state of consciousness.

Brandon opened his eyes. Confusion and anger arose. The confusion was understandable. He lay on a musky berth of hay in a stall, an unaccustomed bed for him. The pungent smell he defined to be that odor peculiar to a stable. Slivers of hay danced amidst dust particles in a narrow slice of sunlight that had the audacity to cut through the rough boarded wall beside him. Why was he in a stable? Furthermore, why was a small kitten meowing to his one side, a baby duck cheeping on his other, while a sleeping fox kit nestled alongside him heedless of a potential meal cheeping nearby?

More important, why was he angry? No doubt it was because he was wounded, hurting like the dickens. Common sense told him that much. Memory, however, obstinately refused to add a jot of detail.

Brandon cautiously with great care turned his splitting head to where he had first heard the voice. A wizened little man, clearly a stable hand, stood at the entrance of the stall. His expression harbored both astonishment and fear. "Dicked in the nob, she is."

"Who is dicked in the nob?" Brandon asked. "And just where am I, by the by?"

"A Lord yet!" The small man gasped. "Unnatural creature, she's gone too far."

"How did you . . . ?" Memory tumbled for Brandon. He had been set upon by two men. They had meant to kill him. No, hold. A hazy recollection sifted into his mind. In the midst of the fight when pistols were drawn, the one had shouted to the other that their orders were to keep him alive. Brandon had been too occupied with dealing out blows to take the full measure of it, but it seemed the two henchmen were in strong disagreement on that head. Their debate might have been comical, if it hadn't been about his life.

Now he understood. They had meant to keep him alive and bring him here, wherever here was. He thought he had driven them off. Then he had lost consciousness. They must have circled back around for him. Common sense made the deduction. His memory could only reconstruct the fight with the two thugs. His rage gained strength with that scene alone. He forced himself to sit. "Who is the unnatural creature? What does she want with me?"

The stable hand stumbled back, raising his hands. "I—I ain't had anything ter do with it, m'lord! I swear it!"

Brandon realized he had moved too fast for both of them. The stable hand trembled like a leaf. Brandon's head swam. "Confound it! I didn't mean . . ."

He never succeeded in his apology. The stable hand spun and ran from the stables. His frightened voice drifted back. "Miss Rosalind! Miss Rosalind!"

"Rosalind?" Brandon whispered. Ah, the name of the unnatural creature to be sure. The man had said she was desperate to be a mother. Brandon shook his head. It made little sense. Unless this woman was so cracked as to have captured him with the intention of forcing him to marry her. Was she that unnatural?

He must escape. He crawled to his knees and struggled to a weaving stance. A bark sounded and a large spaniel came bounding into the stall directly at him.

"No!" Brandon ordered. "Down boy!"

The dog, its brown eyes warm and joyous, did the opposite. It jumped up. Brandon went down. He struggled to maintain consciousness. He subsided into darkness as the spaniel bathed his face.

"Miss Rosalind. Miss Rosalind!" Peters's voice shouted.

Rosalind looked up from the rose bush she pruned to discover her stable hand loping toward her, waving his hands in the air. A sigh escaped her. She recognized Peter's expression and state of frenzy very well. It was spring after all.

"Hello, Peters," she said as sunnily as she could while the small man stopped short, gasping for breath. "What did Jessica bring home to mother this time?"

Peters blinked in momentary surprise. Then ire returned to his features. "I told you that the dog would cause you trouble, real trouble."

"Oh dear, what did she bring home, now? How dangerous is it?" True concern filled Rosalind. Thank heaven all the children had gone on a morning fishing excursion. Logic, however, battled the flood of fears. "Wait. Surely it can't be that dangerous, Peters. Not if it is a baby."

"It ain't a baby." Peters said, his tone rather spiteful. "It's a full grown man, it is. And it also be a lord, to boot, I'll have you know. It only had ter speak and I knew it!"

Rosalind's eyes widened. "Jessica brought home a lord? Impossible!"

"Ain't impossible. I seen it. There it was all sprawled out in her favorite nest, with all those other critters she's stolen."

"She hasn't stolen them. She's adopted them," Rosalind said, her mind boggling over the thought that her spaniel could have actually brought home a full grown man. A nobleman at that, which to Peters would indeed be the worse thing possible. Peters harbored a strong aversion to the peerage. Only she and her family held special dispensation from his rancor. "And *it* would be a he, not an it."

"*It's* a lord!" Peters persisted. "I think *it* put up a fight with Jessica cause it's hurtin' and bloomin' fierce about it. I barely escaped with me life, I'll have you know."

"Gracious!" Rosalind picked up her skirts. "Why didn't you tell me he was injured?"

Without another thought but that a man lay wounded, she ran through the garden and dashed toward the stables.

"Don't go, Miss Rosalind!" Peters shouted, chasing after her. "It's something fierce I tell you. It's a lord!"

Graced (dubiously so, in her opinion) with long legs to match her six-foot height, Rosalind far outstripped Peters in reaching the large half-timbered building. Entering the stables, she raced through it, knowing very well in which stall she would espy Jessica's latest foundling.

She came to a stand at the entrance of the stall. There indeed lay a man sprawled in the hay. Not just a man, but a huge man. Jessica lay curled by his face, offering his bruised cheek a lick.

"Oh, Jessica," Rosalind murmured.

Jessica looked up. Her eyes lit and her tail thumped a greeting. She didn't stop attending to the man's cheek, however.

"Dearest," Rosalind said, torn between fear and amusement. "He is anything but a puppy."

Jessica's tail waved and she barked. Her gaze turned cozening.

Rosalind frowned. "No, you are not going to keep this one. That much I can tell you." Rosalind, drawing in a steadying breath, tiptoed over to the man. Why she tiptoed, she didn't know. Gingerly moving Jessica's other adopted progeny aside, she knelt down beside him.

"You be careful Miss Rosalind! That's a lord, I tell you!"

"Yes, Peters." Rosalind peered closer. "He's unconscious, Peters."

"Good. You wouldn't have wanted to see his black mood. He was something fierce, I tells you. Course, he might have had a right with that unnatural creature dragging him here as she did. I told you ye shouldn't humor the animal like ye always have. If she can't breed the natural way then she ought ter be put down."

"Peters." Rosalind paled as her gaze fell upon the man's arm. "It wasn't Jessica that he fought."

"What do ye mean?"

"This man has been shot," Rosalind said. "No matter what you may think about Jessica, she hasn't taken to carrying firearms."

"Bloody Hell!"

"It looks as if it is a mere graze, thank God, but you must go and fetch Doctor Hillsdale."

"But . . ."

"Go!" Rosalind ordered. "No, first get help from the house, he can't remain here."

Jessica yelped. Rosalind cast her a stern look. "No, you have done more than enough, thank you. I will take him from here."

Jessica whined.

"No, he is mine now," Rosalind said firmly to the dog.

"Gor'!" Peters said. "You shouldn't keep it, Miss Rosalind. It's a lord I tell you. You don't want it. It'll bring nothing but trouble. Better the dog keeps it than you."

"I'm not really going to keep it, I mean him, Peters." Rosalind laughed and looked to him. Her eyes widened. Peters wasn't laughing. He was shaking his head in the saddest of ways. "Just do what I say, Peters. And hurry!"

Peters ran from the stables. Rosalind turned her gaze back to the unconscious man. For a moment, she could only stare at the man's face. It was a strong face, every feature chiseled in bold lines. His brows were raven black, his hair the same. Rosalind wondered about his eyes. What color would they be? Surely they would fall short of such a compelling countenance.

Jessica thumped her tail and offered a woof. Rosalind smiled, despite herself. "You've brought home quite a handsome pup, I will concede that."

Jessica's eyes became eager.

Rosalind changed her voice, knowing she dare not give Jessica an inch. "No, I am not going to change my mind. You can't keep him. He's going up to the main house. He is mine!"

The words "He is mine!" filtered through Brandon's subconscious. More, it shot through his mind like a great dawning light. The voice was low, melodious, but strong. Very strong. And very feminine.

Brandon surfaced to consciousness once more, this time the memory of the old stable hand strong in his mind. Pain returned. With it, so did his rage. This had to be the unnatural creature who had captured him and intended to force him into marriage.

"You cannot help him. Now leave us!" To whom was she talking? "That is an order."

Brandon heard nothing but a bark from a dog. He heard rustling and then silence. He sensed that they were alone. This would be the perfect moment. He knew his strength and his power. The unnatural creature would find herself in for a shock. Brandon opened his eyes, prepared to gain his freedom without much of a struggle.

A woman peered down at him. Her eyes were aquamarines. Copper curls framed a face of ivory perfection.

"Oh!" she said as if rather surprised. "Hello!"

All fight left Brandon. Dizziness flooded him. Not the dizziness of before, but a different kind, a kind he had never experienced before. Rosalind. It was the name of the most beautiful woman he had ever seen. Faith, his very soul was dizzy from looking upon her.

This was the unnatural creature that wanted to be a mother? His heart leapt with excitement. What had appeared a curse before was indeed a blessing. It was his destiny. He laughed from the joy of it.

The beautiful creature smiled. "I am glad to see you can laugh at your predicament, sir."

"Indeed. My dear Rosalind." Brandon smiled. "You have fairly caught me and I will marry you."

"I beg your pardon?" Rosalind said.

Her face was adorably astonished. Brandon smiled. She no doubt had expected opposition. He struggled to sit up. He sucked in his breath from the pain.

"Oh do be careful!" Rosalind exclaimed. She stretched out a supporting hand, and then an arm about his shoulder as Brandon gritted his teeth. "Please lie down until my servants come."

"No." He stared into her eyes. Her concern was balm. "It was bad form for me to have proposed to you flat on my back. That is not what we shall tell our children."

"Oh dear." Her face fell in dismay. "You are not in your right mind, sir."

"Yes, I am," he said softly.

"Sir, you are shot."

"Yes, I remember that." Brandon grinned. "I'll own I was in a rage about it."

"I would be too, I am sure." She smiled wryly.

"You should have employed better men to bring me here, my dear."

"You mean simply men, do you not?" She asked dryly.

He laughed. "Yes, they were not even that."

"They?" She frowned.

"When shall we wed?" he asked.

"We are not going to wed," she said rather gently. "You are not in your right mind, sir. Now please, do lay back down and we shall discuss this later."

"There is no reason to be coy." Brandon laughed.

She lifted a brow. "Sir, do I look like the type of female to be coy?"

The frankness in her eyes that looked directly at him was a delight. No, his lady was neither coy nor flirtatious. Faith, but she was a rare treasure. "No." His heart flooding, he leaned over and kissed her firmly.

"Sir!" She frowned upon him. "That is more than enough."

"No," Brandon said. "Not nearly enough."

"Yes, it is." She said it in a strict tone, as if to a child. "Now do lie down and behave until my servants arrive."

"You will be excellent with our children." He grinned. "But I am not one of them. Kiss me just once more."

"I shall not. And we are not going to have any children. We are not going to marry. Indeed we are not . . ."

"Too many 'nots', my dear." Brandon grinned and kissed her again. Only this time, he didn't draw back. Though he might have jested, he had disliked hearing those "nots" come from her sweet lips. If she thought to change her mind upon this venture, he would offer her the persuasion she needed.

The entreaty took off like wildfire. Such was the kiss that Brandon felt it course through his entire frame. He felt it course through Rosalind's at the same time. A groan escaped him as he heard her moan.

He tore his lips away. "Faith."

"Yes." The look in Rosalind's eyes was dazed.

"A thousand apologies. I—I thought I would be too weak to . . ." Brandon halted. Just what was he about to confess?

"Be of any danger?" she murmured. "I did too."

"We must marry soon, Rosalind," Brandon said rather hoarsely.

"Yes, yes, we will." Rosalind shook her head to clear her thoughts. "I mean . . . please, sir, d-do release me and lay back down."

"Now that you have said you will marry me, I shall." He groaned. The exhilaration of her kiss was wearing off and the pain reasserting itself. He lay back down. Regardless, he chuckled. "Only imagine how it will be like when I am healthy."

"Gracious, no!" she exclaimed, with more fear than excitement.

He frowned. "You shall not change your mind? You will marry me?"

"I . . . Sir, I do not know you," she said with clear restraint. "We . . . we must discuss this later."

"Rosalind." He reached out his hand. What was the matter with him? "Confound it, I feel faint."

"I know. So do I."

"No, I fear I am going to pass out." He gripped her hand. "Promise, Rosalind. Promise me you shall marry me."

"I promise." Rosalind nodded. "Now rest."

"Rest?" Darkness was descending upon him at an alarming speed. "An excellent notion, my love."

Two

Rosalind moved about the bedroom, setting up the bandages and water that she thought Dr. Hillsdale might require. He would arrive soon. She cast a worried glance to the man that the servants had lain upon the bed; Brandon Laith, the Earl of Craymore to be precise. Peters had been correct, he was a lord indeed. The cards they had found upon him testified to the fact.

"Ninnyhammer." She shook her head in disbelief. Had she actually promised to marry the man? She still couldn't believe it. She had known that he was not in his right mind, but what mind had she been in?

She shivered. Granted, his kisses had befuddled her. She had heard from her grandmother about the seduction of kisses, but until now, she had never experienced such a kiss, or indeed, *any* kiss before this one. However, since this was her first, it was quite unfair for it to have bowled her over so.

No, she had been bowled over before that. It was how the gentleman had greeted her. *My dear Rosalind, you have caught me fairly and I shall marry you.* A thrill shook her and she frowned. "Widgeon." His words made no sense, whatsoever. She shouldn't let them affect her as they did. Although, regardless, a smile tipped her lips. Still, for an introductory greeting, it was rather impressive.

She grimaced and straightened her spine and her resolve. She must simply tell this earl the truth, that she would not marry him. She paced the bedroom, astonished that she experienced a fit of the nerves. Why should she? When he awoke she would speak reasonably and firmly. The matter would be settled and that would be that. After all, he was a nobleman. He would be honorable and bend to her wishes. At least, she prayed that he would.

She flexed her hand in instant memory. When the servants came to assist her they had been shocked, and rightly so, that she held his hand. Though in truth, it was *he* who held hers and would not relinquish it. She had discovered that his unconscious strength was far stronger than her conscious strength. There was nothing she could do but to pretend that it was a natural thing, acting as if she were merely being helpful by holding his hand all the way to the house and to the room.

Only when they had laid him upon the bed and left the room and she had whispered that he must release her hand and not to fear for she would indeed marry him, had he actually let it go. That had been three hours ago.

Then the children had arrived home and were agog to hear the story. Unfortunately, Peters had unloaded his version to them first. Next, cook had told them of the stranger holding her hand so romantically. Her two younger brothers, Jonathan and Jeremy, had both reacted like bristling bulldogs. If the earl persisted in his wild behavior, there would surely be a tempest in the house.

Worse, where the two boys led, her three young cousins would surely follow. Faith, but Cassy, Ellen, and Rachel were growing up far too fast, Rosalind thought. Three years ago Rosalind had offered them a home at Treemont after their parents had died. Richard, her oldest brother, was indeed their legal guardian. He was stiff-rumped and a nipfarthing to boot, and Rosalind had known she couldn't leave them to his care. Their lives would be nothing but boarding school after boarding school, and whichever proved to be the most economical at that. She couldn't leave them to a series of cold stone floors, drafty halls, and embittered headmistresses. Furthermore, she couldn't help but remember how she had felt when she had lost both father and mother, and that had been at the grown age of sixteen.

Thus, she had offered to raise them at Treemont. Fortunately, her grandmother had bestirred herself and agreed. Richard, a bachelor and surely to be one all his life, had readily accepted. Rosalind knew she had done the right thing. Only now did she wonder if she were actually up to raising and steering three precocious girls into womanhood. Rosalind swiftly cast that thought from her mind. What mother didn't suffer such concerns?

A high-pitched howl arose from outside the door. Jessica! Now there was a mother with concerns. The French spaniel was about the only one in the Treemont family who doted upon the earl. Rosalind had barred her from the sick room because of Jessica's overzealous administration of motherly affection. The earl's cheek was raw from the dog's devotion.

Rosalind shook her head. No doubt, if the stranger had awakened to the Treemont family assembled about him, five in deep mistrust and one in slobbering affection (that was Jessica of course), he might never recover his sanity. Rosalind hoped for the best, but if not, she had already taken the precaution of sending the children out. If the earl awoke still in the frame of mind that he had been when he had passed out, she didn't want any witnesses.

"Where am I?" a low voice asked.

"Gracious!" Rosalind started. She looked over to the bed. Her mad earl was conscious and studying her with wary eyes. Eyes of silver gray that, alas, were as compelling as his countenance. Perhaps that is what had befuddled her before as well. She summoned up a smile. "You startled me."

"Who are you?" he asked directly. Confusion stamped his face. There was not a speck of passion in his eye. "And where am I, pray tell?"

Rosalind stiffened, feeling as if he had dashed a bucket of cold water on her. This greeting was a far cry from the other, to be sure. Her smile turned wry. "I see that you are in your right mind now."

"Of course, I am." He lifted a brow. "Why should I not be?"

"Because . . ." Rosalind found herself at a loss for words. A laugh escaped her. She *had* prayed that he would be reasonable, had she not? Yet, this kind of reasonable was rather daunting. "Never mind." Another laugh bubbled up. The Almighty had answered her prayer so completely that she was now swimming hard to make the shift. "It is nothing, nothing at all."

"I beg your pardon, Madam?" He smiled, but with strong reserve. "Are you feeling all right?"

"Indeed, my Lord, I am." Rosalind bit back another bout of laughter. Faith, if she didn't watch it he'd be calling her cracked. "Do not fear, I am in my right mind too. You are at Treemont Court and I am Rosalind Treemont."

His gaze did not waver from her. He frowned darkly. "A thousand apologies, but am I supposed to know you?"

"No, of course not," Rosalind jumped to say. "We are strangers, complete and total strangers."

"That is fortunate, for I own that I do not recognize you." He shook his head. "How did I get here? It is all a blank to me."

Rosalind walked over to a chair and fell into it as gracefully as she could, considering she was overset, a condition she rarely permitted. Histrionics employed by frail females might be effective, but for a lady of her stature to indulge in them would be tottyheaded. "I had my servants bring you up from the stables."

"From the stables?" His look of suspicion did not lift. "Why was I in your stables?"

Rosalind bit her lip. "I believe my dog Jessica, er . . . retrieved you. From whence I do not know. She was not forthcoming in that regard."

"I see." He fell into a brown study.

"She has a bad tendency to bring foundlings home for adoption. To date you are the largest of them all. Generally they are baby ducks and kittens and what have you."

He barked a laugh. "Faith. Not only the largest but surely the oldest."

"And the most titled," Rosalind teased.

"You said that you do not know me, then how do you know my title?"

"We found your cards. Also, I am told that Peters found your horse an hour ago as well. It was out wandering in the woods." She frowned. "My Lord, I do hope I am not too forward, but I did hope you might be more forthcoming than Jessica in regard to what has happened to you."

"I fear I cannot be." He frowned. "I cannot remember an infernal thing. About your dog, that is. I do remember that I was riding to my fiancée's place."

"Your fiancée's!" Rosalind exclaimed. It was another bucket of cold, no, freezing water.

"Yes, my fiancée." He cocked a brow. "What is the matter?"

"Oh, nothing. Nothing at all," Rosalind said quickly, very quickly. How odd to have a complete memory of something that had happened, but had not happened. For in effect, since this man did not remember it, it had not truly occurred. Nor did she want him to remember. Surely that would be the best course. He was betrothed. What had transpired when he was not in his right mind should not be held against him.

"Though I suppose I should not say that the lady is my fiancée. Not yet, that is." He smiled. "I was on my way to her estates to officially ask for her hand. Do forgive me for my misrepresentation. My friends all bemoan the fact that I act far too quickly and without hesitation. They claim I am impetuous."

"Yes, you are," Rosalind murmured, relieved that she hadn't actually kissed a fully betrothed man.

"I beg your pardon?"

"What?" She looked up and then flushed. "I was wool-gathering I fear. Who is your fiancée, I mean your soon-to-be fiancée?"

"Miss Amelia Fancot. Do you know her?"

"I have heard of her. Her family seat is quite a distance from here." The Fancots were the ton of the ton. "Do proceed."

"I remember being set upon by two men."

Rosalind frowned. "We have never had highwaymen in this vicinity before."

"They were not highwaymen." His gaze turned from suspicious to guarded.

"They were not?" Rosalind studied him. "Were they poachers, do you think?"

"No, I do not think so."

"Then just precisely who do you think they were?" Rosalind asked point blank, confused by his evasiveness.

"I do not know." His gaze turned with a burning intensity upon her. Rosalind watched as his eyes took on a look of remembrance. She tensed. Was he about to remember the scene in the stables after all?

"Blast, I have this odd memory."

"Do you?"

"Yes. I remember a small man, I think a stable hand."

"Yes. Peters," Rosalind admitted in resignation. Here it was. He would remember. How very embarrassing. "He was the one who found you first."

He nodded. "Yes. I remember. And an unnatural creature . . ."

"Unnatural creature?" Rosalind stiffened despite herself. "I beg your pardon!"

"No, not you, I am sure." He frowned. "Your stable man talked about some unnatural creature who wanted to be a mother?"

"Jessica." Rosalind sighed. "He was talking about Jessica, the dog of which I told you. She has never been able to have puppies, but she does so wish to be a mother. Hence, every spring she . . . well, she goes about, er, gathering babies to foster. Peters believes it unnatural and that we should not encourage her. In fact, he thinks we should put her down for it. He rather confuses his horses with his dogs."

"Are you telling me the truth?" He stared at her.

"Yes." Rosalind bit her lip. Well, she was telling the pertinent part. Suddenly, it all fell into place. "Gracious!" She stared at him. He had proposed to *her* thinking that it was *she* who wanted to be a mother. That is why he told her she needn't be coy. That is also why he spoke about the men she had employed. Could he truly have thought that she had meant to capture him? Demented. Insane. Yet thinking that, he had still proposed to her! "My stars."

"Madam?"

Rosalind reeled. "Nothing, nothing at all."

"You are not telling me the truth, are you?"

"I am, truly." Guilt rose within Rosalind. It was ridiculous to be sure. But to tell this now sane man before her just exactly how insane he had been would not be kind.

"How could a dog drag a full grown man like myself?" He asked, his gaze narrowing.

"That I do not know," Rosalind admitted. "It seems well nigh impossible. Though Jessica is a big dog, she weighs not but four stone at the most. Surely to bring you here would be a feat beyond even her capabilities. Do try to think, my Lord."

"I am," he said curtly. Rosalind watched as thoughts raced across his face. Full outright suspicion is what he finally settled upon.

Rosalind could tell. "My Lord. Do try to remain logical and sane."

"I beg your pardon?" He looked at her, his face shocked.

Rosalind bit her lip. "I mean, do not jump to conclusions. You yourself said you are impulsive. And you are attempting to determine matters without your memory intact."

"Which leaves me rather vulnerable, I would say."

She stared at him. Just how had it turned from her worrying about his sanity, to his worrying about her motives? Worse, if she attempted to explain it all to him now, he would only think her designing.

"Well." He smiled. "I am sure I have imposed upon your hospitality long enough. I must leave."

Rosalind's eyes widened. So that was the tack he was going to take? The man was facile, his style and grace impressive. He promptly sat up and threw back the covers. He looked down at the nightshirt he wore.

"That is my butler's," Rosalind said hastily. "He and Peters put you in it. Mrs. Gadson, my cook, was determined you must be in clean clothes and bed."

"I commend them too." He sucked in his breath and swung his feet to the floor. Rosalind watched, determined not to enter into an altercation.

He stood. He swayed.

"Oh, enough of this tomfoolery!" Rosalind sprung from her chair and hastened to him. She caught him barely in time. They looked into each other's eyes for one still moment. His gaze widened in a stunned manner. He bent his head. Gracious, he was going to kiss her!

Rosalind withdrew. He rather shook himself in astonishment. Which was unwise, for in his weakened state he swayed again. Rosalind clutched him once more. This time they listed together.

Then the door opened. Outraged roars arose. Rosalind turned her gaze. She had just one moment to view her two younger brothers charging down on them.

"Rosalind, beware!" Jonathan cried and grabbed hold of Rosalind.

"Unhand her, Sirrah!" Jeremy shouted and grabbed hold of the earl.

"No!" Rosalind cried.

Jeremy gave the earl a blow to the chin.

"Good work, Jeremy," Jonathan cheered and promptly shoved Rosalind to the side with brotherly rudeness.

The earl miraculously delivered a returning blow to Jeremy.

Rosalind nodded. "Good work, my Lord."

New shrieks arose, high pitched, and feminine. Cassy, Ellen, and Rachel bounded into the room. They jumped up and down and squealed in excitement as young girls are wont to do over anything, let alone a brawl between family and foe.

"B'gads! What the devil!" Dr. Hillsdale trundled in just as the earl, injured though he may be, managed to offer up some rather amazing punches to Jonathan and Jeremy. Though the two youths were lighter of frame, all three males were well-sized. Rosalind was astonished.

"Jonathan and Jeremy, cease!" Her order was drowned out as the girls shrieked and promptly jumped upon the bed for a better view. Jessica entered the room at that moment and gave her presence away by a howl.

Rosalind tried a new tack. "My Lord, please stop!"

Lord Laith paused at her plea. Unfortunately it permitted Jeremy and Jonathan the advantage. They plowed into him. With no resistance, all three toppled to the floor.

"Good heavens!" Rosalind groaned. "Jonathan and Jeremy, get off his lordship this instant."

"Young hellions. Do what your sister says," ordered Dr. Hillsdale, a small, rotund little man.

"He was attacking Rosalind!" Jonathan cried.

"He was hugging her!" Cassy said eagerly.

"He was going kiss her!" Ellen said. "I just know it! He's wicked."

"I told you he was attacking her!" Jonathan supported. "We were protecting her!"

"Don't be daft, boy," Dr. Hillsdale shot back. "Look at your sister. Do you think such a strapping wench as she needs protection!"

"Of course she does," Jonathan spouted.

Rosalind blushed. "Jonathan and Jeremy, get off of the gentleman, now."

"Very well." Jeremy rose. Blood trickled from his lip. "But you did need our protection."

"She sure did," Jonathan said firmly as he drew himself up. His right eye was purple.

"I—I quite agree with the gentleman." Lord Laith groaned and rose very slowly. He sported now, along with all his other wounds, a bruise along the unscathed cheek and a bloody lip. However, his eyes were alight with amusement. Gone was suspicion and distrust.

Rosalind gaped. Faith, the blows from her brothers had apparently knocked his common sense back.

"B'gads!" Dr. Hillsdale sucked in his breath.

Rosalind did too. The three were in dreadful shape. And they warmed her heart with their defense of her strapping womanhood.

"Well." Dr. Hillsdale cleared his throat and looked away. "That's because you are all giants."

Rosalind bit her lip and forced a sternness. "Girls, get off the bed. And you, my Lord, get into the bed. Jonathan and Jeremy, assist him. You should not have jumped to conclusions." She looked at Lord Laith. "It must be something in the air today."

"My salute, Madam." He nodded.

"You can't trust him, Rosalind," Jonathan said as he dutifully took up the earl's one arm.

"He's a lord." Jeremy took up the other arm. "And you can't trust a lord."

"Ridiculous," Rosalind said. "You can trust a lord. You two have titles as well and you know it. Indeed, our family abounds with them so do not attempt to use that as an excuse."

"But we are different," Jeremy said.

"We are your brothers," Jonathan added. "You can trust us."

The earl looked at her. "You did not tell me you were titled."

"I have no need of a title in these parts," Rosalind said sharply. "But if it will help ease your suspicions, I will tell you I am of the peerage."

"What!" Jeremy exclaimed. "What suspicions?"

"His lordship thinks that we sent two men after him to abduct him."

"Two men?"

"Yes," Rosalind said.

"But why would we do that?" Jonathan exclaimed. "We don't even know the fellow."

"True. But he *is* a lord," Rosalind responded, despite herself.

"A well-trounced Lord," the earl murmured. "Who . . . appears to have lost more of his wits than he had first thought."

"Precisely. Now do get into the bed," Rosalind said more gently.

He frowned. "No. I must leave here."

"What?" Rosalind said. "Whatever are you thinking of now, my Lord?"

His smile glimmered. "I was set upon by two men who were commissioned by someone, either to kill me or abduct me. That is the one strong memory I do have."

"Really?" Jonathan exclaimed.

"Well which was it?" Jeremy frowned. "Did they want to kill you or abduct you?"

"I do not know. The two chaps were in disagreement. I must confess, I was rather too occupied with fighting them off to pay particular attention to what was the final vote."

"Blast," Jonathan exclaimed. "A mystery."

"How jolly," Jeremy exclaimed. "I enjoy mysteries."

"He's a hero!" Cassy exclaimed.

"Not a villain." Rachel nodded. "Peters was wrong."

"The others are villains." Ellen clapped. "How exciting."

"Gadzooks, my Lord," Jonathan cried. "You must get in the bed."

"Oh yes. Do hurry!" Cassy said. "We don't want you to die."

"Yes, we want to hear more," Rachel said. "Who wants to kill you?"

"I'll lay odds those two rum customers intend to follow you here," Jonathan said and all but shoved Brandon to the bed. The indestructible Lord Laith finally showed his weakness and went meekly.

"That was my thought." He cast Rosalind a weary smile. "And now that I have been, er . . . made aware of the extent of your hospitality, I would not care for those two villains to cause any trouble for you."

"We'll take care of them." Jeremy puffed out his chest. "Bloody their noses we will."

"We'll roll them up, see if we don't," Jonathan boasted.

The earl grimaced. "Yes, I was rather afraid you would feel that way."

"They won't slip by us, I vow." Jonathan nodded.

"You mean we could be in danger?" Ellen asked, her eyes wide. "How famous! Nothing like this has ever happened to us before."

"But I want to know who wants to kill him." Rachel frowned. She was the most orderly of all the children and the deepest thinker. "The two men aren't important."

"Here now." Jeremy looked offended. "When they come knocking on the door with pistols in hand, you'll think they are important."

"They weren't all that brave," Brandon said. "Indeed, they were rather bungling. I mean, I did escape them, though I don't have much memory of it."

"Bungling?" Jonathan's face fell.

"Yes," Brandon said firmly. His lips twitched, however, and he cast Rosalind a look of commiseration. "Positively so, now that I come to think of it."

"That is not good, Lord Laith." Rachel chewed her lip.

"Why not?" Brandon asked. "I should think we can relax. Those two bunglers should be far away by now."

"Yes, but if I wanted to kill you and the first two bungled it," she said, "I would hire better men to do the job the next time. Wouldn't you?"

"B'gads, she's right!" Jonathan said in awe.

"She is rather daunting," Brandon said to Rosalind.

"I know." Rosalind smiled, despite herself. "I fear she takes after her great grandmother."

"Hello!" Jeremy smiled. "We'll have better fare than two bunglers coming at us."

"Maybe they'll send four more," Ellen said.

"Or six." Cassy nodded.

The girls squealed with delight. Jessica jumped up on the bed. She took a stance over the paling earl and proceeded to growl and bark. All the children backed away in astonishment.

Rosalind laughed and stepped forward. "Jessica is quite right, you know. We must leave Lord Laith. Dr. Hillsdale must attend him."

"Not if you don't take that dog with you!" Dr. Hillsdale said with a dark frown.

"Very well, I will." Rosalind cast the earl a wry look as the children protested. "You have sealed your fate, I fear."

His look was just as wry. "Forgive me. It was my blunder. Regardless, I shall be pleased to have the good doctor tend me, and then but direct me to the nearest inn."

"There isn't an inn for miles around!" Cassy said, her voice jubilant. "You will have to stay with us."

"Are you married then, Madam?" he asked forthwith.

"No." Rosalind said. "However, grandmother resides with us. She can act as chaperone. She is Lady Wroxeter, I would imagine she should be considered acceptable."

"Lady Wroxeter?" The earl's brows shot up. "Faith!"

"Yes," Rosalind said rather grimly.

He smiled. "I see why you have no need for a title, then."

Rosalind nodded. "You are quite correct. Grandmother holds enough titles for us all."

They looked at each other and broke into laughter.

Rosalind sat at her escritoire attending the Treemont accounts. The door opened and she looked up. Ignoring the tension within her she smiled as the earl of Craymore entered the room. He moved stiffly and was still bandaged, but all things considered, since just six days ago he had not only been shot, but a lump the size of a robin's egg on the back of his head testified to him having been struck, he was doing miraculously well. She was forced to admit that her brothers had added to his list of wounds.

Rosalind sighed. According to Dr. Hillside, the blows to

his head that he had received from her two hellion brothers would have killed a lesser man. He went on to assure her if Lord Laith died it would be because of them.

"Hello," she said.

"Hello." He nodded and smiled in return. He paced to a chair and sat down. He sat and watched her, a puzzled expression upon his face.

She frowned. "What is it, my Lord?"

"Why are you always on the fidgets while I am about?"

"Gracious." Rosalind started. She lowered her gaze. "Whatever do you mean? I—I am not on the fidgets, I assure you."

"Do not attempt to be coy, Miss Treemont," he said seriously. "You are not a coy woman."

Rosalind's gaze flew to his in astonishment.

He paused. Then he smiled. "Well, are you?"

She laughed. "No, my Lord, I am not. Forgive my paltry attempt at it."

"Certainly. And I do hope you do not think it is something I desire. I find it refreshing that you are always forthright and honest with all. You are a composed woman. Indeed, very peaceful."

"A great accolade. Thank you, my Lord."

His eyes lit with amusement. "You don't care a fig for that. But I've been watching you and I am the only one you are on the fidgets with. Why?"

"Perhaps it is because you *are* watching me," Rosalind returned with great truth.

"A home point," he said, his tone rueful.

Rosalind waited. He still did not speak. She drew in a deep breath. If they were going to speak without the bark on it, she had her own question to ask. "Why *do* you watch me so closely? Do you still fear that I am in some way involved in a devious plot against you?"

"No." His voice took on a drawl. "The only female about here with designs upon me is Jessica, and that only to mother me."

Rosalind laughed. "But you are her fair-haired pup, to be sure."

"True. For which I am grateful. Else I would lose all my male confidence, I am sure. I fear without her support I would go to Miss Fancot a crumbled shell of a man without enough confidence to ask her to dance, let alone ask her to marry me."

"What?" Rosalind blinked. "Surely we are not that bad!"

"I have yet to see your grandmother, Miss Treemont."

She smiled. "Which, Lord Laith, you should consider a blessing. Grandmother has lost all interest in society. Mine included. She only cares for the children, I assure you."

"Ah is that it?" His voice was light. "I had begun to wonder if she actually lived here."

"Oh, she lives here.' Rosalind's smile tightened. "She may not be seen to the ready eye, my Lord, but it is never wise to overlook Grandmother's presence."

"Yes. So I have heard." He studied her once more.

Rosalind gave up. She laughed in exasperation. "My Lord, if you do not wish for me to be on the high fidgets, you simply must stop watching me so minutely."

"So you have told me." He cocked his head in a considering way. "Why have you not married?"

Rosalind blinked, nonplussed. "Why, because no one has asked me!"

"Gammon. Certainly some gentleman has proposed to you."

Rosalind bit her lip. "Very well, one gentleman did."

"Only one?"

"Yes, only one. Now do not put me to the blush." Rosalind laughed. "My Lord, not only am I a big girl, but my nature, the one *you* are kind enough to call refreshing and peaceful . . ."

"It is."

"Others have considered disconcerting, managing, and quite unbecoming in a female. Furthermore, even if they were to take a shine to my sterling qualities, I do not care to wed."

"That is the conclusion I have drawn." He frowned.

"Have you?" Rosalind asked with astonishment.

"Women who are desirous of marriage are far more conciliatory to the opposite sex than I have noted you to be. They do attempt to employ some of the feminine arts." His frown only deepened, the silver in his eyes turning to charcoal. "But why do you not wish to wed? You are famous with the children."

"Indeed. I do not deny it. I love the children and I am blessed that they love me back. But five is the top of my bent, I assure you."

A glimmer lit his eyes. "Nonsense. You need five more."

"What?" Rosalind gasped. "Are you cracked?"

"No. I am a strong proponent for a large family. I come from a family of eight, you see. I, myself, intend to have ten children."

"Ten!" She stared at him. "Have you discussed this with your fiancée? Excuse me, your future fiancée?"

"Of course I have." He smiled. "It is not a thing with which you should surprise a lady, I believe."

"And she did not faint upon the spot?" Rosalind asked. She shook her head. "Now I know who sent those men after you. *She* did. Ten children indeed."

"No." He barked a laugh at that. Then he sobered. "No. I imagine the men were sent by some other source."

"Do you have that many enemies?"

"I have lead an active life in society."

She frowned. "And for that you have made enemies?"

"I was once considered a rake, I fear." He said it rather gently.

"A rake?" Rosalind blinked. So, there was her reason! That was why she had been so bowled over by his kiss. It was his expertise that had made the difference. "No wonder!"

"I beg your pardon?" he asked.

"Hmm?" She looked at him. Then she flushed. "Did I say something?"

"You said, 'no wonder.' "

"Did I?" She attempted an innocent look.

"You are truly hopeless at coyness, Miss Treemont." He grimaced. "And I have reformed, which means I cannot give you lessons in the arts of flirtation."

"Reformed?" Rosalind smiled. "Is there not a saying that leopards do not change their spots?"

"Ah, but leopards do grow up." He smiled. "Or perhaps I am a deer instead. A fawn has spots until it grows into a stag, you know?"

Rosalind broke into outright laughter. "Faith, I cannot see you as a fawn."

"I am going to settle down, I vow. I intend to become most unfashionable, in fact. I will have my ten children and I intend to take a most attentive, and thus unconventional, role in their rearing."

"Beware, my Lord." Rosalind teased. "Soon you shall go wandering about your country seat pronouncing to strangers that you have no need for a title."

"There, you have it."

"My felicitations. I myself admit to enjoying being unfashionable." She turned her gaze back to the ledger. "I can but hope that you can lose your spots."

"For shame," the earl said. "Have I not been most circumspect with you? I have done everything in my power to insure that I did not frighten you."

"Have you?" He was a jot too late for that in her opinion.

"Come, Miss Treemont. Have I in any way importuned you? Even with such a conspicuous lack of chaperonage."

"I would have thought the fact that you are engaged, or soon to be, was the reason for that."

His grin was irreverent. "If I were not reformed that would not have stopped me one whit."

"But you are my guest!" Rosalind exclaimed.

"Once again, that would not have mattered were I not reformed."

"Surely you jest, my Lord!" Rosalind gasped.

"Surely I do not." He laughed. "I can tell that you have not had any experience with rakes."

"I have met some, I will have you know."

He raised a brow. "I cannot believe it."

She laughed. "Certainly. And I know they were rakes because Grandmother always told me, and I do believe I could depend upon her knowledge."

"And her protection." He nodded. "Then with your great experience, you must confess that you did not know by my behavior in these past six days, that I have at one time been a rake."

"Very well, I do own it. Does that please you?"

"Not completely." His gaze narrowed. "Despite my excellent behavior, you accepted far too quickly that I was a rake. Furthermore, you truly don't believe I can change. I want to know the why of that, pray tell."

"And why would you want to know the why of that, my Lord?" Rosalind returned, pressed.

"Because that surely is the root of it, I vow."

"The root of what?"

"Why I make you fidgety." A sincerity entered his gaze. "What have I done, Madam, to cause this? Do I not deserve an explanation?"

Rosalind stared at him. A sigh escaped her. "Very well, my Lord. I have not wished to tell you this. However, the simple truth is that you and I, er . . . well, we did meet before, but you do not remember."

"Impossible. I would not forget a woman like you."

"Yes, I stand head and shoulders above the rest," Rosalind said, her tone dry.

"No." He frowned. "That is another appealing thing about you. You are precisely my height. You cannot know how tiring it is to always be bending down to . . . to speak to a lady."

Rosalind flushed. Both from the compliment and the one pause in his declaration. "Thank you."

"You are welcome. I am sure I should not have said that because I am reformed and well-nigh engaged. But, the point still stands, you say we met and I say we have not. I would not forget you, Miss Treemont."

"Thank you, but not only did you forget meeting a woman like me," Rosalind said with good humor. "But you also forgot kissing a woman like me."

"Impossible." His face was so incredulous that Rosalind found comfort in it. "When, and where? Was I foxed?"

"No, no. It was in the stables. Peters went for assistance. You regained consciousness and you kissed me."

His brows shot up. "Gads, you don't say?"

Actually Rosalind breathed her first sigh of relief in six days. She wasn't good at secrets. And following their conversation, she now felt she had discovered a reason for what had happened. "My Lord, you were all about in your head and no doubt your old . . . er, ways, came back. You didn't know."

"I see." He appeared nonplussed. He looked at her. Then he laughed. "Miss Treemont, you are the most amazing of ladies. Why did you not tell me?"

"My Lord, I considered it a rather unnecessary scene to relate to you, considering that once you had regained your full faculties you did not remember it. After all, you are engaged, or soon to be engaged."

"Most ladies would have been up in the boughs rather than in the fidgets if I had done such. All I can do is beg your pardon."

"You are pardoned." Rosalind smiled.

"Well, I certainly received more enlightenment than I expected." He stood abruptly. His lips twisted in a wry smile. "I fear you are right, Miss Treemont. I still need work. It appears my subconscious self has not reformed to the same degree as my conscious self."

"Do not be disheartened." Rosalind smiled. Some encouragement was surely in line. "It shall follow, I have no doubt. After all, you *did* do the proper thing and propose beforehand."

He stiffened. "I beg your pardon!"

His expression was so unreadable that Rosalind hastened to assure him. "Do not worry about that. I assure you, I do not. You were not in your right mind."

"Miss Treemont. You must be honest with me. Did I truly propose to you?"

"Yes." He was scrutinizing her in a new fashion. She found herself stumbling to speak fast. "Though it was Jessica you meant to propose to, I believe. You evidently had heard Peters talking about how she wanted to be a mother and how she had brought you here. Therefore, when you awoke, you proposed to me directly. It is a very lowering thing to confess, that the only proposal I received was meant for my dog." She laughed.

He did not. Her smile faded. She didn't know why, but she felt that she was digging a huge hole of some sort. She hoped it wasn't her grave. "You do not find that amusing?"

"I have never proposed to anyone. No matter what kind of rake I have been or how impulsive. I have never proposed."

The feeling persisted. "What about Miss Fancot?"

"I proposed that I would propose to her," he said softly. "I took this journey alone and by horseback in order that I could screw my courage to the sticking point as it were."

Rosalind shivered despite herself. "Your proposal to Miss Fancot shall be excellent, my Lord, I promise you. Perhaps that is how it transpired. You . . . you thought I was she."

"Did I call you by her name?"

"No. You called me by my own."

"What did I say?"

" 'My dear Rosalind, you have fairly caught me and I will marry you.' I didn't understand at the time why you proposed, but it makes sense in regard to what you thought Peters had said."

"No, Miss Treemont. It does not make sense. You do not know me. I have never proposed to anyone. Why would I propose to you directly upon first sight?"

"I do not know, my Lord. As you said, I do not know you." Rosalind shifted in her seat. "No doubt you were still suffering from being knocked on the head. Now, all apologies have been made. The scene should be forgotten or I will regret that I ever confessed it."

"How did we kiss?"

"My Lord!" Rosalind gasped.

"Please, Miss Treemont. Rosalind. This is no time for coyness."

"I'm not coy. We have both agreed on that point. But surely you cannot expect me to relay the details of our kiss to you!"

"I need to know how we kissed."

Rosalind sprang up. The fire in his gaze was bringing back the memory too fast and furiously. "No, you do not."

"I am about to propose and marry, Miss Treemont. I need to know how we kissed," he said, rising from his chair.

"Why? So that it will help you with Miss Fancot?"

"I have kissed her. I know exactly how that went." He waved a dismissing hand.

"Gracious!"

"I told you I was a rake." He sounded positively stern. "I cannot remember how we kissed. Now . . . how did we kiss?"

"Why do you need to know? If you do not remember the kiss, that should certainly speak for itself, should it not?"

"No. It is not enough."

"My Lord." Rosalind glanced at the door. She considered herself a brave woman, but she was going to cut and run without apology. "You cannot ask me. You simply cannot."

"You are right." He strode up and put his arm about her waist.

"What?"

"I need to know," he said.

He kissed her. Rosalind struggled for a moment, but then groaned, melting into him.

He drew back. "Now I remember."

"Do you?" Rosalind bit her lip.

"I also remember why I proposed." He said it softly.

"Do you?" Rosalind couldn't keep her train of thought

in line. Gracious! She could barely breathe from the sensations coursing through her. Kissing could be a quite potent matter it seemed.

The most wonderful smile crossed his face. "I want to marry you."

"My Lord!" Rosalind stared at him, stupefied.

"You, Rosalind. Not Jessica. Not Miss Fancot. You."

"Talk about impetuous. One kiss and you've decided this?"

"Indeed. I've waited for just such a kiss. I want to marry you."

"You cannot want to marry me. You do not even know me."

"I have been trying for six days not to know you. But I could not help but study you, knowing that I had forgotten something important. Apparently I think better when rapped on my thick skull. I want to marry you."

"But I do not want to marry you!" Rosalind said firmly. "I do not want to marry anyone."

He grinned. "I will simply have to show you just how wrong you are then. You do want to marry me, my dear Rosalind, you do."

Three

"So you want to marry Rosalind, do you?" The Most Honorable Lady Wroxeter, The Countess of Alverstoke, The Dowager Countess of Chedworth, The Dowager Viscountess Monmouth, Dowager Lady Ramsey of Sawtry, asked from her mammoth wing-back chair that looked suspiciously like a throne. Set on an ornate parquetry floor within a curtained enclosure raised a step up from that of the salon, it had the effect of the lady being ensconced on a dais, rather than in the comfortable reading chair it was meant to be, surrounded as it was by shelves filled with books. An Indian silver tiger-headed cane rested against the chair. On the table beside her a tea tray balanced amidst several books.

Her suite that Lord Laith had invaded was spacious, with large mullioned windows bringing light to art treasures of great value and beauty. If it were true that no one but the children were freely invited into Lady Wroxeter's presence, he could not help but think it a shame that so few had ever beheld the splendor. It was clear that her retreat from society was quite comfortable.

"Yes I do." Brandon nodded.

Lady Wroxeter quirked a brow. "Humph. She doesn't know you came to see me, does she?"

"Certainly not. This infraction is no one's fault but my own." Brandon smiled at the old lady, a peeress in her own right having succeeded to one title, who had married and buried three titled noblemen as well; a lady who was considered a myth now, though few dared to speak her name with malice in fear of retribution. "I decided to take my life into my own hands and come for an audience."

"You're a brave lad." Lady Wroxeter nodded. Her eyes turned piercing. "Didn't I just write to that totty-headed Andrea Fancot that you would be detained for only a few days?"

"Did you write that?" Brandon asked, astonished.

" 'Course I did. Rosalind intended to write it, but I told her she'd make a mull of the message and then we'd have Andrea and her widgeon of a daughter down upon us, determined to protect their claim upon you. I didn't want that."

"But you wouldn't have seen them, would you, so why the worry?"

"What affects my family, son, affects me." She cracked a smile. "I'm like a spider in a web. You jostle any part of it and I feel it."

Brandon tensed. It had been whispered amongst the *ton* that she was the black widow incarnate. Even at seventy, bent and rheumatic, the force of her personality still let one know she held power. It was not, however, like her to have confessed it so completely.

She laughed. "I frighten you, don't I, lad?"

Brandon laughed. "Dreadfully, my Lady."

"Ha. It is Rosalind you should fear," Lady Treemont said. "She's learned the secret and at too early an age."

"The secret?" Brandon frowned.

"Of how to be happy, you dolt," Lady Treemont said. "Me, it took me two husbands before I found one that made me happy. And God rest Rolly's soul, I still didn't learn how to be completely happy until he passed on to his reward. That was when the Almighty and I buried the hatchet, I suppose. But Rosalind, she has been blessed with everything and she dosen't take it for granted. She enjoys it."

A fear did course through Brandon. "I see."

"She has wealth. She has Treemont. She has the children. There's not much need for you now, is there?"

Brandon clenched his teeth. "I'll make a reason for her to need me."

She laughed. "Before you go off half cocked, I'm going to warn you that if you try to seduce Rosalind, I'll poison you."

Brandon stiffened. "I beg your pardon?"

She smiled. "You thought I was lax in my chaperone duties, eh? Well, I have just taken care of them. You're a brighter man than most. You want Rosalind. Most looby's look at Rosalind and are offset. I confess, I didn't think I would need to bestir myself, but now that I know you've an eye for her, I'm warning you. I'm too old to be toddling after the two of you to insure that you behave yourself."

"Certainly. That is very understandable." Brandon swallowed hard, whether from indignation or amusement he did not know.

"Now I have reformed, I'll have you know."

"So have I," Brandon said.

She cracked a grin. "Then you know it's rather easy to stray off the path once in a while. And so I will, I vow, if you even so much as kiss Rosalind. My first husband seduced me. He got his just deserts for it, but I'm not going to have that for Rosalind, do you hear me? She'll not be forced into marriage. Truth is, I don't think she'll marry you. But just in case you think you can get her by your wiles, I'm warning you not to try it."

"I'll make her love me without that," Brandon said. "We were meant to be together. She is my destiny."

"Huh. Did God tell you that?"

"What?" Brandon blinked. "No. Of course not."

"Well then don't try that line upon Rosalind. She's no nickninny. She won't accept hearsay. Unless you got it from Him, she won't be swayed."

Brandon stared. After processing her words he barked a laugh. "Are you saying I would need an authority that high to hold sway with her?"

"Yes." She smiled. "Perhaps a vision would do the trick."

"A vision?" Brandon drew back. Suddenly he could see Rosalind in armor with a bright light shining down upon her. "Gads. Like Joan of Arc?"

"Yes."

Brandon shook his head. "You *are* quite lowering."

Her grin was not kind. "I'm just laying the odds out before you."

"Vision or not, we are going to marry." Brandon rose and bowed. "I will be proud to be a member of your family, Lady Wroxeter."

"At least you've got bottom, that much I will say. Though I don't think it will do you any good." She lifted a hand. "But I'll not put my oar into this yet. I'm laying my money on Rosalind. With that said, I'll send another letter to Amelia, telling her your condition has not improved. That should give you more time."

"What of Rosalind?"

"I'll tell her that I'm giving you protective asylum here at Treemont until your enemies have been found. Which is the best choice for you after all. The way you arrived with our dog, I doubt your enemies will look for you here. And if they do know you are here, I think they will think twice before crossing me or mine."

"Thank you," Brandon said.

"Don't thank me, son," she said. "I mean what I say. And I expect we will be shot of you fast enough without me having to come out of retirement, as it were."

"Confess it," Brandon said, strolling alongside Rosalind at a leisurely pace. Considering it was a beautiful morning and they had only to join the children at the stream to fish, their pace was most suitable. "You do like me, do you not?"

Rosalind laughed. "Indeed, I do."

"Then marry me."

"I said I liked you." Indeed, Rosalind did. Within one week it was an undebatable thing. She liked Brandon. "But that is no reason to marry you."

A sudden seriousness crossed his face. "In truth, it might be the best reason in the entire world to marry." Before Rosalind could pull that thought to pieces and examine it, Brandon laughed. "Very well, in that case, tell me your secrets."

"I beg your pardon?" Rosalind asked, confused.

"And your dreams of course," Brandon persisted.

"Secrets and dreams are two different things," Rosalind said. "And why should I tell you either?"

"I have a feeling that your dreams and your secrets are the same. And you should tell me them in order that I might grant them to you and thus make you love me."

She laughed. "Ridiculous."

"Do you wish to travel? I shall whisk you away and show you the world."

"You know I am very happy right here. Treemont is my domain and I like it."

"I know. Your domain is most pleasant." She flushed for he nodded to her in both a silent salute and compliment. "Shall I save you from peril, do you think? Would that do the trick?"

"Perhaps." She gave it due consideration. "However, I do hope I am not totty-headed enough to fall into peril."

"Alas, a heroine who refuses to wander into a dragon's lair in order that I might slay it for her."

"Or into a strange tower that I might be locked within?"

"Indeed. Or make a dark and powerful enemy of any sort. No, you must be obstinate and be upon good terms with everyone."

"I know. So very disobliging of me." A small twinge passed through her. "I do wish that you had done the same."

"Yes. I know," he said. "It is very lowering to start considering just who might hold such a grudge against me that they wished to kill me or abduct me."

She forced a laugh. "It is the children's list that should have you sunk into the doldrums. One hundred suspects does seem alarming."

"Yes, I told them they should at least scratch off my

family. First, it would subtract seven from the list. Second, I have told them that I am not that offensive a sibling that all seven would wish me dead."

"No, no. They have narrowed it down to your brother, Trenton. After all, he would gain the title."

Brandon shook his head. "You do not know Trenton. He is the most unprepossessing of men. It would not be him."

She schooled her look to be serious. "And I do not think it is those six pirates that you tangled with years ago and who now follow you about, seeking revenge."

Brandon's eyes twinkled. "Your Cassy has an excellent imagination."

"Which you have completely encouraged with your own faradiddles."

"Perhaps. But what am I to do when she asks me to tell her a story?"

Rosalind sighed. "I rather wish it *were* all a story."

"I know. It is another very good reason for me to reform and settle down." He lifted a brow. "You wouldn't care to save me from myself, would you?"

"No, I do know better than that. Besides, you were already set upon reform. And you have already tendered that proposal to another."

"No, I proposed to tender that proposal. There is a difference." He nodded at her, his look discerning. "You fear I cannot be true to you, do you not, since I was so very fickle to have considered offering for another just two weeks ago?"

"Yes." Rosalind knew better than to deny it.

Brandon possessed the talent of knowing what she thought. She should have considered it disquieting, but in truth, it was a relief. Despite what others thought, she did attempt to be discreet. Brandon boldly presented her questions to her without her being forced to ask them. "I own I have thought that."

"I did not know about you." He said it simply. "I knew that it was past time for me to settle down and finally make my own dream a reality. I have sown my wild oats. I have done my duty to society." He frowned. "In truth, as the eldest of so many, I followed that path as a rebellion, I believe. I no longer feel that need. Indeed, I have been positively bored to flinders the past few years."

"How can you say that?"

"Easy." His eyes lit. "I wasn't building anything of substance. Going to do the pretty with society, spending hours in idle talk that for the *ton* is as malicious as it can be. No, in the end it all became too predictable. I finally lost my spots, or gained my spots. I am not sure which, but I knew I wanted to have more family. I wanted to create what my parents did, and as my siblings have already." He grimaced. "The rub is, since I never expected that I would so very instantly fall in love with you and to such a degree, I did what I could to accomplish my goal. I set about and decided upon a lady that would have and should have sufficed." He grinned. "I put the cart before the horse, I fear. Or the dream before the lady, as it were. I simply didn't know that you were my destiny." He had an odd, waiting look upon his face.

"Perhaps because I am not your destiny," Rosalind returned dryly.

He laughed. "Your grandmother said you would not accept that line from me."

"You talked to my grandmother in regard to this?"

"Of course. I had a suspicion that she was the one I had best apply to for your hand."

"Gracious!" Her mind whirled.

"I suppose you wouldn't believe me either, that God told me that you were meant for me?"

"No, of course not. Why ever should I?"

"Oh nothing. I just thought I would save you a vision."

Rosalind frowned, amazed that he had dared to approach her grandmother. "You do have the tendency to go after dragons, don't you?"

They both paused equally to stare at each other.

"What vision?" she asked him.

"What dragons?" he asked her.

A bellow of male origin far off in the distance interrupted them.

"Oh no! The children!" Rosalind picked up her skirts and began to run. Brandon followed directly behind her.

When she was halfway to the stream, the bellows only increasing, the three girls came crashing through the thickets.

"Rosalind!" Cassy cried.

"Brandon!" Rachel cried.

"Come quick!" Ellen gasped. "The boys have caught your villains!"

"Have they?" Brandon frowned.

"Oh, no!" Rosalind's heart turned over.

Brandon was off at a pace faster than hers. He reached the stream first. Rosalind came in a panting breath behind him. They both froze.

The two boys sat atop a man and a large, bullish boy.

"Gracious!" Rosalind said.

Brandon's look turned wry. "Even *they* don't need saving, it appears. This family is far too self-sufficient."

"We caught your villains!" Jonathan said.

"I'm not a villain!" the older man snapped from beneath Jeremy. "I'm a tinker, I am."

"And I'm his apprentice!" the boy squeaked from under Jonathan.

"You were sneaking through our woods!" Jeremy accused.

"We weren't sneaking!" the tinker said.

"We were chasing a dog!" the boy said.

"You lie!" Jonathan said, though the eagerness faded from his face.

"I am afraid he does not, Jonathan." Brandon's tone was gentle. "Those two are not my villains. I've never seen them before in my life."

"They aren't?" Jonathan asked.

"What a pip!" Jeremy exclaimed.

"Will you two young fools get off of us now?" the tinker asked.

"Yes," said Brandon, and looked at Rosalind with the most teasing of gazes. "I may at least save the tinker, may I not?"

"Be my guest, my Lord." Rosalind chuckled. Then she frowned and looked to that unfortunate individual. "What did the dog steal from you?"

"He stole my bird," the apprentice howled. "I've got me a pigeon and he stole it."

"Is that your dog?" the tinker asked.

"Yes, she is," Rosalind said. She looked to the apprentice. "Do not worry. She will not harm your bird. She just wants to be a mother."

"Then it's *your* dog, and these here are *your* children?" The tinker actually smiled. A rather interesting view, considering he was still flat on the ground beneath Jeremy.

"Yes," Rosalind nodded.

"They are mine," Brandon said at the same time.

Rosalind gasped and stared at him. "I beg your pardon!"

He grinned. "I figure I might as well proceed as I intend to have it."

Rosalind turned back to the tinker. "They are not his children. Jessica is not his dog."

"Why would you say we were your children?" Cassy asked, her brow puckered.

"Well I'll be hanged!" Jonathan said. "He wants to marry Rosalind."

"Zounds!" Jeremy exclaimed.

"He's proposing to Rosalind!" Cassy jumped up and down.

"I demand restitution," the tinker cried to Brandon.

"Do you mind if I marry her?" Brandon asked all at large.

A full pause ensued.

"I've no objections." The tinker was the first to speak. "But I warn you, I am going to go to the authorities about this . . ."

"I will buy all you wares sight unseen," Brandon offered smoothly.

"My Lord!" Rosalind gasped. "I shall buy his wares, not you."

"Sold to his Lordship and his Lady-ter-be," the tinker said.

"I think it would be rather nice," Rachel said in a cautious tone.

"Yes." The two other girls nodded.

"Sold." Brandon's eyes brimmed with laughter.

"What about my bird?" the apprentice cried. "I don't want to sell it."

"A hitch, my Lord." Rosalind laughed despite herself.

"Hold a moment," Jeremy said. "What about grandmother?"

"I have already asked her," Brandon said. "She did not say no."

"But she did not say yes, I'll wager," Rosalind parried.

"Well, no of course not. That is up to you."

"I am so glad to hear that." Rosalind laughed. "I was afraid for a moment that I didn't have a choice."

"You don't." He said it with confidence. He offered a slight bow. "I merely wish to make it an easy matter for you."

"Zeus!" Jonathan exclaimed. "You will be our brother-in-law, won't you?"

"Yes." Brandon nodded.

"In that case, my Lord . . ." Jonathan said.

"Call me Brandon . . ." Brandon smiled.

"Brandon." Jonathan grinned. "Will you teach me and Jeremy more about fisticuffs?"

"No," Rosalind exclaimed.

"No to what?" Brandon grinned.

The boys looked at her, in inquiry.

Rosalind threw up her hands. "No. No to it all!"

"There, now Jessica, your family this year is as large as it should be." Rosalind stood towering over the dog and her brood of chicks, kittens, one fox, and the newest addition, one pigeon. "Enough is enough."

Brandon's heart warmed as he watched her. "I believe Jessica and I agree in that respect. The more the better in a family. You still lack five, you know?"

"You both are too optimistic, I fear," Rosalind returned.

He frowned, a disquiet filling him. "Would you truly object to having more children? Cannot you find it in your heart to have perhaps three young Brandons, and two Rosalinds? Or we could have it the other way around. We could have three Rosalinds and two Brandons. Or would you prefer that they are perfect blends between the two of us . . ."

"Do stop." She chuckled.

"Only imagine . . ." He warmed to the subject.

"No, I cannot."

"Very well." Brandon frowned. He could no longer jest and found his voice thickening with intent. "Would you settle for three children? I am willing to compromise, Rosalind."

"How very kind of you, my Lord." Rosalind laughed. "That is more manageable, to be sure."

Brandon's heart raced. "Then it will be only three children as you wish."

"My Lord . . ." She stopped. Her eyes widened and she blinked. Then she shook her head quickly.

"What?" Brandon asked. She had taken on a far off look. "What is it?"

"Nothing." Rosalind's smile was weak. "Nothing at all."

"It must be something. You look as if you have seen a ghost."

"No. It is nothing, I assure you."

"Very well," Brandon said. "Then do let us return to my fantasy, which has been properly revised, only imagine if you will . . ."

"No," Rosalind said sharply.

Brandon frowned. Such was not Rosalind's manner. Then his heart leapt as understanding struck. It was there in her gaze. She *had* imagined it. She refused to meet his look directly, which was proof positive. She could not hide her thoughts and he loved her for it.

"My dear Rosalind!" Brandon strode over to her. She started and looked up at him with a beleaguered gaze. Chuckling, he pulled her into his arms and kissed her with full ardor. She stiffened but a moment, and then she melted into him.

Every time they kissed, there was no need to know who did the leading or the following, for it was something completely unified, something Brandon had never experienced with any other woman, and something he knew he would never have to seek from any other woman. Rosalind was his with each breath, touch, and embrace.

He drew back, shaken as much by that knowledge as from the hot blood thrumming through him. "Faith! But I cannot wait to marry."

"My Lord, I do not . . . !" Rosalind flushed deeply.

"Be quiet, dear." Brandon lowered his lips just above hers. He smiled in amusement. "Death by poison is not that bad a notion after all."

"What?" Rosalind whispered.

He claimed her lips and the wild sweetness of them. Fire flared through him and the need to know her completely. That forced him to draw back. Then step back. "Faith, but you are hard to resist. Poison. I must think on that."

Rosalind stared at him. Her gaze was passion dazed, her manner rather bereft. How he wished to take her back into his arms, to make her completely sure of his love. He knew better. Surely, he knew better. "Poison. Why do you think my kiss poison?"

"I do not. Indeed, I'm sure it would be the antidote." He moved toward her, for her wrinkled brow was his undoing. "Hang it. If I am to be poisoned and die, you need only to kiss me, Rosalind, and I shall be brought back to life."

"I am not a hand at this." Her voice showed confusion. "But I do not see how talk of poison and death should be considered conducive to it all."

Brandon laughed as he put his arms about her once more. Faith, but it was right, so very right. "Your grandmother vowed she would poison me if I dared to seduce you."

"She did!" Rosalind stiffened. Her face paled.

He rocked her gently, cherishing the gesture. "Though that is not why I refrain. I would never dishonor you, Rosalind, and I would not have you even think it."

Rosalind scrambled from his arms, leaving him bereft now.

"Rosalind?"

Her chest rose and fell with fast breaths. "You should not kiss me, Brandon. I mean, my Lord."

"You mean Brandon." Brandon paused. "You are afraid of your grandmother, are you not?"

"No, of course not." Rosalind smiled. For a moment it appeared she told the truth. "I merely possess a strong respect for her."

"Faith." Brandon attempted to lighten the heavy atmosphere. "Here I thought you only feared God."

"I do only fear God." Rosalind's natural calm and poise was returning. ". . . and steer clear of Grandmother."

Brandon suddenly realized what dragon it was that he needed to slay for Rosalind. "She'll not frighten me off, Rosalind. That is what she has done to the other men, isn't it?"

"No." Color returned to her face. "There were never any that cared enough to cross her." A glint entered her gaze. "You truly are the only one that has pressed for my hand."

"Then kiss me, Rosalind," Brandon said with determination. This dragon was not going to come between them. "Now."

"No, I shan't," she said firmly.

"Your grandmother has changed," Brandon said. "No matter her past, she has changed."

"Leopards don't . . ."

"Change their spots," Brandon said gently. "But they do grow up. Now kiss me. Take a chance. I am willing to do so, and it is my life after all."

"That is the difference between you and me. You are a risk taker." She smiled. "Besides, it is fine for you to say such things, but only imagine my quandary to have a dead Lord of the Realm upon the premises."

He barked a laugh.

"Rosalind! Lord Laith!" Rachel's voice called out to them from the stable.

"We are here!" Rosalind called out.

Rachel arrived at the stall's entrance, frowning.

"Faith, I can tell the look." Brandon sighed. "What trouble have the boys gotten into now?"

"Is it Jessica?" Rosalind asked.

"No, it is Jonathan and Jeremy," Rachel said.

Rosalind raised her brow. She nodded to Brandon. "Your trick, my Lord."

He grinned. "I know boys. I was one once."

"They have caught another villain."

"Not another one!" Rosalind groaned.

"I do not think the man is anything but what he says he is."

"What does he say he is?"

"The butcher from town."

"Gads!" Brandon laughed. "I will go and tend to this, since I make no headway here."

Rosalind's face flushed. Brandon brightened considerably. He strode off, determined to help her in every way possible until she knew she could depend upon him completely.

Four

"You look tired," Brandon said, his gaze upon her, from across the breakfast table. The children had left quite early for an expedition to the village.

"Only slightly," Rosalind said. She was tired. Ever since four days and four more villains ago, she hadn't really slept. It was not the exorbitant amount of money that Brandon was paying out in regard to the boys. It was a certain mental picture that appeared before her eyes at odd moments and in her dreams. Indeed, it was a painting. In it, she and Brandon posed together, she sitting and he standing, with his hand upon her shoulder. Six children of various sizes and ages posed with them.

She sighed in exasperation.

"What is bedeviling you?"

"The children," Rosalind murmured. She knew that it was Brandon's silly chatter about having five children that had prompted her imagination to take whimsical flight. That did not disturb her. Yet why in heaven's name had she added a sixth child to the portrait, and why did two of the boys look like Brandon, while the third looked like her father? And why did one of the girls look like her, one look like her grandmother, and one look like Brandon?

Brandon chuckled. "They are doing a bang-up job of capturing the neighborhood hereabouts, aren't they? It shall pass, no doubt. Pray, do not let it tax you."

"No. I shall not." Rosalind shook her head to clear her straying thoughts. The simple and appalling truth was that

Brandon's talk of marriage was beginning to affect her. She had never been wooed before and therefore had never known the strong effect it could have on even the most reasonable of ladies.

Yet she had been raised to be far more discerning in the matters of the heart than her grandmother or mother before her. Having both their examples set before her, how could she have not been so? Both had warned her of the missteps of romance. Her mother had chosen well and reasonably, and had had a faithful and fortunate marriage because of that. Yet she had admitted to boredom far too often.

Her grandmother had had three marriages and her advice on such matters was overwhelming, to say the least. Though no one in the family would have ever asked her directly about her husband's deaths, the underlying question was always there. Had she killed her husbands? She had never denied murder, and at certain times would allude to the fact of it.

Rosalind forced a smile. Faith, it was time for her to put such thoughts aside for they could be nothing but defeating. Marriage simply did not have as much to offer as many were wont to think. She thanked the Almighty regularly for blessing her with wealth and a full family of such that she had no need to seek it in marriage. "Now, what were we talking about?"

"I don't know." Brandon's eyes lit with amusement. "But I vow, I would give my fortune to know what has your sweet mind in a whirl, for surely you are in a brown study."

Rosalind laughed. "You have already given that fortune away to pay off the boys' victims."

"True."

"Madame," Rosalind's butler stepped into the breakfast room. "There is a gentleman here wishing to speak to you. He seems highly irate, I fear."

"Gracious. I shall go and see him."

"I'm here, I am!" A small man charged into the room. His lined and reddened face was aggrieved. There could be no other word for it.

"That will be all, Thompson." Rosalind nodded and turned her direction to the man. "Sir, how may I help you?"

"I can't find your hellion brothers anywhere. Your butler says they shall be gone for the day. I can't have that, I tell you. I can't!"

"Really? Why is it so important that you see them?" Brandon asked. "Faith, most individuals in the vicinity are wisely attempting to avoid them."

"That they might. But I have to pay my landlady this eve and I want to be caught by them quick. I have no time to waste."

"What?" Rosalind gasped.

"Faith." Brandon's eyes gleamed. "But of course. You have heard that you shall be paid off if they catch you, have you not?"

"Of course I have. It's my turn, it is. I won the lottery at the Bores Inn all right and tight. But after today someone else will jump my claim, I'll lay odds. Now I've looked all over for those boys. What are they doing leaving at a time like this?"

Rosalind looked to Brandon. "You've been had, my Lord."

"So it seems." Brandon's eyes showed deep amusement. It was a wonderful trait of his, that he never became angry, and indeed always chose to see the enjoyment of life rather than the displeasure that many would. His look turned speculative, wickedly so. "I say, old man, how would you like to make triple what you expected to make with the boys capturing you?"

The man licked his lips. "What would I have to do?"

"You would have to take a blow or two, that is all."

"What?" Rosalind gasped.

The little man actually nodded in pleasure. "Good. Good. I was trying to figure out how I could go back with the ready and nothing to show for it. But I simply have to have it. I'm not leaving anything to chance."

"Either am I." Brandon rose. "We shall attend to that part of the business outside. However, when you return to the village I want you to bruit it about that I turned you up short. You weren't paid for anything. Furthermore, Miss Treemont has turned as cross as crabs and vows to bring the next trespasser upon her land up on charges."

The man grinned. "I sees what you want, m'Lord. That I can do quite deedily, I promise. Especially if you triple my pay. Then I can pay the landlady and have enough for drink fer the next sennight, I will."

"If you will excuse us, Miss Treemont." Brandon nodded to her and the two men left the breakfast room.

Rosalind sat and waited for Brandon's return, partly stunned, partly amused. When he returned, his smile showed devilish satisfaction. "Well, I believe we have spiked Jonathan and Jeremy's guns. As well as the denizen at the Inn."

"I would think so." Rosalind chuckled.

At that moment they heard voices from outside the room. Then, lo and behold, Jonathan and Jeremy entered.

Rosalind well nigh choked on her laughter. "Heavens. What are you two doing here? We thought you were gone to the village for the day."

Jonathan grinned. "We gave the girls and Mrs. Johnson the slip."

"We came back to keep a watch out for your villains," Jeremy said with great importance. "Got to be on guard, what?"

"Who wants to kick about in the village when one can be here?" Jonathan concurred.

"Star crossed lovers, I would say," Brandon murmured sotto voce.

"Indeed." Rosalind laughed before she could stop herself.

Brandon managed to keep a straight face far better than she. "Only too true, gentlemen."

"What did you say before? And why is Rosalind laughing?" Jonathan frowned.

"Oh, it was nothing you would care for." Brandon said,

his voice bland. "I had been telling her a joke before you entered, that is all."

"Well, why stop then?" Jonathan said. "You can tell us."

"No." Brandon said. "It is a secret joke. One between just your sister and me."

"Here, now." Jeremy said. "What kind of joke did you tell her that you couldn't tell us? It wasn't improper, was it?"

"No. It was simply something that should be shared between adults," Brandon said solemnly.

Rosalind smiled. "That is the truth."

"Well, I don't think that fair," Jonathan said, indignation strong in every feature. "Here we are, doing all that we can to protect you, and you won't let us in on your secret joke."

"Ungrateful I would say," Jeremy said.

"Very well. The joke is from the pen of Shakespeare," Brandon said.

"What?" Jonathan asked with alarm.

"Oh no, that's that fellow," Jeremy said with dismay. "That writer chap we were suppose to learn about."

"Gads." Jonathan jumped. "Thought his name was familiar."

"We got to go," Jeremy said. "Best start looking for your villains."

"Yeh." Jonathan waved a staying hand. "You two keep telling each other all that chap's jokes. You are right, just keep those a secret between the two of you. We'll be going."

The two boys were gone from the breakfast room in a wink.

"My Lord, you are simply Machiavellian," Rosalind observed.

"Machiavellian? Oh no, not that chap too?" Brandon's imitation of Jeremy was precise. "I say, keep that a secret, won't you?"

Rosalind let her delight free in laughter. Brandon's deeper chuckles only refreshed her own. The thought passed through her mind then, clean and pure. No one—not her mother, not her grandmother—had ever told her how very nice it was to share laughter and a secret with an adult man whose thoughts were similar to hers, and who understood her.

She couldn't help thinking that surely was the best basis for marriage that she had ever imagined.

Brandon watched Rosalind from across the breakfast table. It was a pleasure. The children had already set off for a foray into the woods for berries. The day lay ahead of them. "What is on your schedule for today?"

Rosalind's eyes turned dreamy, a look he enjoyed. "I do not know. It is odd, but I cannot think of one particular task that is of any importance."

Brandon nodded. After two weeks of effort, he fully expected the answer. Rosalind ran Treemont with great ease. Yet Brandon had quickly found the areas she didn't manage well and had applied himself to them most quietly and readily.

She turned those beautiful aquamarine eyes upon him. "What shall we do?"

Brandon strove not to lean over and kiss her right there over the coffee cups. Rosalind hadn't noticed it, to be sure, but he did. She said *we* naturally and unconsciously.

"I do not know. What *shall* we do?" He acted as if he was in deep meditation. If he had his way they would take the carriage to a quiet setting for love.

"Rosalind!" Cassy's voice shouted from outside the breakfast room. "My Lord!"

"Rosalind!" Both Rachel's and Ellen's voices chorused.

"Gracious!" Rosalind said, her face surprised. "We haven't had one alarm for a well nigh on a week."

"We do now," Brandon muttered, instinct telling him that his plans might just be on the way to being cancelled.

"Rosalind!" Cassy burst into the breakfast room. "Come quick. You must come quick."

"The boys have caught your villains, my Lord!" Rachel said as she entered behind with Ellen.

"Who are they this time?" Brandon asked her.

"I am not quite sure, my Lord," Rachel said. "But they are quite poor sports. When Jonathan and Jeremy came upon them at the stables they did not resist a jot."

"Hurry!" Ellen squealed. "Hurry!"

"Someone didn't get the message apparently." Brandon sighed. Forcing a smile, he rose and offered his arm to Rosalind. "Shall we go see the latest marvel in the way of villains, Madame?"

"Certainly." Rosalind laughed and rose to place her arm in his. "Though I do believe these villains should be paid from my purse this time."

The girls squealed once more and ran ahead. Brandon and Rosalind proceeded at a slower pace. He decided not to give up hope. "After this, could we perhaps take the coach and go for a private luncheon, just the two of us?"

Rosalind looked up at him as they left the house, her eyes flaring with anticipation. "Indeed, My Lord, I believe I would like that."

Brandon had not thought it would be so easy. He found he could not resist asking. "You sound far more adventurous than I had anticipated. Dare I hope that you have grown to trust me more? Or is it that you have you decided your grandmother wouldn't poison me because of a mere kiss?"

A flush painted her cheeks. "I believe it is a bit of both. Perhaps I am considering your notion that your spots, respectively, have worn a bit thinner than I first thought."

"Music to my ears." He winked at her and led her across the expanse of lawn toward the stables. The girls had turned the corner and were gone from sight, though not from hearing, their excited calls and chatter like a beacon. "I shall make a great addition to your household, sweet Rosalind. I promise."

Her flush deepened. "Though I do not wish you to kiss me, my Lord, if I do go with you upon this jaunt."

"No, indeed," Brandon said with deep sincerity. "I do not intend to do so. I want your trust as well as your love.

Unless you believe completely in me as I do in you, I know we cannot marry."

"Thank you, my Lord," was all Rosalind said.

He halted a moment, smiling sardonically down upon her. "Of course, I will own that my belief in you is far simpler than your belief in me. But I am not an average leopard. I will never be dangerous to you, Rosalind." He shook his head. "No matter what I say sometimes to the contrary, it shall and must be your decision. I shall abide by it and I will not press you."

"Once again, thank you, my Lord." Rosalind's eyes actually twinkled now. "To stand and deliver so early in the day is far too demanding I admit."

"Very well, sweet vixen." Brandon chuckled. "Not another serious word shall I speak. Let us join the children, else they will be quite displeased."

A tension suddenly crossed Rosalind's features and she looked swiftly about. "Yes, we must hurry."

"What is it?" Brandon frowned. Before she answered, the tension rose within him. The reason was obvious. "Blast, it is far too quiet."

He let loose her arm and they both lengthened their stride. He and Rosalind turned the corner of the stables at the same moment. He bit back a curse at both the scene and Rosalind's frightened gasp. Instinctively, his fists clenched.

The three girls stood in a huddle, deadly silent, their gazes all fixed as if mesmerized upon two men. They were, indeed, his two villains. They held their pistols upon Jonathan and Jeremy.

"Hello, Brandon," Jonathan said, his face twisting in misery. "Sorry about this."

"We were caught by surprise." Jeremy grimaced. "None of the other chaps had pistols."

"It's all right," Brandon said with a reassuring smile.

"No it ain't!" The first villain said staunchly. " 'Cause we will use these poppers if we have ter, don't you think otherwise."

"We ain't suppose ter kill him, Casper," the other said. "I keep telling you that."

"Blast it, Seth. I told you not to use my name in front of our victims," Casper growled. "How many times do I have to tell you that?"

"I forgot." He blinked. "And you just used my name."

"I did not," Casper bellowed.

"Did too," Seth muttered, flushing up.

"Seth is right, Casper, you did," Brandon said.

"I did?" He looked belligerent. "Well I wouldn't have if the numbskull had done what he was suppose ter do and guard my back while I locked up your bloody dog."

"I did guard your back," Seth muttered. "They caught me by surprise."

"The dog is not mine," Brandon said.

"The dog is mine," Rosalind said.

"Why would you wish to lock up our dog?" It was Rachel who spoke in a calm voice.

"Because your dog is fierce," Seth said. "That's why, Missy."

"It bit me in the arse, I mean, in the bum," Casper said.

"Enough talking. We are taking you, my Lord! We are going ter get our money, confound it!"

"Who is going to give it to you?" Jeremy asked.

"Why, that gentleman that talked to us," Casper said.

"Hold your gaff," Seth ordered. "We ain't going ter talk about that."

"Yeh. And we ain't going to conk you on yer head either," Casper said. Clearly he thought himself clever. "So don't think we'll fall fer that trick of yours."

"Trick?" Brandon frowned. "What trick?"

"Trying to gull us again," Seth snorted. "Well, we ain't that green."

"Not anymore we ain't." Casper grinned, gap-toothed.

Brandon frowned. "I truly do not know what you are talking about."

"Right!" Casper said. "You didn't pretend ter be unconscious like, only ter sneak away when yer dog attacked us."

"Jessica attacked you?" Rosalind exclaimed.

"Jolly good of Jessica," Jonathan exclaimed.

"Her bite wasn't jolly good, I'll have you know," Casper said. "And himself sneaking off on us with his horse when we thought him out cold was low down."

"I don't think so," Rachel said. "I think it terribly clever."

"I do not remember it." Brandon shook his head. "I am sorry for such er . . . delirious behavior, but I was not conscious of it at the time."

"Go on with yer!" Seth said.

"No. It is true," Rosalind said. "He is a rather different man when he is unconscious."

"Well, he left us fair be-twattled," Casper said, aggrieved. "When a man is down, he's suppose ter stay down. And he shouldn't have left us with his biting dog the way he did either."

"Forgive me for doing that. However, you need not fear that this time. I am conscious now." Brandon said it quickly. It seemed that Casper was working himself into a true grudge. "If you will permit the young gentlemen to go free, I will be your captive. You may take me where ever you wish. You want me, and the gentleman will pay you for me, is it not true?"

"I know. I know. I ain't dumb," Seth said, his tone indignant. "I was just about to suggest that, I was."

"Yeh. He's up to all the rigs," Casper said. Then his eyes crossed. "How we going to do this, Seth?"

"Easy. You hold yer pistol on both of the young whelps." Seth ordered. "And I'll hold mine on Himself. Got it?"

"Got it." Casper grinned. He promptly waved his pistol in a wild arc. Seth yelped, unprepared for such swift action. Jonathan, from whom the pistol had swung away, moved even more swiftly. He rammed his elbow into Casper's stomach. Casper groaned as his pistol discharged. The shot went off wild.

Brandon growled and sprung at the doubled-over man.

"Stop!" Seth swung his pistol toward Brandon. The girls all shrieked.

"No!" said Rosalind and lunged toward Seth.

"Blimey!" Seth, shocked, swung the pistol in her direction. Brandon roared in fear and rage and kicked out at him. Seth fell back and his pistol discharged into the blue of the sky.

"Run, Casper!" Seth said without one jot of bravery. His order was too late. Casper was already running in a crouched lope toward the waiting horses. Seth proved to be an amazingly fast runner. Indeed, he reached the horses at the same time as Casper, though, granted, his course had been easily open, since there was confusion within the Treemont clan. The boys were hampered by the girls, who ran toward them, screaming. The boys were forced to disengage from them before they could give chase to the men.

The girls immediately ran to Rosalind, who was standing stock still, the oddest expression upon her face. Rosalind looked to Brandon as she put her arms about the girls, her gaze as one totally stunned. Brandon's heart wrenched in pain, such was her look of fright.

"Do not let them, my Lord," she said softly.

"Jonathan and Jeremy, stop!" Brandon raised his voice, ignoring his own thought of following Seth and Casper. "Let them go!"

"What!" Jeremy and Jonathan paused, giving Seth and Casper their chance to mount their horses.

"Let them go!" he repeated.

"Blimey!" This came from Seth.

"Aw!" Jonathan complained.

"You sister wants it. Now come back here!" Brandon said sternly, while he himself strove to deny the blood lust thrumming through him at the same moment. It took all of his power to stay still as the two men, the knowledge of their freedom dawning upon their faces, took full advantage and spurred their horses into a gallop.

Only turning his gaze back to Rosalind gave him the strength. He smiled. "I'm sorry."

Her smile wavered pitifully. "That is all right," she said, yet what lurked in her eyes frightened Brandon.

"I can't believe it," Jonathan complained, stalking back, his expression one of complete disgust. "We had them in the palms of our hands."

"No, we didn't," Brandon said, since it appeared Rosalind would not or could not speak. "It would have been far too dangerous with the ladies present. Now, please take the children to the house." He drew a deep breath. He wished to comfort Rosalind, just as she was comforting the girls who clung to her, but instinctively knew that he would not be permitted to do so. "I am going to follow them."

"What!" Jonathan cried. "Don't we get to go with you?"

"No. You must remain here and guard the family."

"Blast. That won't be any adventure."

"I certainly hope not. Haven't you had enough danger for the moment?"

"I promise after I have caught them and dealt with them properly, I shall return to you." He turned his gaze to Rosalind, his love flaring within him. "I promise."

"No." She finally spoke. Her gaze turned anguished, but determined. "You need not return, my Lord."

"What?" Jonathan asked.

"Why?" Jeremy asked, frowning.

The girls all added their objections. Only Brandon did not. This time he could not find it in himself to speak.

"He may write you of his exploits," Rosalind said. She looked away. "That will suffice."

"But what did he do wrong?" Jonathan, true to youth, asked it with anger.

"She does not need to explain herself, Jonathan," Brandon said. Faith, what hadn't he done wrong in his past? He looked at her, her arms spread protectively about the girls that had been threatened because of him. "My presence here can be nothing but dangerous."

"Yes," Rosalind said, her voice choked. "Precisely."

"But how are you going to marry him, Rosalind, if he doesn't come back?" Cassy clearly frowned at the logistics.

"We are not going to marry." Rosalind looked directly at Brandon again. The resolve in her gaze did not waver.

Brandon's heart failed him. She had been forced to stand and deliver this morning whether either of them wished it or not. And she was delivering. She would not trust him. She would not love him. She would not wed him.

Anger filled him. Anger at himself. Why should she, after all? Who ever had sent those men after him, no doubt had a just cause to do so. He wanted to believe he wasn't really a leopard, but why wasn't he? Nothing proved otherwise. He probably couldn't change.

Rosalind already lived with one leopard in the family, why should she volunteer for another? "I understand. Your wish is my command." He bowed low to her and then turned, striding away without saying anything more and before Rosalind said any more. He already despised himself enough. To hear more from her lips would not be necessary.

Five

Rosalind sat in solitary splendor in the breakfast room. The children had already eaten and departed. She attempted to focus upon what she should do for the day. Only, she didn't want to do anything.

Except cry, perhaps. Faith, how her heart ached. She missed Brandon. She missed him especially now. With whom was she to plan the day? With whom was she to discuss matters? There was no laughter to share. No secrets to tell.

She tried to tell herself to be strong. She tried to tell herself that this would be a passing thing that she must fight through. After all, surely it could not be as frightful as that moment when that villain had pointed his pistol at Brandon. At that moment, Rosalind's entire world had come crashing down upon her.

She had discovered in a split second, a new dimension in her spirit that she had never known existed. It was a dimension that loved more deeply than she could have ever imagined. Its revelation was shattering.

All of it had been danger. Danger if she loved Brandon to that degree. Danger to her family that had faded for a moment in her fear for him. Danger to the blessed life that she knew and enjoyed.

Her mother and her grandmother had warned her this could happen, of course. So she had tried to pick up the pieces as quickly as she could. She had sent Brandon away knowing it was the best way to protect all involved. To protect her and the children. Indeed, Brandon himself. After all, if he survived the gentleman that was after him, he might not survive her grandmother. He jested, but Rosalind's grandmother was not an enemy to make.

This was what she had told herself for the past three days.

Only, new evidence was presenting itself. New pieces of the picture that she could not deny. She might very well be in more danger than she had first surmised. She was in danger of her heart never mending. She was in danger of losing an even fuller and more wonderful life than she now had. It seemed to whisper through her mind that if she refused this great love, her life would forever be less and never more.

She sipped her tea and her hand shook. Faith, what had she done, turning Brandon away? Everything her mother and grandmother had said did not matter anymore to her. Their lives were theirs alone. Hers was hers. For all the wisdom they had imparted, she could hope to employ it, but surely add her own to it as well.

She set her cup down. Was she being reasonable? Could she truly believe in a love that had sprung up so fully, so quickly?

She smiled. Why not? Nothing had been reasonable in this entire time. It had not been reasonable the way Brandon had come to them. It had not been reasonable how he had looked at her and swore immediately that he would marry her. He had jested that it was their destiny.

Now Rosalind didn't think it a jest. That was far more reasonable to assume than anything else, because love was reasonable. Fear was not. Not in the grand and glorious scheme of life.

Rosalind lifted the bell and rang for Thompson. She sipped her tea far more calmly. She also gave him orders to prepare the coach and to send Tilly, her maid, to her. Not even a tinge of a qualm arose. The peace within her told her that she had just grasped her destiny by the coattail.

By heaven, she would hold on to it. Chuckling, she

leaned back and truly enjoyed her tea. Faith, it tasted so much better now. Though her mind did race. She now considered the exact opposite of the coin. Her love was impetuous. When Brandon had left, his face was as resigned and determined as hers. Nor had they received any sort of missive from him.

She had best move as swiftly as possible before he did something life-changing, like becoming engaged to Miss Fancot. She could not count upon Brandon to sit about, not chasing his dream. She knew without a doubt that love could overcome all obstacles, but if she could avoid certain obstacles, she would.

"Hah! There you are!" said Lady Wroxeter as she entered the breakfast room, her cane tapping.

"Grandmother!" Rosalind exclaimed. Speak about obstacles! "What are you doing here?"

"I figured since you wouldn't come and see me, I would come and see you." She came to the table and lowered herself into a chair.

Rosalind raised her brow. "I would have come to see you if I had known that was your wish." Amazing, of a sudden, she was looking forward to breaking the tether of her dread of Lady Wroxeter. She would marry and her grandmother wouldn't dare to hurt Brandon. Here was the dragon to be slain! Brandon had sought to do so for her, but Rosalind knew it was something she must do herself.

"Well, yes. You are an obedient child." Lady Wroxeter pursed her lips. "Rosalind, it is time for me to tell you something."

"No, Grandmother. I believe it is time for *me* to tell you something."

"Let me talk," said her grandmother, her voice short and querulous.

"Very well." Rosalind nodded. Lady Wroxeter was the elder. "As you wish."

Lady Wroxeter drew in a deep breath. "I need to tell you and tell you right now. I never killed my husbands. I never killed anyone."

"What?" Rosalind strove hard to keep her jaw from dropping. One should not look so very astonished at such a disclosure, after all. Yet she was, completely so. Lady Wroxeter stared at her in expectation. Rosalind stumbled to say something. "That is good to know. Er . . . very good to know." She shook her head in bemusement. "But, but why have you never said this before?"

"Because I have been a coward, that is why," Lady Wroxeter said. "When my first husband passed and the rumor began to spread, people became afraid of me. I gained a reputation. It was power. Life became easier for me for no one wished to cross me. Then my second husband met with another accident that looked suspicious and my position was complete."

Rosalind stared at her grandmother. She was not a dragon to be slain after all. She was merely a woman who had tried to make it through life as best she could. Faults a-plenty to be sure, but just a woman. Rosalind sighed. She truly saw her grandmother for the first time.

The dragon had been her fear of her grandmother and not her grandmother herself. With that, a sudden question crossed her mind. "Why are you telling me this now?"

"Because confession is supposed to be good for the soul, confound it." She sounded frightfully disgruntled.

"I see." Rosalind's lips twitched.

"And . . ." Lady Wroxeter looked away. "I don't want you to be afraid of me anymore. I've . . . I am afraid I have ruined your life. Ruined your chance to love. Just because my experiences with men were not all they should have been, it doesn't mean that yours should not be good. You already know how to love. It is no small thing, that talent, child. I don't like to admit it often, but the unvarnished truth is I didn't have one clue about how to love. When I got married I was completely at sea. After all, in fashionable marriages you weren't suppose to need to love." She snorted. "Faith, but I was naive. Now you, you love everyone so far as I can tell, so I don't see why adding one more to your list should hurt you one jot."

"You mean Brandon?"

"I mean Brandon." Lady Wroxeter nodded.

Rosalind chuckled. "If I add him, I won't be adding just one. I will be adding six more to the list. He wishes to have five more children."

Lady Wroxeter waved a hand. "Five, six, what does it matter? The more the merrier." She drew in an obvious breath. "Well, Rosalind. Now you know the truth about me. I—I won't stand in the way if you wish to marry Brandon."

"I see," Rosalind murmured.

Her maid, Tilly, entered the room at that moment. She dipped a curtsy. "Mr. Thompson said you wished to see me?"

"Yes, Tilly," Rosalind said. "I wish you to start packing for a journey to London. I shall be there for a few days. I do not care much what you pack just as long as you do it speedily. I wish to catch My Lord Laith before he decides to propose to another lady."

"Yes m-mum," Tilly stammered and quickly left the room.

If the look on her maid's face was comical, the look on Lady Wroxeter's was in the realms of divine farce.

Indeed, she remained silent for a goodly minute. Then she lifted a brow. "What did you just do?"

Rosalind smiled. "That is what I wanted to tell you before. I love Brandon and I am going to marry him. I had already ordered the coach before you entered."

Lady Wroxeter's mouth fell open. "You mean that I . . . I just confessed for no good reason?"

"Yes."

Lady Wroxeter looked toward heaven. "That was not fair. Not fair at all. I was gulled into it."

"But confession is good for the soul." Rosalind laughed.

"Yes, yes it is," Lady Wroxeter said.

Rosalind started, for such a sweet smile like she had never seen before crossed her grandmother's lips.

"Besides," Rosalind said as she rose, "it will save me from the rest of the speech where I was going to tell you that you could not frighten me anymore. And that if you dared to hurt Brandon I would have to do something dreadful."

"Like what?"

"I don't know." Rosalind laughed.

"No, no. That is no way to threaten people," Lady Wroxeter said, then she paused. She flushed. "Faith, you don't need that kind of advice one jot. Now do make haste and catch the lad."

"You truly do want me to marry him," Rosalind gasped in full realization.

"Yes," said Lady Wroxeter. "I want all those grandchildren you've been talking about. I want to see you happily married to a loving mate. It is my absolution, child. I don't deserve it, but I'm glad of it. Now do make haste. Go catch your man. He's your destiny, child, and I have that on good authority."

"I do not see why we cannot go with you!" Jonathan objected with force.

"Do you not?" Rosalind smiled and gazed about at her family. She then looked pointedly at the waiting coach. "We would all be rather cramped do you not think?"

"There is no time for your complaints, young man," Lady Wroxeter said. "Do not detain your sister."

"Stop! Stop!" A voice cried out.

Rosalind looked up in surprise. Peters came running up. "Please, Miss Rosalind. Don't go get that lord. *It's* gone and that is the way it should be."

Lady Wroxeter tapped her cane upon the ground. "Don't be insubordinate, Peters! Faith, if I am not going to stop her, you best not try. Else I will . . ." She grimaced. "Oh, confound it. I don't know what I will do."

Rosalind laughed, her heart filling with excitement. She turned to go. However, the thunder of horses' hooves stopped her. She halted. A coach was advancing toward them from the side road. Its speed was alarming.

"Lud! What now?" Lady Wroxeter exclaimed in exasperation.

Rosalind felt very much the same. She maintained her composure, however, as the coach drew up before them. She recognized its coat of arms. It was that of the Fancot's family. Her heart raced. She wasn't sure she wanted to receive any news from that quarter.

As the driver jumped down from the box, a shout was heard. A lone rider appeared now, waving a hand and crying out. Clearly he was in desperate pursuit.

"Just what in blazes is going on?" Lady Wroxeter barked.

The door to the coach opened and a petite and teary-eyed blonde tumbled out. She appeared slightly stunned by the crowd watching her, but it did not deter her. "Please . . . please, may I see Lord Laith? I must see him. I must confess. I cannot bare the guilt anymore. I must make restitution."

"Gads. For what, you ninny?" Lady Wroxeter asked before anyone else could react.

She reared back. "I—I beg your pardon?"

"You shouldn't be here, Amelia Fancot," Lady Wroxeter said, her tone stern. "Have you no consideration or respect?"

"Forgive me. I know that his Lordship is at death's door. That . . . that he contracted scarlet fever from his weakened condition . . ."

"What?" Rosalind asked, nonplussed. She looked to Lady Wroxeter, who appeared to have some understanding of it all.

She shrugged pettishly. "Very well, I embellished somewhat when I wrote the Fancots about Brandon. You know how I detest company."

The lone horseman arrived by this time. He sprang from his steed. Short of stature, he wore a bright peacock blue wasp-waist jacket. "Do not do it, Amelia! I shall confess. It is all my fault!"

"No." Amelia broke into fresh sobs. "I asked you to do it."

"Do what?" Rosalind asked in confusion.

"I sent the two men who shot and beat Lord Laith," she sobbed.

"No, I did. I sent them. I vow it," he persisted. "I sent them. No one else did. I did."

"Very well. You did," said Lady Wroxeter. "But just who are you, Sirrah?"

"My name is Lord Fargate," he said. He lifted a rather weak chin. "And I am in love with Amelia."

"Horace only sent those two men because I asked him to do so." Amelia's voice rose in hysteria. "It was my notion. It is all my fault."

"Do calm yourself," Rosalind said soothingly. The child was close to fainting.

"Calm herself? Rot," Lady Wroxeter said. "Loosen your budget, girl. Why did you send those men after Lord Laith?"

"Because I didn't wish to marry him." She broke into a fresh squall of tears.

"Why didn't you simply tell Lord Laith, No?" Rosalind asked. Logic required her to do so.

"Because she is a Cheltenham tragedy miss, I'll wager," Lady Wroxeter said.

"My father told me he would *force* me to marry him. He vowed to lock me in my room and feed me on bread and water until I agreed." Her eyes began to roll dangerously. "But . . . I could not. Lord Laith wants . . . wants. . . ." She hid her face in her hands and broke into uncontrollable sobs.

Lord Fargate put his arm about her. "Don't cry, my love."

"Wants to what?" Lady Wroxeter raised an interested brow.

"Grandmother, do not press the child," Rosalind said.

"Well, what depraved thing does the lad want of her? You best learn about it now, Rosalind."

"He wants children," she sobbed. "T-ten of them!"

"Gracious," Rosalind gasped, "I was right after all."

"Right about what?" Lady Wroxeter asked.

"When he told me that he wanted ten children I told him it surely had to be Amelia who had sent the men after him." She shook her head. "At the time I was speaking in jest."

Lady Wroxeter peered at Amelia. "Hmm. You have more sense than I thought, girl. I doubt you can manage one child, let alone ten. You ain't good breeding stock."

Amelia shuddered. Lord Fargate puffed out his chest. "I will not permit it. I will kill Lord Laith before that happens."

"So you did order Seth and Casper to kill Lord Laith?" Rosalind asked.

Lord Fargate flushed red. "No. No. I never ordered them to do that. I mean . . . that I shall enter into a duel of honor with Lord Laith. I bent to my love's wishes and hired those men to abduct Lord Laith. They were to take him and put him on a ship for the Americas so that he would be out of the way until I could convince Amelia's father that I am a proper candidate for her hand."

"That was your plan?" Lady Wroxeter asked Amelia.

"Yes. I would never have hurt Lord Laith. It is not his fault that he adores me."

"Sound's toddyheaded," Rachel said.

"Rachel." Rosalind said, "respect your elders."

"She's right," said Lady Wroxeter. "Glad I'm the elder here because respecting that chit would stick in my craw. And I'm glad Brandon didn't marry her. The world don't need ten more want-wits like her."

"No, he will never marry my dear Amelia," Lord Fargate said. "I shall challenge him to a duel."

"Well, you will just have to wait. Lord Laith isn't here," Rosalind said. "Only permit me to go to him and I shall relay your message."

"That's my girl. Now be off with you." Lady Wroxeter waved her hand. "I'll take care of Miss Widgeon and Lord Popinjay."

"At least I know he hasn't become engaged yet."
Rosalind smiled in relief. She turned toward the coach. Yet
two more shouts, but from another direction, occurred.

"Just go, girl," said Lady Wroxeter. "This day is full of
too much infernal ruckus and rumpus."

Rosalind knew she should proceed, but curiosity lured
her into looking. Curiosity got a flabbergasted eyeful. Casper and Seth were pounding toward them, their hands raised
high in the air. Disheveled and wearing twigs and vines,
they appeared to be on their last legs.

"Hello! There are those two villains now," Jonathan announced rather unnecessarily.

Only Lady Wroxeter peered at them. "Ha! Idiots if I've
ever seen any. Lord Popinjay, you are a clodpole."

It said much for the oddity of the situation that Lord
Fargate did not object. As the two came to a puffing stop
before them, his refusal to defend himself was far too understandable.

"Wh-what are you doing here?" Amelia turned pale.

"Bloody hell! You mean what are *you* doing here?" Seth
panted.

"Yes," Casper said. "Don't seem right you paying a social call on the man you want to kill."

"Yes, you blundering fools." Lord Fargate stiffened.
"You weren't suppose to kill Lord Laith! I never ordered
you to do that."

"I told you that Casper," Seth growled. "But you never
listen."

"I do too. Only, well I shot at him out of self defense,
and I'll confess it. He scared me." Casper turned desperate
eyes to Rosalind. "And he's still scaring me. Will you help
us? He's after us."

"Do you mean Lord Laith?" Rosalind said.

"Ha!" Lady Wroxeter grinned. "It saves you the journey,
girl."

"Please, Missus, save us from him will you?" Seth said.
"He's been after us for three days. We are gutfounded."

"He'll listen to you," Casper said.

"Why should he do that?" said Lady Wroxeter

Casper shook his head. "I don't know. But he did the last time. And he won't kill us in front of the children, that I know."

"You have a point." Rosalind smiled, though her heart began to pound. She looked from whence they had come. To be sure, Brandon appeared, riding his horse at a slow, meandering pace. He rode directly up to the enclave. His gaze moved across them all with a precision void of his usual humor.

Rosalind's throat constricted as he did not pause to meet her gaze.

"What is going on here?" He frowned, directing his look to Casper and Seth. "You have bungled again. I didn't follow you for three days straight for you to lead me back here. I had hoped you would lead me to your employer."

"But they did!" Cassy squealed. "They did!"

"By Jove, so they did." Jonathan smiled. "Jolly good work, Brandon."

"Thank you." The frown did not lift. "But who of you all is it?"

"My Lord." Lord Fargate stepped forward. "I sent them."

"No, I sent them," Amelia cried.

"What?" Brandon said.

"I confess," Amelia said.

"No, I confess," Lord Fargate said. "And I challenge you to a duel for the hand of my beloved Amelia."

"No. Please." Amelia broke into more sobs. "Horace I— I could not bear it if he killed you."

"Tragedy airs, I tell you," Lady Wroxeter said with disgust.

Amelia drew in a breath. "I shall marry you, Lord Laith. Only do not kill my Lord Fargate."

"Faith, I did not know I was such a catch." Brandon's tone was self-deprecatory. It sliced through Rosalind.

"She does not wish to have ten children," Rachel explained with precision. "She wants to marry Lord Fargate instead. They sent Casper and Seth after you, but they were only to put you on a boat to the Americas so that you were out of the way so that Lord Fargate could convince her father that he was a candidate for her hand."

"Forgive me, Lord Laith," Amelia cried. "I shall make restitution. I shall marry you, I swear it!"

"No." Rosalind finally found her voice. She stepped forward. "It is I who will marry Lord Laith."

"What?" Amelia gasped.

"I beg your pardon!" Lord Fargate gasped.

Rosalind looked directly at Brandon. His gaze was cool and reserved. She forced a smiled. "After all, it is *I* who have received an *actual* proposal from him and I accept." She looked to Amelia, who was gurgling somewhat. "He only tendered a proposal that he would propose to you. Whereas he proposed to me direct. Therefore, I have the right and I claim it."

"Why?" Brandon asked. "Are you sacrificing yourself in an effort to stop me from dueling with Lord Fargate or some such rot?"

"No." Rosalind's heart pounded. "It is because I changed my mind and I want to marry you." She received strong applause from her family. Only Peters wailed and objected. Brandon, however, said and did nothing.

Rosalind swallowed. "I love you, Brandon."

"Perhaps." His smile was gentle, all things considered. "But you do not trust me, and I fear you should not. Leopards do not change their spots."

"Poppycock!" Lady Wroxeter said. "They do. Now stop being difficult and accept Rosalind. This is my absolution we are working on, confound it."

"Indeed?" Brandon did laugh at that.

"And yours as well, you young whippersnapper," Lady Wroxeter said, thumping her cane. "She is your destiny and you'd best get down from there and kiss it, I mean her, confound it."

"She is not my destiny," Brandon said. "I have realized that."

"Yes she is, and I have it on good authority."

"You said she'd not accept that line unless it was from God himself. Why should I?" Brandon looked at Rosalind. "Or did you have a vision? Faith, how lowering that the only way a female will accept my hand is if the Almighty himself appears."

"No," Rosalind said, feeling both helpless and wounded. "I had no vision. I just realized I love you and I want to spend the rest of my life with you. And you are wrong, I do trust you."

"You want ten children?" Amelia gasped.

"I already have five wonderful ones. And yes, I want five more, each and every one of them." Brandon showed no relenting. Rosalind smiled as sadly as he had. "I suppose it is only fair. I did not believe in you before, and now you do not believe in me."

"Please, Brandon, will you marry her?" Jonathan asked. "We like you."

All the children joined in the clamor.

"Marry her young man, else I will . . . I will. . . .I will . . . oh, never mind, just marry her." Lady Wroxeter turned purple from temper.

And then, loud and clear, a howl arose. Rosalind tore her gaze away from Brandon and watched in fascination as Jessica appeared as if from out of nowhere. Why she was so fascinated she could not say, except that Jessica had a crusading light in her eye, or to be more precise, perhaps that of a mother coming to the rescue of her young.

Regardless, she was full of undeniable purpose. She charged down upon the group and circled through it. The exclamations, shrieks, and bodies jumping about did not phase her in the least. Jessica found Casper, alas, and promptly bit him in his posterior.

Rosalind watched, still unable to move. It took both Jonathan and Jeremy to grab hold of Jessica and confine her. Unfortunately no one saw fit to confine Casper. He leapt about, shouting and cursing. A final bound of his slammed him up against Brandon's horse. Apparently neither the horse nor Brandon was prepared for such behavior. His horse reared and he was flung from the saddle.

"Brandon!" Rosalind was finally shaken from her distraction. She ran to him and knelt down beside him, lifting his head to her lap. His eyes were closed and he appeared deathly still. "Brandon, are you all right?"

Brandon opened his eyes. The light that filled his wonderful silver gray eyes Rosalind recognized. It brought her to tears. She had feared she would never see that look again. "Brandon, you do forgive me!"

He gazed at her a moment. "Madame, I am sure I would forgive you anything, indeed I would, but what is your name and who are you?"

"God! He's been conked on the head again," Seth was heard to say. "Come on, Casper. Run fer your life."

"My name is Rosalind," Rosalind said softly. She drew in her breath. This was her second chance and she knew it. "And I have abducted you."

He blinked. "Forsooth. Why?"

"Because I want to be a mother and I want to marry you."

Brandon stared at her most steadily. Rosalind held her breath. He then smiled his wonderful smile. "My dear Rosalind. You have fairly caught me and I will marry you."

"Ah-ha!" Lady Wroxeter shouted. "We are all witnesses! We all heard it! He will marry her."

Rosalind didn't wait. She leaned down and kissed him. She continued to kiss him as she heard her grandmother tell the children not to gawk, but to go on up to the house.

He kissed her in return as her grandmother gave Amelia Fancot, Lord Fargate, and Peters a thorough piece of her mind and sent them all packing.

She kissed him once more as Lady Wroxeter then said something about a most excellent piece of intervention and departed herself.

Only a concerned whine close to their heads caused Rosalind to draw back. Jessica had found her way to their side. Rosalind's mind whirled as the passion coursed through her. Now she would confess, since it clearly was a day for confessions, such wild desire was indeed another good and beneficial reason for marriage after all. "Heaven's, we must wed soon, my Lord."

"Yes, yes we must." Then a frown passed across his face. "Do you know how many children I would like to have, Rosalind? If not, I must warn you . . ."

"You need not warn me." Rosalind laughed. "I know exactly how many children you would like to have and I look forward to our bounteous family, I assure you."

"Do you? Thank God." He sighed. "So do I. We are destined to be together, do you know?"

"I know that as well, my Lord." Rosalind nodded.

"Rosalind. You are a treasure." Brandon smiled warmly. Then he turned his head and passed out once more.

Rosalind smiled and gently ran her fingers through his hair. Jessica leaned over and licked his cheek. "Your fair-haired pup is going to be my husband, Jessica. Thank you for bringing him home to me."

Six

"Well, you wanted to be a mother and you have succeeded far past any of our expectations. Eight is quite impressive." Brandon smiled and held out a bone. "This is for the mother."

Jessica barked, her eyes alight with adoration, as she lay nestled in a mat of hay. Puppies, some looking very much to be spaniels, others retrievers, crawled close to her, around her, and over her, yapping for their supper.

Brandon lowered himself to sit beside them, leaning his back against the stall's boards. "I must admit I am just as pleased to be a father. Though one for us was just perfect. *He* is just perfect." Brandon smiled with complete satisfaction. "Could life get any better than it is now, do you think?"

Jessica barked her own wonderment. Brandon chuckled. Then froze. Then blinked. He shook his head to clear it. "Faith!"

"Brandon?" Rosalind's voice called out from outside the stables.

"I am here with Jessica," he called, his voice rather weak.

"I thought I would find you here." Rosalind appeared. She smiled wryly and came to sit beside him. "Grandmother has banished me for the nonce. She demands her own private time with our darling son. And she says that *I* coddle him."

"Of course not." Brandon absently put his arm about her, drawing her close.

"The pups are growing so very fast," she observed. She leaned over and kissed him. "You were brilliant when you thought to bring Rufus from London. All poor Jessica needed was a better dog, as it were, than those around here."

"Yes. We London gents are champion stock."

Rosalind frowned. "What is the matter? You seem in a brown study."

Brandon looked at her. He shook his head. "I do not know, but I believe I have had a vision."

A delighted smile crossed Rosalind's lip. "Was it of a painting? Only we have six children, not five. Three boys and three girls. Did you notice the one girl looked like grandmother?"

"Yes. But how . . . ?" His brows shot up. "Do you mean you have had the same vision?"

"Yes, I have."

"Why didn't you tell me?" He frowned deeply. "In fact, I think you told me you never had a vision."

"But I married you regardless, didn't I, my love?" Rosalind shook her head ruefully. "At the time I had it, I didn't know it was a vision. I thought it was my imagination run amuck."

"You didn't know it was a vision?" That unsettled Brandon as much as the image that had just flashed before him minutes ago. "How could you not know it was a vision?"

"I did wonder about that myself after I married you, and I certainly knew it for what it was after I had had our sweet child." Rosalind laughed. "But all I can say is that I do not think a vision can be worth a farthing until you have found and followed your destiny. Indeed, I am now of an opinion that we all probably have visions, but they mean naught to us until the time is right."

"Faith!" he muttered.

"And I was determined not to follow my destiny." Her aquamarine eyes twinkled. "If you can remember that, my Lord."

"I seem to have a hazy recollection, yes," he chuckled.

"Though it became very hazy after we were married. Now why was it you did not want to marry me, my Lady?"

This time she laughed. "I have no recollection. Indeed, since I am so blissfully happy, I am rather mortified to think of my resistance before."

"Yes." He frowned. "Like never telling me about such a fantastic vision."

"Why are you so very upset, my dear?"

"I am not sure why. Though I would have liked to have known, I believe."

"I love you, Brandon." She smiled. "Surely that was the truest of all visions. And though we both can look forward to posing for that particular painting some time in our future, I also know that it will be love, every day, that will bring us to it."

The weight fell from Brandon. The vision now could settle deep within his heart. He kissed her slowly, deeply.

She flushed. "Heavens, I presume that means you are not upset with me anymore."

"No. Your grandmother told me that you knew the secret, and you do, fair Rosalind."

"What secret?"

"The secret to being happy." He nuzzled her neck.

She squirmed slightly. "Beware, my Lord, your leopard spots are appearing."

"Are they?" Brandon grinned down at her. "Imagine, we are going to have *six* children."

"Yes." Rosalind's voice was both breathless and full laughter.

"It will take an extreme amount of love to fulfil that vision."

"I am not too worried about that, Brandon dear." Desire flared within Rosalind's gaze. "That is something of which we have plenty, is it not?"

"It takes plenty to make plenty?" He smiled. "Is that part of the secret as well?"

Jessica barked at that moment.

Rosalind looked to her and nodded. "You've taught your fair-haired pup well, dear."

"No, dear." Brandon's heart filled with emotion. He would cherish her forever. "You have. Only you."

The Runaway Duchess

Mary Kingsley

It was the note that set Katherine off, the note that was so carelessly worded and delivered with equal carelessness by her husband's secretary. It was the note that sent her stamping to her rooms and demanding of her maid her plainest walking gown, while announcing at the same time that she was going out. Alone, she added, to her maid's astonishment. Yes, she insisted a few moments later to the butler, when he suggested that perhaps her Grace would like a footman to accompany her. Quite alone.

It was a different note, delivered by a small, grubby boy sometime later to the mansion on Grosvenor Square, that made his Grace frown. "She did not say where she was going?" he asked.

"No, your Grace," Cressy, the butler, replied, craning his neck in a vain attempt to read the note. "She said only that she was going for a walk."

"Damn," the duke swore softly, so rare an event in this house that Cressy raised his eyebrows in surprise. "Without her maid?"

"Yes, your Grace. Without a footman, either, though I asked." He cleared his throat. "If I could be of some assistance?"

"Hm?" Robert, Duke of Trent, looked up at last from the note covered with his wife's neat handwriting. "No, Cressy. Yes," he said, wheeling about to face the butler again. "Have the tilbury put to."

"Yes, your Grace," Cressy said, bowing, and went off, not only to transmit the duke's order to the stables, but to share this delicious tit-bit with the rest of the staff.

Damn! Robert thought again, before catching himself. Swearing was expected in a man of the *ton,* but he had been brought up to guard his tongue. This, however, was an occasion that called for oaths. What had gotten into his wife, to make her act in such a way? Ordinarily she was the most placid of women, running his house, raising his children, and aiding his career in the most serene manner. Yet she'd gone haring off on this mad start, and with no more reason than that she wished to be by herself for a few days. She was quite all right, she'd written. She was simply tired, and needed some time alone. She had enough money with her, she added, though he knew she hadn't taken so much as a bandbox, and she imagined she would manage quite well. She didn't expect to be gone above five days.

Five days! That raised Robert's ire again. Did she not remember that they were to attend a soiree at the Prime Minister's on Thursday next? It was vitally important that he be there. And had she not had his note, asking her to arrange a dinner for several of his associates for that evening and to invite whomever she wished to make up the numbers? She was needed here, damn it, he thought, indulging himself again. She had no right to do such a thing.

Georgina, his eldest child, chose that moment to come pounding down the stairs. Another time, he might have remonstrated with her on the proper decorum for a young lady making her come-out, but this time he was too distracted. "Is it true?" she demanded.

"Is what true?" he answered, though he knew what she was asking.

"Has Mama bolted?"

"Georgina!" He frowned at her. "I do not know where you got such language, but I wish not to hear it from you again."

Georgina, her brow furrowed in annoyance, simply stared at him, so much like her mother had been at that age that for a moment he was young gain, and so in love . . . "Has Mama left?"

"I am sure it is all a hum. Doubtless she will return this afternoon."

"This afternoon!" It was a wail. "But she was to accompany me to Madame Celeste's for a fitting!"

"Hardly the most vital thing in the world, Georgie."

She stamped her foot, reminding him again of Kate, and the tempers she had once fallen into, before she had grown up. Before he had taught her that such conduct was unbecoming in a duchess and the wife of a politician. "But I particularly need that gown for the Carpenters' ball."

"With all that is in your wardrobe? Your come-out is costing us a fortune, Georgie."

"It is not as if we cannot afford it, Father."

"Georgie—"

"Pray don't call me by that horrid name! And even you must know I cannot wear the same gown in public twice."

"I beg your pardon?"

Georgina fell back a pace at his tone of voice. "I am sorry, Father," she said, sounding chastened. "I meant no disrespect."

"I hope not." He looked down at the note once more and then crumpled it up. "She will be home by this afternoon," he said again. "Now, back upstairs, Georgina. Haven't you lessons to do?"

"I wish you wouldn't make me keep on with them—yes, Father, I'm going!"

Robert watched as Georgina ran up the stairs, light, impetuous, tempestuous. So much like Kate as a girl, he thought again, this time startling himself. Surely he didn't really wish her to be that way, did he? The qualities that might be considered exciting, perhaps even desirable, in a flirt were surely not suitable for a duchess with three children, one grown and another two nearly there. And yet . . .

"Your Grace," Cressy said, and Robert turned. "Your tilbury is ready."

Robert nodded. "My hat." He held out his hand imperiously. "And my driving gloves," he added, and stalked out.

Out in the square he startled his groom on this already surprising day. "No, I will not be needing you."

"But, your Grace," the groom remonstrated. "Just to have someone to see to the horse—"

"I shall find someone."

The groom visibly recoiled. "You'd surely not trust this beauty to just anyone, your Grace?"

Robert bent on him the look he had earlier given his daughter. "I can and I will. Now, let him go."

"Yes, your Grace." The groom stepped aside, scratching at his graying head in bewilderment as the duke drove off at a spanking pace. First the duchess, and now the duke, he thought, turning to go back to the stables. Was the quality all running made today?

It proved, Robert found, to be surprisingly easy to trace the movements of a lady of quality, despite the great many inns from which coaches—common coaches!—departed. For one thing, there were not many which had a coach leaving so late in the morning. Yes, your lordship, the innkeeper said, bowing obsequiously. There had been a lady such as his lordship described here earlier. Not too tall, with red hair, dressed in clothes that were plain but of good quality—oh, yes, he remembered her well. She'd had no baggage with her, had she? Mark my words, North, he'd said to himself, he had, there was something havey-cavey there, and he hoped he hadn't done anything wrong in selling her a seat on the Oxford stage? Robert, his mouth tightening in annoyance, merely tipped the man and turned away, striding back toward the tilbury, where a young boy held his horse. Oxford, eh? He'd be bound she didn't have enough with her for the entire trip. Nor was she as prepared as she'd thought, not if she'd gone without luggage. Likely no respectable inn would take her in, a woman alone. Someone would have to rescue her. He would have to rescue her.

The thought startled him so much that he pulled up on the reins, drawing up with a start. Behind him a heavy cart

barely stopped in time to avoid a collision, the driver cursing him loudly. Robert paid no heed. But he had a dinner
tonight, an important one, he thought, if Wellesley, fighting
so valiantly on the Peninsula, had any chance of procuring
the extra funds he needed during this session of Parliament.
The men he had so casually invited needed to be persuaded
to his point of view. True, another voice inside him, rarely
heard these days, argued, but surely Kate came first? No,
that was the wrong way to look at it. He could not allow
his wife to be a runaway duchess. It simply would not do.

"Will you be requiring evening dress, your Grace?"
Menton, his valet, asked, packing a bag for him when he
returned home.

"I don't believe so, no," Robert said absently, pacing the
length of his room. Never before had he realized how con-
fining it was.

"No evening dress?" Menton sounded shocked.

"No, Menton," Robert said, smiling slightly in spite of
the situation.

"Might I inquire, your Grace, where we are going?"

" 'We?' I am traveling alone this time."

"Alone, your Grace! It will not do!"

"Will it not, Menton?"

"Who will tie your neckcloths for you, sir, or polish your
boots, or shave you?"

"I daresay I can muddle through tolerably enough."

"But, your Grace—"

"Enough, Menton," Robert said, not so much angry as
suddenly weary. Menton, apparently knowing the look on
his Grace's face, subsided. Robert's day, which had begun
much the same as any other, had taken an alarming turn
toward the unusual, and now he faced unknown hours of
travel. It was only because Menton had been with him so
very long that he allowed the man such liberties. "Ask her
Grace's maid to pack a bag for her as well."

That really took Menton aback, Robert noticed, and
wanted to laugh out loud. He didn't, however. Dukes didn't
do such things, not in the face of such disasters, and cer-

tainly not before servants. There was, however, an oddly pleasurable feeling at behaving so unpredictably, even to himself.

His groom seemed stunned when told that again he would not be needed. "But, your Grace," he remonstrated with Robert. "Who will see to the horse?"

"I found someone before, Griggs. Doubtless I shall do so now," Robert said as he climbed into the tilbury. His valise and Katherine's bandbox were already within, he noted automatically. He wouldn't have expected less.

"At a country inn? But, your Grace—"

"Are you implying, Griggs," he said in his most bored voice, "that I am not capable of judging a good stable?"

"No, your Grace," Griggs stammered. "But—"

"Then step aside."

"When do you expect to return, your Grace?" Griggs asked, as Cressy had.

"I really couldn't say." He looked meaningfully at Griggs's hand, and the groom at last stood back. Taking up the reins, Robert drove off at a spanking pace, leaving behind him the Grosvenor Square mansion and all the responsibilities with it. Strange. He felt as if he were doing something strangely, pleasantly illicit.

His Grace had taken only one bag, Menton later reported belowstairs, and that with no evening dress. Aye, and who was to see to his horses, that was what Griggs wanted to know? The whole lot of them had run mad, a footman, very young and very new to his post, dared to put in, and Cressy drew himself up quite as tall as possible. It was quite one thing to discuss the events of the day, he opined, but who were they to judge their betters? The footman made a face behind his back, which, in another situation, might have been reported. As everyone in the household rather agreed with him, however, not a thing showed on anyone's face. They had run mad abovestairs, and where it would end— well, there was just no telling.

* * *

"No, ma'am," the third innkeeper said for the third time, in a voice which clearly implied that he doubted her tale of a carriage broken down and luggage left behind. "There's no room for the likes o' ye here."

"I beg your pardon," Katherine said in her frostiest tones, learned from her mother-in-law, but all that earned her was to have the door of the inn slammed firmly in her face. Frustrated, she kicked at it, and then hopped upon her good foot for a moment. Stupid man. Couldn't he see she was of quality? True, she had neither carriage nor bags, but it wasn't until after she had set out on her adventure that she had realized that such disadvantages might hinder her. As it was, the night was growing steadily darker, even this late in the spring, while the quality of the inn at which she tried to get a room went steadily down. If she didn't find a place soon, she was likely to find herself sleeping out-of-doors. Oh, why had she not stayed on in the coach to Oxford, no matter how unpleasant a mode of travel it was? It would, at the least, have offered shelter. She could have traveled through the night, getting that much farther away from London, and then have used the day to find suitable lodgings. Instead, she had given in to the same impetuosity that had made her flee her home in the first place, the very quality she had been told years earlier would make her an unsuitable duchess. That, and some pressing physical needs.

One of those made itself known now, as her stomach growled. She had not had a good meal since breakfast. One could certainly not count the overpriced, greasy food served at coaching inns at which they had stopped, and which she barely had time to eat. It looked, however, as if she would go hungry this night, she thought glumly, limping along the verge of the road leading out of Thame, where she had decided to stop. Ahead she could see a bridge. She would rest there on its parapet for a moment, to assess her situation and perhaps find a solution.

The low stone wall, golden in the late evening sun, still held some warmth from the day, which was some comfort, even if sitting there was a thing she knew a duchess just didn't do. But then, a duchess didn't kick at doors, or travel on a common stage, or bolt from her home, for that matter, even if she did think she had cause. No. A duchess preserved her dignity at all cost, and did what was expected of her.

That thought fortunately raised her ire again. Most of the time she didn't mind following what society or her children or Robert expected of her. When she felt as resentful as she had this morning, though—as she had for some time, she realized with surprise—it was a different matter. All season she had accompanied her daughter to Court and assemblies and routs, along with staging what even she admitted was a truly splendid come-out ball, with nary a thanks. All during the time when Parliament was in session, she had accompanied Robert to various parties and dinners where he could meet and mingle with his associates, and had arranged dinners and parties herself, thus demonstrating again and again why she was considered a brilliant political hostess, with not a word from him. All this, and not even taking into account her anxiety over William's entrance into Oxford, or her supervision of Pamela's education and the time spent with her. Altogether, she spent far more time with her children than most *ton* mothers ever did with their offspring, and until recently she hadn't minded. Until recently, the emotional satisfaction she took from her role had compensated for a certain lack she had sensed in her marriage for many years. Only gradually had she begun to feel dissatisfied, a feeling she tried to ignore. Until Robert had sent her that note through her secretary.

A carriage drove by at that moment, and from inside came masculine jeers and catcalls, returning her to a sense of where she was, and her precarious position. Coughing a little from the dust the carriage had stirred up, she rose, and then abruptly sat again. In the few moments she had been inactive, her foot had gone numb. It was preferable to pain, perhaps, but as limiting. She wished she dared take off her low walking boot to assess the damage, even if it were likely no more than bruises, but that was another thing a duchess didn't do. In this case, it made perfect sense: she was outside, open not only to the elements, but to the dangers of anyone passing by.

The rumble of wheels warned her that another carriage was approaching. Not a coach this time, she guessed by the lighter sound, but that didn't mean she was safe. Injured foot or not, she had better try again to find a place to stay, she thought, and was about to rise when she heard the carriage pull up before her. Frightened, she looked up to see the last person in the world she wanted to see. Her husband.

Robert looked down at her from the superior height of his tilbury, just as it seemed he had looked down at her for so many years. "Well, Katherine?"

She glowered at him. "What are you doing here?"

Unhurriedly he let the reins drop and pulled off his driving gloves; unhurriedly, he climbed down to the road. "More to the point, what are you doing here?"

"Enjoying the evening."

He laughed, sounding, to her surprise, genuinely amused. "So I see." He settled on the flat stone wall beside her, and she edged away. " 'Tis getting dark," he said, conversationally.

"Then I imagine you won't want to keep the horse standing." She examined the carriage for a moment. "The tilbury, Robert? For me?"

"Why not?" he asked, apparently not catching the irony in her tone.

"I'd fully expect you to be driven in the traveling coach."

"I'd never expect you to take the common stage." He shook his head. "Not even the Royal Mail, Katherine?"

He'd surprised her again with his own use of irony. "It had already left."

"Ah. A small difficulty." He shifted on the wall, and she could sense his gaze on her. "As I imagine you're facing now."

"Why, what could that be?"

"Finding some place to stay."

"Oh, I did that ages ago," she said, airily.

"Liar," he said, but without heat. "In a bit of a spot, aren't you?"

She stared stonily ahead. "I shall come about."

"Shall you? How?"

"I shall tell the next innkeeper—"

"The next one?"

"—that I am a duchess," she finished, and compressed her lips. Drat. She hadn't meant to let that out, that she had been refused a room.

"Ah. Of course, this one will believe you."

"Oh, they all did. There were simply no rooms available."

"Of course not." He rose suddenly and held out his hand to her. "Come."

She didn't move, but looked up at him instead. "Where?"

"To find a place to sleep."

"In a common inn, Robert?"

"Why not? Do you think I'm too high in the instep for that?"

"I'd think it was beneath your dignity."

"As it's getting late, I think we have little chance of reaching London before nightfall."

"I've no intention of returning to London with you."

"We will discuss that later. Well?"

"Well?" she replied, mimicking his tone. "I don't expect we'll have luck. Each inn where I tried turned me away."

"I doubt that there will be a problem."

The cool arrogance of that made her catch her breath. "Of course not," she said. Of course, no one would refuse the Duke of Trent a room, she thought bitterly. Of course, anyone with him would automatically be afforded the same courtesy, and that was the problem. Facing some part of what she'd faced today would do him good. Not that he was likely to travel incognito, as she had. No. He'd come to expect respect, simply because of who he was. He expected everyone around him to jump to his bidding, including her.

"Katherine." She could hear in his voice the same note

of patience he used when he was remonstrating with one of the children. That was something else that annoyed her about him, she thought. He never had to raise his voice to compel anyone to obey him. "What did you expect? You're a woman alone, without luggage. Whereas, I brought a bag."

"I didn't need you to bring anything of mine."

"I didn't," he said, coolly, and again held out his hand. "Well?"

She regarded it. This was the Robert she knew all too well, the implacable man who would be obeyed, no matter what. Once he had been young, smiling, open, but that had been long ago. She let her breath out. Her mad dash for freedom had ended, almost before it began. "Oh, very well," she grumbled, and, pretending his hand wasn't there, rose on her own, letting out an exclamation when she put her weight on her foot.

Robert's hand shot out to steady her. "What is it?" he asked.

"I hurt my toes," she said grumpily, forgetting for a moment her grudge against him.

"How?"

"It doesn't matter."

" 'Tis not like you, Katherine, to be clumsy."

"I wasn't clumsy!" She glared at him and shook off his hand. "Oh, very well. If you must know, I kicked a door."

To her immense surprise, he laughed. "At the first inn, or the second?"

"Neither."

"Ah. The last one, then. I suppose that makes sense." His hands at her waist were firm and matter-of-fact as he lifted her into the tilbury. "You'd hardly be able to hobble to another one."

Katherine stared stonily ahead as, whistling softly to his horse, he set the tilbury into motion. "I'm sure I'm pleased to be providing you such amusement."

"Oh, indeed. I haven't been so diverted in ages." His voice sounded dry. "Not since I received your note."

"I hope you don't expect me to apologize for that, because I won't."

"I hardly know what to expect of you anymore, Katherine." He pulled the tilbury to a halt with a flourish in the yard of the first inn she had tried, the best the town had to offer. "Stable him," he said with his usual arrogance to the groom who ran forward. Though no one in this village could know who he was, the groom obeyed with alacrity, holding onto the bridle. "Well?"

Once again, he was waiting for her to move. Katherine studied his hands, held up to assist her, considered for a moment mutiny, and then, like the groom, gave in to the inevitable. She let him swing her down to the ground, aware, again, of his hands at her waist. Once his touch hadn't been so impersonal; once just the feeling of his hand on her back could cause her to catch her breath. Yet, when she was safely on the ground, he didn't release her. Instead, he threaded her arm through his, making sure to support her so that she wouldn't have to put too much weight on her foot. Say what you would about Robert, she thought, in some ways he always had been considerate. Drat the man. She would feel better, in some ways, if he weren't.

"We'll take two rooms, of course," she said, as they approached the inn's door.

He looked down at her, his eyebrows raised. "Shall we?"

"Yes."

"We shall see. Innkeeper!" He pounded on the counter, and the same man who had earlier refused her a room stepped forward from down the corridor. He narrowed his eyes when he saw her, but, at sight of Robert, held his tongue. For now. "Two rooms, please."

"Oh, aye? And you be?" the innkeeper said, his voice bordering on insolence.

From an inner pocket Robert withdrew his card case and took from it an engraved square of pasteboard. She didn't have to see it to know what was on it. Thus she was surprised when the innkeeper didn't immediately start bowing and scraping in deference to her husband's rank. "And this is my wife."

The innkeeper again sent her a narrow look. "I'm afraid, Mr. Hawthorne, that I have only one room," he said.

Katherine involuntarily glanced at Robert in dismay; he met her look with an impenetrable one of his own. "No matter," he said. "We will take it."

"Just the one?" Katherine demanded. "Are you quite certain?"

"Yes, Mrs.—Hawthorne." The innkeeper smirked. "That I am."

It struck her, then, the name that Robert had used. Hawthorne? And plain "mister," when his rank would surely have procured what they wished? It was the family name, of course, but why was he using it?

"It matters not," Robert said, crisply. "We'll take it."

"Very good, sir. If you'll sign here?" The innkeeper slid the register across to them. Robert scrawled his name. She wondered if the innkeeper was aware that he deliberately sent an ink blot across the page, to cover his title, which he had automatically begun to write. For the first time since arriving at this benighted village, Katherine's spirits picked up. She suspected it would not be easy for her husband to accustom himself to being thought of as a plain mister.

"Good. If you will follow me? I am Tanner, by the way," the man tossed over his shoulder, holding up a candle to light the way up stairs gone dark, now that evening had fallen. "Will you be staying long, Mr. Hawthorne?"

"Just the one night. My bag—our bags—are in my gig. See to it that someone brings them in."

Tanner muttered something under his breath. Katherine didn't hear it all, but she did catch something about people getting above themselves. Again, she felt cheered. If this kept up, Robert might just receive the taste of humility he deserved.

At the top of the stairs they turned left, and then left again, to climb up another staircase. Under her hand, she could feel the tension in Robert's arm. They were not, ap-

parently, being given one of the better rooms in the inn.
What Robert must be making of that, she could only
imagine.

"Here it be," Tanner announced, throwing open a door.
The light of his candle illumined a small room, with rafters
at the farther end that would prevent even Robert, who was
not very tall, from standing upright. This would not do, she
knew.

It didn't. After a cursory survey of the room, Robert
swung back toward Tanner. "Surely you must have something better."

"No, sir." Tanner sounded almost satisfied. "All I have.
It's late, you see? Most people who are going to come
through here have already, on the stage." At that, he glanced
at Katherine again, his look almost a leer. She drew herself
up. If Robert could draw on his rank and his upbringing,
she could use hers, as well. She met Tanner's gaze with a
cool, assessing one of her own, and, after a moment, the
innkeeper looked away.

"I see," Robert said, his voice crisp, cool. "Very well.
We shall want hot water for washing. And send someone
up with some food. Unless you are not hungry?"

This last was addressed to Katherine, who was happy
enough to forget her annoyance with him in the alliance
they had formed against Tanner. "Quite hungry, Tre—Mr.
Hawthorne."

"Tea for the lady," Robert continued, laying extra stress
on the last word. So he, too, had noticed Tanner's sneers.
"And a bottle of your best brandy for me."

"Yes, sir," Tanner said, bowing, though he appeared disgruntled.

"Good. That will be all," Robert said, and turned, dismissing the man from the room and his thoughts. "What
bumblebroth have you landed us in this time, Katherine?"

"I? If you had just let me be—"

"And leave you by the side of the road, to be accosted
by who knows what manner of person—yes, what is it?"
he broke off sharply at the sound of a knock on the door.

"Excuse me sir, mum," a timid voice said from the hall. "Mr. Tanner said as how you wants something to eat?"

"Yes, yes, bring it in." Both he and Katherine were quiet as the maid came in, bearing a heavy tray, which she placed upon the room's battered table. At the sight of the mutton stew, Katherine's mouth began to water, even though it was not one of her favorite dishes. Without saying a word to her husband, she ladled some stew into a bowl, tore off a piece of bread, and sat on the only chair in the room.

"Well?" Robert, having poured some brandy into a thick glass goblet, frowned down at her. Her mouth full of bread, Katherine could only stare at him. He looked thoroughly annoyed, thoroughly arrogant as he stood there, silently demanding reasons from her for her flight. She also thought she caught, just behind his characteristic self-possession, a hint of uncertainty. Why, he was unsure of what to think of what she had done, she thought, her eyes widening a trifle. She relaxed. For the first time in a very long time, she felt as if she had some control in their relationship. And just when had that happened that she had become so subservient, she wondered?

Robert was still glaring at her. Ignoring him, she took a small bite of bread, sipped her tea, and then patted her lips with a napkin that, though clean, was worn and frayed around the edges. Oh, no, definitely not the kind of service the Duke of Trent was used to receiving. She wondered when he'd rebel against it. "I noticed you did bring a bag for me," she said, answering at a tangent. "When you said you didn't."

"I lied. Do you intend to answer my question?"

She returned his look, levelly. Once she would have ripped up at him, declaiming passionately all her sense of ill-usage and hurt. She was older now, and, with any luck, wiser; she knew quite well that that approach never had worked with Robert. "I don't consider that we're in any sort of bumblebroth at all, sir."

"No? We are here in this God-forsaken village, on an

evening when I had hoped to be having an important dinner—"

"Ah."

"What is that supposed to mean?" he asked, peering at her suspiciously.

She pressed the napkin to her lips again. "Nothing."

His frown deepened. "You can ask such a question, when you know that your actions have landed everyone in the suds?"

"Everyone?" She drained her tea and then set the cup down. With food inside her, she felt strong, fortified, ready to face anything. Even an angry husband. Make no mistake about it, Robert was angry, no matter how quiet he might be. Doubtless his temper would be terrifying to behold, if he ever loosened the rein he held so tightly on it. If he ever loosened his hold on any of his emotions. "I believe, sir, that I am the one who left home. I am the one who came to this village, not you. By my own choice, that is. Why you are here, I cannot imagine."

"Katherine," he growled. She could practically hear him grinding his teeth. "Have you forgotten that you have children, madam? Not to mention a husband who needs you."

"No, I've not forgotten anything. I believe, though, that what you need isn't so much a wife, as it is a hostess."

"Of course I need a hostess. You have been a partner in my career—"

"Have I, indeed?"

"Yes. You have been of great help to me."

"Oh, really." She rose to face him, becoming angry for the first time. "Are you truly speaking of me, or would any woman have done? You are a duke, Robert," she went on, when he would have spoken. "Furthermore, you are landed and wealthy. Do you really believe you would have had trouble finding a suitable helpmeet."

"No, but I chose you, instead."

Somewhat to her own surprise, she laughed, at what she suspected had been an unintentional slight. "Oh, Robert. You really don't know, do you?"

"Know what?"

Still smiling, she rose. "What your life is really like."

"My life is as I wish it to be."

"Is it?" She searched his face. "Have you ever considered that mine might not be?"

"You enjoy the way we live, Katherine."

"Do I?"

"Have you forgotten that you were the one who wanted to live in London and socialize?"

She bit her lip. There was something to what he said. When she was young, the prospect of being free of her family, of being able at last to enjoy herself at balls and soirees and routs as an adult, had been enticing. Doing so because she wished to was one thing, however. Entertaining, and being entertained, in the name of duty was another matter. "This isn't about living in London."

"What, then?

"I don't think you'd understand."

"You owe me some explanation, Katherine." When she continued to stay quiet, he went on. "Why did you leave?"

She did, she suppose, owe him something. "It was the note."

"The note?"

"Yes. The note."

"Which note?"

"The one you had your secretary deliver this morning."

He frowned. "The one I sent you about arranging a dinner party for this evening?"

"Yes."

"For pity's sake, Katherine. I have sent you notes before."

"Mayhap I've grown tired of receiving them."

"Should I have summoned you to my study instead?"

She considered that. "That may have been better, yes."

"For pity's sake," he said again. "You are not an errant child, to be dealt with in that way."

"No, Robert. I am your wife." She paused. "Something which you seem to have forgotten."

He frowned. "It's unlikely I'd forget such a thing. I wouldn't be where I am, were it not for you."

"Nor would I be where I am," she muttered.

"Excuse me?"

"I wouldn't be here." She glared at him, where he stood across the room, the goblet held negligently in his hand. "I wouldn't have left."

"I don't quite think I understand."

"No. I know you don't." She raised a hand, brushing back the curl that would never stay off her face with the back of her hand. "I'm tired, Robert. Must we brangle over this tonight?"

Still frowning, he crossed the room, deliberately poured himself another glass of brandy, and took a sip, curling his lip at the taste. "No. But I would like to understand."

She put her hand to the small of her back, grimacing. Hours of travel in the dubious comfort of a public coach had left her exhausted and aching in every joint. "I don't think you ever will."

"Oh, for pity's sake, Katherine." He banged the goblet down on the table. "You could at least give me a chance."

"I have." She made herself face him again. "I've already told you. 'Twas the note."

"Then we are back where we began." He drained the goblet and made another face as he set it back down. "As I said. 'Tis nothing I haven't done before."

"And I could try to explain to you all night, but it would avail us nothing." She eyed the bed. "It doesn't look very comfortable."

Robert bent upon her the stern look he gave the children when he wished to scold them, and then turned away. She hadn't heard the end of this, she thought, but for tonight, she had a reprieve. She wasn't quite sure she could deal with much more. "I wonder how often they air the sheets," he said.

She stared at him in undisguised alarm. "Surely you do not mean to sleep there."

His glance at her was mild. "As there's only the one bed, I don't see we've a choice."

"I will not share the bed with you, Robert."

"And I don't intend to sleep on the floor. Have mercy, Katherine. I've a bad back, remember?" he snapped, knowing he sounded as irritated and annoyed as she. Truth to tell, he didn't want to share the bed with her, either, a startling and dismaying thought. But then, he was tired. What had seemed like adventure when he'd left Grosvenor Square now felt like sheer folly. Travel was tiring, even if he had been in his own carriage. His back ached from the hours of driving in the tilbury, and the thought of the work he'd left behind to go after his wife was disheartening.

"Oh," she said, blankly, averting her head. "But I don't wish to sleep on the floor, either."

"I'm not asking you to." He leveled his most ducal look on her, the one that cowed most people into submission. "Well, madam? What do you suggest?"

Katherine's brow wrinkled in the frown that always meant she was deep in thought. "I don't know—ah, yes!"

"What?"

"Bundling."

Now it was his turn to react blankly. "I beg your pardon?"

"Bundling. I'm sure you know what that is. We would need to put a bolster of some sort between us on the bed."

"As a barrier?" Some of his good humor was returning. "Katherine, I hardly think that would be a deterrent—"

"Ordinarily, no. I do believe, though, that usually the man is restrained in some way."

At that, he laughed outright. "And I do believe you'd enjoy that, wouldn't you?"

"As things are now, yes."

He nodded. "I see. Ah, but Kate. There was a time . . ."

"Yes, well, not tonight." She studied the bed, lips pursed. " 'Tis warm. Surely we don't need a counterpane, or all the blankets I am persuaded are there. If we roll them together, they should serve."

"Hadrian's Wall," he murmured.

She stopped in the act of stripping the bed of the counterpane. "I beg your pardon?"

"Hadrian's Wall." He gestured toward the bed. "I believe that is what we're building. A border between us, Katherine?"

"Hadrian's Wall has stood where it is for centuries."

"Except where it's been breached," he shot back.

"This one will not be breached," she said.

He watched as she tugged the counterpane from the bed and began rolling it, making him feel reluctant admiration for her. She hadn't been trained to this kind of work, and it showed; no matter how she tried, she could not make the bulky quilt roll evenly. He would have helped her, but some unknown streak of humor in him was enjoying this too much. "Unless we want to breach it."

"We're too tired," she retorted. "At least, I am. Well?" She stood back, glaring at him with her hands on her hips. "Do you plan to help, or not?"

He faced her across the bed, and then, resigned, picked up a blanket. She reached for it at the same time he began trying to wrap it around the quilt. It was perhaps inevitable that their hands would meet; her reaction, however, was more unexpected. Her cheeks turning pink, she jumped back, as if they had never touched before, as if they had not shared their lives for all these years. That same unknown streak of humor made him reach farther over, though he was doing most of the work and his back protested at the movement, simply to see what she would do.

"Well," she said, and he looked up to see her watching him with a small smile on her face, startling him. "I wonder what our servants would think could they see the mighty Duke of Trent now."

" 'Twould be only one more odd thing for them to discuss. There." He placed the bolster on the bed and stepped back to examine his handiwork. "What do you think?"

Katherine, holding another quilt, eyed the lumpy, makeshift bolster he'd placed in the center of the bed dubiously. "I suppose it will serve."

"It will have to." Yawning hugely, he began to strip off his coat. To his vast amusement, Katherine hastily turned away, as flustered as she had been when their hands had touched. Someday he would tease her about this night. "Do you want help with that?"

"What?" She turned back, and he noticed, with interest, that she had begun unfastening the top of her dress. "No! I hardly need you to act as a maid."

"I meant folding the quilt."

"The quilt." She stared at him, dumb. "Oh! The quilt."

"Yes." He lounged back against the sloping wall. "What did you think I meant?"

"I thought—never mind," she said, hastily. "No. I can manage, I think."

"Very well," he said, and this time began to unbutton his pantaloons. Katherine again wheeled away, making him bite back a grin. "Though I think that if we both do it, 'twill be easier."

"Both do—oh. The quilt."

"Yes." This time he did smile, though he suspected that if she had been looking at him, her temper would have flared again. "Otherwise, we'll never get to bed, will we?"

"The bolster will be between us," she said, sharply.

"Of course. Katherine, my dear, why do you persist in misinterpreting what I say?"

She looked up at the ceiling, her lips set. He wondered if she realized the picture she made, with her dress not quite fastened and her hair not quite pinned up as it should be. Quite a difference from the impeccably groomed woman who presided over his home, making sure that all ran smoothly, from the rearing of his children to aiding his career. "Shall I blow out the candle, or will you?"

"I will." Hastily she turned away from him, and a moment later the room was plunged into darkness. Though he was occupied with removing his own clothes without the aid of any light, an unusual state of affairs for him, still he was deeply aware of the little rustlings of fabric that told him Katherine was doing the same thing. Strange, but he somehow found that more intriguing than he might have, had the candle remained lighted. Perhaps Katherine had a point. Perhaps he had been taking her for granted.

He heard a further, louder rustling a few moments later, and it filled him with dismay; when he climbed into bed at last, his worst fears were realized. The mattress was stuffed with straw. "Dash it," he muttered.

Katherine stirred next to him. " 'Tisn't precisely what you're accustomed to, is it, your Grace?"

"Katherine—"

"All you need do to obtain a better room is tell the innkeeper who you are."

"And chance the scandal? I think not."

"Oh. Now I know why you registered under a different name."

"Yes. What did you think?"

"I didn't think anything. I didn't wish you here, Robert."

"Yes, I know." His voice was dry. "You made that clear enough."

"Yet you didn't once consider my wishes."

"In this situation, madam, your wishes are unimportant."

"Unimportant!"

"Yes."

"The innkeeper thinks we are unmarried. What scandal will that cause, should it get out?"

"If that happens, people will already know the truth of the matter," he said imperturbably. "Do you not think that the servants have spread the news of what has happened today?"

Katherine pressed her lips together. Their actions today had been extraordinary. Of course the servants would talk. She could not let that sway her, though. "I'm not returning home, Robert. Not yet."

"We shall see," he said, as he had once before.

"Huh," she said, and they both subsided, Robert wondering if she were as tensely aware of him as he was of her, on the other side of the bolster. Hadrian's Wall, indeed. Frail though it was, it might as well be. Certainly it was serving its purpose.

Depressing thought, though he could hardly expect her to turn to him, not after all that had been said between them. More dispirited than he had expected, he turned onto his side, facing the center of the bed, at the precise moment that she did the same. What he had not realized, and what he suspected she hadn't, either, was that the mattress had a decided sag in the middle. He found himself facing her, mere inches away, across that ridiculous barrier she had insisted they build.

For the merest second, he felt her breath soft on his cheek, and then she twisted away, presenting, he was certain, her back to him. "Well, madam," he said dryly. "Had Hadrian's builder constructed such a wall, I suspect he would have suffered greatly."

"We still both know 'tis there," she retorted.

He stayed where he was for a few moments. If he reached out he could touch her, but he didn't. Not just because of her restrictions, but because of something in him: something that had always held him back.

"Then I will bid you goodnight," he said, and turned away himself, lying stiffly and still. This was absurd. They had been married for eighteen years, for God's sake, he thought. From the beginning they'd shared a bed, even if it was true, more recently, they tended to sleep apart. Surely this shouldn't be so awkward. Surely they should at least be able to talk. As matters stood, he had no more idea now than he had before as to why she had run away. When had he stopped being able to talk to his wife?

Katherine's breathing had, without his realizing it, settled into the relaxed, easy rhythm of sleep. He turned his head on the pillow, though the room was too dark for him to see her, and wondered if he dared reach out and touch her hair. He wondered why he didn't do more of such things. He never had, though Lord knew he wanted to. Oh, how he wanted to. The marriage may originally have been a planned marriage, and it may be very much a political partnership, but that was never what he had wanted. Not that he'd fallen in love with Katherine at first sight, but he'd certainly been enchanted enough by her that he'd tumbled head after heels soon after. He had always thought she felt the same about him. They simply had never said the words.

Frowning, he turned over. He didn't quite understand why they hadn't, or why they hadn't shared a bed in—how long? His frown deepened. He couldn't remember. He went to her room, as he always had, but when was the last time they had spent the night together? Nowadays both were too busy, too tired, and they each needed their sleep. At least, that was how he rationalized it to himself. Now he wondered. Something was very wrong with his marriage, else Katherine wouldn't have bolted as she had.

So. He studied the problem analytically, as he usually did. True, he wasn't someone who could express his feelings easily, not with words or with touches. It wasn't how he had been raised. Maybe if he hadn't succeeded to the title so young, things would be different. Certainly from an early age he'd had it drilled into him that, as the heir to a dukedom, he had duties that other people didn't have. From his mother he'd learned that he always had to think of what was owed to his title, to his station in life. There were certain standards to be upheld, something he must never forget. He never had.

His father's lessons may have been less verbal, but they'd been no less potent for all that. From him Robert learned about his responsibilities to his estate and to his tenants. No matter that those estates were vast, or that his income would, one day, be correspondingly high; no matter, even, that he would someday bear one of the first titles in the land. He must always comport himself with dignity and yet with a certain humility, and he must never waste his money, or his time, in such foolishness as gambling or drinking or other high-spirited adventures, such as most young men in his class did. With the notable exception of a prank he and a few friends had played at Oxford, resulting in a severe dressing-down both from the Dean and his father, as well as being sent down for a time, he never had. He had never again had the chance.

Again Robert turned over, restless, uncomfortable. The prank had killed his father, so his mother had always claimed, his death following as quickly as it had, and so he had come to believe. It wasn't true, of course; his grandfather had died of an apoplexy, just as his father had. If he weren't careful, the same thing might happen to him. It was one reason he kept such careful rein on his temper. His father, he knew now, had been young to die. He wished to live a long life. With Katherine.

Which brought him back to his original problem. He shifted onto his back, wishing again that he dared reach out and touch her, just touch her, her hair, her cheek. If Katherine could leave him once, then she could easily do so again. The only way to prevent it was to keep her from going outside the house, and how was he to do that? She had her duties, just as he had his. She had to see them through.

Duties. He made a face. For once, he'd like to forget about all the pressures of his life, about the various political issues in which he was involved, even about his title and estates. For there was a time, once, when he had just been Robert. Not the duke, not even a marquess, though that had been his title. He had simply been himself, just as his wife, his Kate, had been herself.

He went very still. That was it, of course, the heart of the problem. They'd each forgotten that one important fact about the other, that they were husband and wife first, and that everything else came after. No wonder that Katherine had bolted; he rather thought he would have, had he been in her place. He certainly hadn't given her the support she needed, given his preoccupation with his career. Combine that with the way he kept his emotions inside, and there was their marriage, in the state it was in. What he had to do was find some way to know her again, as once he had.

Lord knew he wouldn't if he forced her to return to London with him.

Good Lord. He took a deep breath and turned toward her, this time reaching out, barely touching her hair. *Ah. Katherine, what have I done to you?* he thought, and turned back, thinking furiously. What faced him was going to be difficult, but that didn't matter. He knew now what he needed to do.

Katherine stared at her husband across the table in the sunny private parlor Robert had convinced the innkeeper to let them have, her knife stilled in the act of buttering a muffin. "You've decided what?"

Robert unconcernedly speared a piece of ham. "That I'm not returning to London."

"But you have to," she blurted out. "You've people to see, plans to make—"

"All canceled," he said cheerfully.

She set down the teapot with a thud that made the cover rattle. "How on earth did you do that?"

"I sent a message home, saying we are at this inn."

" 'We'?" she said, sharply. "I don't recall asking you to come here, Robert."

"No." He cut another bite of ham. "Now that I am, though, it occurs to me that I could do with a bit of a holiday."

"I've been telling you that for years now. But," she went on, watching him eat as if nothing of great moment were occurring between them, "never while Parliament is in session."

"Parliament can hobble along without me for a few days."

"Yes, but can you hobble along without it?"

That made him stop, if only for a second. "We shall see, shall we not?"

"Yes." Lips tight, she returned to her own breakfast, any pleasure she might have taken from it gone. It wouldn't last, she knew. Politics were the breath of life to Robert. Sometimes she thought his career meant more to him than she did; certainly more than the children ever had. Even the one they had lost. "Then they'll know at home where we are."

"I hardly wanted them to continue worrying."

"If they were," she muttered.

Robert's lips tucked back in a dry smile. "We shall see, shall we not?" he said again.

She frowned. "Robert, I know you are always busy or away from home, but I'm persuaded the children do notice your comings and goings—"

"I wasn't thinking of myself, madam."

"Me?"

"Yes, why not you?"

"Oh, Robert. Don't you know?"

"What?"

"No, you honestly don't."

"What? I don't understand you, Katherine."

"Why I ran away."

He let out his breath and set down his coffee cup, untasted. "Because I dared to ask you a favor by note."

Her exhalation was quieter, more of a sigh. "Oh, Robert."

"If not that, what? I don't understand."

"I know." Nor did she think he ever would; not when he was so distant from the life she led, from her. "If you don't return to London, what will you do here?"

He appeared to accept the change of subject. "What did you plan to do?"

"I . . ." she began, and stopped, her voice faltering. "I don't know. I didn't think."

"Mm-hm. You didn't, did you?" This time, he did sip his coffee. "Precisely the sort of thing my mother was concerned about in you."

"Your mother! What has she to say to this?"

"Uh—nothing," he said, eyeing her warily.

"Oh, really? I know her opinion of me isn't high."

"She liked you," he protested.

"But not as a wife for you."

"Not that, Kate," he said, finally. "As duchess."

"Kate."

"I beg your pardon?"

"I don't know when it was you last called me that."

He went still, the look in his eyes arrested. "Nor do I. Too long, I suspect."

"Yes, well." She busied herself with pouring another cup of tea, as uncomfortable with the subject as he must be. They were coming perilously close to discussing happier times, and neither of them was comfortable with that topic. " 'Tis all beside the point. How long do you plan to stay?"

He crossed his forearms on the table and leaned forward, giving her the smile that was always her undoing. He wasn't precisely handsome, her Robert; his height was not above medium, his features were ordinary, and his hair was a plain brown. But when he smiled, he was all she ever had been able to see. Were he to ask her to return home with him at just this moment, she might agree. "That depends," said he.

"On what?"

"On events."

"On me, I presume," she said, sitting back to allow the maid who had come into the parlor to clear their dishes away.

"Mayhap. You, there."

The girl glanced down, looking startled at being addressed. "Me, sir?"

"Yes, you. What is there to do in this town?"

She glanced from Robert to Katherine, her eyes avid. Oh, they must be the cause of much lively speculation at this inn, Katherine thought, perhaps in the entire town. She wondered what people were saying about them. "Well, sir, some people think as how the church is nice. Suppose it is, if you're fine London folk," she said, her voice rising as if in question.

"Ah." Robert's face was absolutely solemn, but his eyes

danced with a light that told Katherine, if not the girl, that he was considerably amused by this. Quickly she brought her napkin up to cover her mouth and turned away, lest her expression betray her. "I gather you don't agree."

"Well, sir, haven't been in it but the once. I'm chapel, you see. Naught to see in there but a lot of pictures of dead people."

"No. Really?"

"Really. 'Struth, sir."

"I see. Is there aught else, miss—what is your name?"

"Michael, sir. 'Struth," she added, when even Robert couldn't keep his countenance. "My father wanted a son."

"Oh," Robert said, blankly. "Well. Is there anything else for us to do? Besides walking."

"Why would you want to do that, sir?"

She sounded so incredulous that Katherine again quickly looked away. "We can hardly stay indoors all day. And it looks a pleasant enough town."

"If you say so," Michael said doubtfully. "There is Thame Park, sir, where Miss Wykeham lives. Do you know her?"

"No, we've not that pleasure."

"Oh. I thought—she does go to London, now and again. Then there's Scotch Grove Hill. The squire's home, you know."

"Mm-hm. What would you recommend, Michael?"

"Don't know as I would, sir, particularly not today."

"Why not today?"

"Because it's market day."

Market day. So that explained the bustle of carts and horses; of people talking and calling to each other that Katherine had heard early that morning. "Thank you, Michael," he said gravely. "You've been a great help."

"If you say so, sir," she said, again doubtful, and, after hefting the tray on her shoulder, went out.

Left alone, Katherine and Robert stared at each other for a speechless moment. " 'Struth," he said.

She let out a laugh. "Oh, Robert! 'Tisn't fair to make a jest of her, for the way she talks."

"No, I suppose not. 'Twas worth it, though, to see you smile again."

"Oh, nonsense."

He considered her. "You've not smiled much of late," he said. "And I still don't know why you left."

"I told you. It was—"

"The note. Yes, I know. It doesn't seem like enough."

Frowning again, Katherine toyed with her teacup. "It did at the time."

"At the time?" he said quickly.

"Yes." Her frown was ferocious, daring him to disagree. "And it still does, Robert."

"So very bad that you would leave behind not only your husband, madam, but your children?"

She looked away, biting her lip. The children. Unfair of him, seasoned debater that he was, to find so unerringly the weak point in her actions. They didn't deserve to be punished in her private rebellion against Robert. And yet. . . . For the moment she forgot Robert's presence in the room. They made their own demands on her, no less pressing than his, if not as serious. Lately, those demands had become more insistent. Georgina's debut Season was proving to be arduous. The girl had to be shepherded and chaperoned everywhere, from shops and Venetian picnics; to balls and routs. William worried her, as well; so poor a scholar had he been at Eton that there was a very real chance he would not make it into Oxford. Nor was Pamela, their youngest, any easier. Ordinarily the most sunny of children, lately she had been quiet to the point of sullenness. Pamela likely needed her the most of all, even if she did feel drained, empty, with nothing to give. Combine everything with her duties as Robert's hostess, and perhaps it was no wonder that she was so tired all the time; no wonder that she felt more and more like a wraith, less and less like a person. There was simply too much she needed to do.

Perhaps she could have gone on if she'd seen one sign,

just one, that all she did for her family was appreciated, but she hadn't. It was all taken for granted, all assumed that she would do whatever anyone wished of her. Somewhere along the way, she'd lost her sense of self. She was no longer Katherine, a person with dreams and hopes and feelings, and an identity of her own, but was, instead, Robert's wife, his hostess, her children's mother. She was tired of putting everyone's needs before her own. For once, she wanted to be selfish. "I'm not going back yet, Robert."

She wasn't certain, but she thought he sighed. "So be it. What shall we do today, then?"

Katherine blinked, startled at the abrupt change of subject. "What did you say?"

"Do you wish to pay a call on Miss Wykeham or the squire?"

"Not particularly. Do you?"

"No, not particularly." They looked at each other, sudden conspirators against the constraints of their lives that would ordinarily have them pay such courtesy calls. "Let us see instead what the market has to offer."

Outside, it was a changeable day of bright sun and dappled clouds, with a breeze that was cooling one moment, merely cold the next. The sense of adventure Robert had had yesterday returned as he gazed around him, intrigued by all he saw, greedy to take it all in. It was so different from his usual life. Thame's wide main street, with fine old houses set back from the road on either side, was lined with carts and barrows and booths, all set up by local farmers come to town for the weekly market, to sell their various produce. There were eggs and chickens, cheese and cream, last year's grain and this year's first vegetables. The town's baker was doing a brisk business at a booth he had set up, while the tavern was, as was to be expected, bustling. Some farmers had abandoned their wares to visit the different shops, there to replenish supplies or, in the case of the women, to purchase fabrics at the linen draper's or perhaps a new hat from the milliner. Robert was amused to notice his wife eyeing the latter with interest. Katherine could choose from the finest shops London had to offer, from the most exclusive modiste to the most fashionable of mantua makers, and yet even she, apparently, could not resist the lure of the town's shops. "Do you wish to go in?" he asked, after catching her looking longingly at the milliner's for the third time.

She seemed to collect herself. "Why, to buy a hat? But, Robert, I am persuaded I can find much better in London."

"Most likely."

"Besides, I've more than enough hats."

"Mm, yes, but I believe you'd like to look, would you not?"

She cast one more look at the shop's small-paned window. "Yes," she said suddenly. "If you don't mind."

"Not at all," he said, convinced he was earning the goodwill of heaven as, his hand under her elbow, he escorted her into the shop.

Therein followed one of the most enjoyable hours he had passed in years, watching his wife shop. The milliner, as quick to recognize people of quality, as the innkeeper had been, bustled over to wait upon them, the movement of her hands as quick and as fussy as the trimmings on the various bonnets she presented for Katherine's approval. Under his amused eyes Katherine tried on first one and then another, tilting her head critically as she studied her reflection. When her gaze met his in the mirror the milliner held up for her, she quickly glanced away, he suspected to prevent betraying the laughter that lurked there. In the end, though, she purchased a hat trimmed with ruched ribbons and braid, though he was convinced she would never wear it. When they left the shop at last, they were more in charity with each other than they had been in many a long day.

At the baker's booth they stopped to purchase some sponge cakes, light and airy and sweet; at one farmer's cart, they added a basket of ripe, red strawberries, and at another's thick, golden cream. Then, their treats in hand, they retired to find a quiet, shady spot where they could eat in peace. They stopped finally near the bridge where Robert had found Katherine the night before, perching on the dry stone wall. It never failed to amaze him, Robert thought, watching his wife, how quickly she could eat and in such quantity, though her figure was as slim as Georgina's. There was much he had forgotten about her, much he had failed to notice recently. If he hadn't, perhaps he would have seen the signs that led to her remarkable disappearance.

Dangerous thought. "I've never been to a market before," he confessed.

Katherine's head shot up. "Never?"

"No. Not once."

"Why ever not?"

He collected his thoughts before answering. " 'Twas seen as frivolous."

"Frivolous! Robert, these people work hard to earn their keep."

"And well I know it. I've seen the tenant farmers on our land."

"Then fairs must have been out of the question, as well."

"Without doubt. Which is not to say I never went to one," he said, his eyes twinkling.

"You did? But if it wasn't allowed—"

"I managed to get away from my tutor one day and go with the son of one of the tenants. A crime in itself," he added.

"Your friend?"

"Yes, in spite of everything. Sometimes I wonder why."

"Why in the world weren't you allowed such things?"

Again he considered his answer. "I was brought up knowing I'd be duke one day, and that my duties and responsibilities must always come first."

She stared at him. "Oh," she said, and fell silent. *Frivolous,* she mused, feeling sympathy well within her for the lonely boy he must have been, understanding a little better the distant man he sometimes appeared.

He turned toward her. " 'Tis why I sent you that note, Kate."

Katherine glanced away. "No one knows more than I that your career is important, Robert."

"Yet you balked at arranging a dinner party."

"I've told you. It wasn't just that."

"Tell me, Kate. I do wish to know."

She gazed down into the waters rushing below them under the bridge. "You wouldn't understand," she muttered.

"You mean I wouldn't care. I do, you know," he went on, as she looked up at him. "Why would you think I wouldn't?"

"Because—oh, because."

"A cogent argument, madam. Were you to take a seat in Parliament, I doubt you'd succeed."

"But that's it," she burst you. "Parliament."

"Your belief, that 'tis all I care about? 'Tis not true." He spoke quietly. "I care about you, Kate, else I wouldn't have come after you."

She turned away, heaving a gusty sigh. "I know you care, Robert. I just think that—well, to be honest, I believe other things matter more to you. Your career, for one."

"It doesn't," he protested.

"No?" She looked at him inquiringly. "But then, when are you ever home? Except for the dinners we give, or such? The dinners I give," she rushed on. "The soirees and routs I plan, the balls I squire Georgina to and the shops I escort her to—no, you don't see such things, do you? You comment that she's rigged out fine, with never a thought as to how such a thing happens."

"I do pay the bills," he said, with what she presumed was an attempt at humor.

"And that is all your involvement in her come-out has meant to you."

" 'Tis quite a bit, madam."

"Very well, let's leave that. What of William?"

"What of William?"

"Did you know there's a chance he may not get into Oxford?"

"The devil!" he exclaimed.

"Oh, yes. And so he must have a tutor."

"But why didn't you tell me?"

"I didn't want to worry you, because—"

"Because I was so busy with my career. You may as well say so. You were about to."

" 'Tis true," she said, defiantly.

"I suppose next you'll be telling me Pamela's up to some sort of mischief."

"No. I rather wish she were. She's become too serious of late."

"Mayhap 'tis just her manner."

"She was a sunny-natured child, Robert. But children feel tension. They know when all is not well."

"So," he said, after a moment. "You are saying this is all my fault?"

She took as long to answer as he had. "No. The children bear their share of the blame. They don't stop to think."

"Children usually don't. You know that."

"And neither do you," she shot back.

"Unfair, Kate. I've some idea of what's involved in what you do."

"Oh, really." She shot to her feet, glaring at him; he followed suit, more slowly. "Do have any idea what 'tis like to invite several hundred people to a ball—"

"You've your secretary to address the invitations."

"But who must needs make up the list? I must, of course. Who does the planning, orders flowers and food, makes up menus, decides on the decorations? I do. Yes, the servants do a great deal of the work, but were it not for me, they'd not know what to do. And all this is just for one ball," she continued earnestly, trying to make him understand. "We have routs and soirees. We attend balls and routs and soirees and dinners. And always I must be the perfect hostess, the perfect wife, I must be perfectly gowned and coiffed, I must know what is happening in politics and who are the people with the most influence. Always, Robert." She held up her hand, forestalling any protest from him. "Yes, I knew what it would be like when I married you. I saw my mother do much the same. But she liked it!" she burst out, and spun away, appalled at what she had just revealed.

"Are you saying," Robert said quietly after a moment, "that for all these years you have hated your life?"

"No, oh no, Robert, I didn't mean that at all!" She grasped his sleeve and gazed up into his face. "I wanted to marry you. I wanted—I still want—to help you with your career. I love our children. But . . ."

"What?" he said impatiently at the pause.

"But I'd like it if someone thanked me once in a while."

He looked down into the stream below, as she had. "Yet it's the life you chose."

Katherine made a noise of exasperation. He just didn't understand. "Are you being willfully obtuse?"

"I hardly think I deserve that!"

She glared at him, and they faced each other from a gap that, though only a few feet wide, might as well have been a chasm. "Then pray don't act it," she said icily, and stalked away.

She had not got above a dozen feet, however, when her arm was caught from behind. Truly angry now, she twisted free, only to have him catch at, and this time hold, her other arm. "Katherine," he said, his voice subdued. "Don't."

"Don't what?" She gazed stonily beyond his shoulder. "Don't be upset?"

"Don't leave like this. Lord." He raked his free hand through his hair. "I've made a mull of it."

"Yes, so you have."

"But if I have, so have you," he said, his temper flashing again. "No one asked you to take on all that you have."

"No one asked—!" She stared at him. "No one had to! 'Twas simply expected of me."

" 'Tis the way of things in our world," he defended himself.

"And you have just contradicted yourself, my lord. Not a very cogent argument, either," she retorted.

"Kate, you are enough to confound the angels themselves," he began through gritted teeth, when the sound of wagon wheels penetrated into their absorption. Startled, they looked up to see a pony cart sweep by them, its occupants apparently deeply interested in the well-dressed couple arguing by the bridge. *Oh, the devil,* Katherine thought, echoing Robert's words in her mind. Knowing country people, she suspected the news of their disagreement would be known, and misunderstood, everywhere in the district by evening.

"Go home, Robert." Tired now, she brushed her wrist across her forehead. "Go, and let me have some days in peace. I promise I will come back of my own accord."

"Yes, but when? Dash it, Katherine—"

"Doubtless in time to plan your next dinner party," she said, and walked away.

That stopped him. He watched her go, dismayed. Oh, the devil. Last night everything had seemed so clear. He'd truly thought a few words from him today would be enough. Now, however, he knew better. Now he realized that the roots of her resentment had begun growing long ago, perhaps as early as their wedding. For if she were unhappy, he thought, so was he, though he had not, until just now, realized it. But then, he'd always known that his marriage had never been quite what he had hoped it would be. Why that should be, he wasn't sure.

There was one thing he did know, however. Katherine would not be coming home soon, not if things continued as they were. Obviously there was more he must do to make amends. Lips firming, he set off toward the inn, following her. Though he didn't quite understand the reasons for her unhappiness, still he could do something to alleviate them. He could try to bring back some of the sparkle that had so attracted him to her from the very beginning. He only hoped it would be enough.

Georgina looked up in puzzlement from the letter in her hands. "But I don't understand," she said, yet again. "Why should Papa and Mama stay in some poky little village?

Surely Mama remembers that Lady Durrell is holding her ball this Friday."

"Oh, forget your dratted ball." William, lounging sulkily in a battered armchair that was badly in need of re-upholstering, ran a hand through his hair quite as his father did, and then self-consciously smoothed it down again. "Now look what you made me do," he fretted. "This took me ages to achieve this morning. I don't know how Papa does it."

"Your hair is of no consequence," Georgina said, with the scorn born of her lofty position of being his elder by one year. "I am making my come-out, I might remind you—"

"As if anyone could forget."

"—and that is a vastly more important thing."

That made him start up from his chair. "More important than my getting into Oxford?"

"Perhaps had you paid some mind to your books in school, you'd not be in such a fix and Mama wouldn't have left."

"Perhaps if you cared about something other than yourself and your precious come-out—"

"It's my fault," Pamela interrupted from the window seat in the nursery, which was the only place where all three could gather with some assurance of privacy, now that Georgina was considered a young lady and her brother was no longer allowed admittance to her room. Across the room from them Pamela's governess nodded over her knitting, but even had she been awake, all three knew they could speak before her without constraint. She was, besides being a most amiable creature, quite deaf, adding to Katherine's problems immeasurably.

"Your fault?" Georgina raised one elegant brow at her, as Katherine occasionally did. "How could you possibly do anything important enough for this to be your fault?"

Rather than taking umbrage at this remark, as she would have in the past, Pamela hunched into herself. "I don't know," she offered feebly. "But you've said yourself I'm forever in the way."

Georgina sniffed. "I am persuaded Mama takes no more notice of you than I do."

"Leave her alone, Georgie," William said, unexpectedly coming to Pamela's support. "So you're in the way, brat? What is new about that?"

She grimaced at him, and his grin widened. Oh, it was a trial being so much younger than both her brother and sister. Georgie awed her, and she frankly adored William, who sometimes deigned to pay attention to her, but they refused to see her as an equal, someone who had feelings and opinions and, sometimes, knowledge. For she knew something they could not possibly know: she knew the real reason for Mama's flight.

Georgina had returned to the letter. "I really do not understand this at all," she complained. "Papa wants us all to behave in certain ways."

William, one leg now thrown carelessly over the arm of his chair, looked up from admiring the shine on his boot. "Such as?"

"Really, this is too much!" Her attention was still on the letter, rather than on them. Georgina, Pamela suspected, thought her brother and sister far below her notice. "He believes I am putting Mama in a pelter about my come-out. A pelter!" She laid down the letter. "He knows how important this Season is to me. So does Mama. They wish me to marry well."

"But not yet, if you don't wish it. I heard Father say so," Pamela put in.

Georgina glared at her. "You know nothing of such matters," she said loftily. "A pelter! But I am persuaded Mama is enjoying the Season."

"Squiring you about?" William said skeptically. "A dead bore, I'd think."

"Do you?" Georgina's voice was cool. "But you've not heard what he wishes from you."

He grinned again. "Nothing much, I suppose."

"No, nothing, except that you're to study harder and pass the exam for Oxford."

"I say!" he exclaimed, straightening up. "I would study, except Mama isn't here to arrange for a tutor for me, as she promised."

"There are books aplenty in the library. As for you," Georgina looked at Pamela over the top of the letter. "You are supposed to come out of the sullens."

"I'm not in the sullens," Pamela protested.

"Hmm." William was studying her. "Come to think of it, brat, you've been quiet of late."

Georgina frowned at the letter one more time, and then folded it again. "A pleasant change, I must say."

"So he wants us to become pattern cards of behavior, does he?" William said. "Well, he's fair and far out there. You're not likely to change."

"Neither are you," Georgina retorted. "As for my behavior, I must make my come-out. That means I must attend *ton* events, and that I must look my best. Mama knows that. Why it's suddenly become trouble, I've no idea."

"Mayhaps she's tired," Pamela said.

Georgina's look was withering. "Mama's never tired. Why, I've seen her go from one ball to another and not turn a hair."

"Stop thinking of yourself, Georgie." William sounded irritated, though he was looking at Pamela with interest. "What makes you say that, brat?"

Pamela shrugged and pretended to be studying the view outside the window, though all she could see was the back garden of the house next door. Not for the world would she disclose what she knew, not with Georgina there. She could just imagine what her sister would say. William, though, might take it rather differently.

Georgina rose, tossing the letter on her chair. "I don't intend to give up my come-out, and I am persuaded Mama will agree with me." She paused at the doorway, looking back at William. "Are you coming?"

"No." Lazily he swung his foot, again apparently admiring the shine of his boot. "Might be I'll find a book in the schoolroom to help me study."

"Well I, for one, am not going to remain in such juvenile company," she declaimed, and swept away.

Silence fell in the wake of her departure, so heavy and thick that, almost against her will, Pamela turned to look at William. He was regarding her steadily, making her want to squirm. As always, when she felt she had to defend herself from one of her siblings, she attacked. "What?" she demanded.

"You know something, brat," he said, still watching her. "Come on. Tell me."

"There's nothing."

"I know that look." He rose. "Do I have to tickle you?"

"No!" Pamela shrank back, though she did, for the first time since the conversation had begun, smile a little. "Don't you dare!"

"Then empty the budget," he demanded.

"Well." She looked down at her hands. "It was really all my fault."

"Huh. Doesn't surprise me."

"But I've never done anything to make her act like that before!"

"Like what, brat? You've not told me yet."

"I know." She took a deep breath. "Promise you won't tell Georgina?"

"Not a chance, brat. Not that she'd listen if I did."

"I know." She glanced at her governess, to make certain she was still dozing. "Very well. It was raining, I remember that, because I couldn't get out to the park. So I was playing with Tommy," she indicated the dog lying before the dark hearth, "and, well, we were running, and—"

"Let me guess. She told you to behave like a lady."

"Worse."

He tried, as his father did, to raise one eyebrow, and failed. Of all Mama's reprimands, the admonition to act either as a lady or a gentleman, always spoken in a sorrowful voice, was somehow the worst. "What could be worse than that?"

She squirmed on the window seat. "We banged into a few things."

"Huh. I'm not surprised. You're remarkably clumsy, brat. So? Out with it. What did you do?"

"I knocked over her Dresden shepherdess."

"Good gad!" He stared at her. "The one Father gave her, that she likes so much?"

"Yes," Pamela said miserably. "And it broke."

He whistled through his teeth. "I can just imagine what she said."

"No, you can't." She looked him directly in the eye. "She said that sometimes she wanted to wash her hands of the whole lot of us." Now she averted her head, lest he see the tears that had gathered in her eyes. "So, you see, it's my fault, and I don't know what to do."

"Sprite, you're being foolish, even for you."

That made her bring her head up, ready to defend herself again, when she saw the gleam in his eyes. "Stop teasing me!"

"D'you really think you made Mama run away?"

"What else could it be?"

"How should I know? Mayhap she and Father had a quarrel!"

That made her draw in her breath, and they looked at each other in growing dismay. "Do you think—"

"I think we don't know what happened. But Father's there, and if anyone can bring her back, he can."

"But—"

"Stop worrying, brat." He ruffled her hair. "It'll turn out right, you'll see."

"Are you going to study?"

"Don't be more foolish than you can help. Of course not."

"But Father said—"

"Father's not here. How am I to find a tutor by myself?"

"His secretary—"

"Can't give permission to hire anyone. No, brat. It's end of term, and I intend to enjoy it."

"But, William—" Pamela ran after him. "Mama might never come back, ever."

"Of course she will. She knows we need her," he said, and, grinning at her, went out.

Pamela frowned at the door. Didn't they care? she thought, incensed at her brother and sister. Mama and Father might be away forever. Well, not really forever; but if they didn't do as Father said, things likely would never be the same again.

Well. If they weren't going to do anything about it, she certainly could, she thought, her mouth set in the mutinous pout it wore more often these days. Maybe she couldn't go after her parents—she didn't have the least idea of how to begin the search, for one thing—but that didn't mean she was completely helpless. Father needed to know how matters stood. It appeared she was the only person who could tell him.

Pamela picked up the letter Georgina had left so carelessly on her chair to note again his direction, and then stalked toward her desk. Sitting down, she drew a piece of paper toward her. "Dear Father," she began.

Morning brought no counsel to Robert. He could only hope his children would heed his message; hope it would be enough for Katherine. Matters were still at an impasse. Hadrian's Wall continued to separate them at night; during yesterday, her wall of icy politeness had kept them apart, with very little to divert them. Not for the first time he wondered what he was doing in this rural hamlet. Clearly he'd made no progress with his wife. Only the knowledge that he might damage their marriage irrevocably should he leave kept him there. "I wonder what's going on in town," he said idly.

Katherine looked up. "Can you not leave politics behind for even a few days?"

"It is my career."

"And sometimes I think you love your career far more than you ever loved me."

"Kate." He stared at her. "That's not true."

"Oh, really."

"Yes, really." He rose and crossed to her, his hand out-stretched. "We really can't go on like this, you know," he said quietly. "Sooner or later one of us will have to give in."

"And I assume that will be me."

"No, not at all."

"Whyever not? It always has been."

"Perhaps this time 'twill be different."

"I don't know how."

"Kate." He dragged his hand through his hair. Lud, if his valet could see him, with his hair, usually arranged in the apparently careless windblown style, now merely care-less, and with boots badly in need of polishing, the man would hand in his notice on the spot. "Cry pax. I don't want this any more than you do."

"Who said I don't want it?"

"I know you need some rest, but—"

"I need things to change."

"I know," he said quietly.

It took her a moment to realize his meaning. When she did, her eyes grew wide. "You'd give up politics?"

He frowned. " 'Tis unfair of you to ask that of me."

"Then I don't see what we have to discuss."

"I believe, however, that you're likely right that I spend too much time on my career."

"How handsome of you to admit such a thing."

"Do you not grow tired of this, Kate? This coldness be-tween us?"

She opened her mouth, hesitated, and then nodded. "Yes."

"That's a start." He crossed the room and grasped her limp hands in his. "I don't deny we've problems between us, Kate, but every married couple does. I'd say, in fact, that we're closer than most."

She was frowning. "As to that . . ."

"What?"

Her eyes were troubled when they rose to his. "I've always felt you're distant from me. No, please, I don't wish to quarrel, either, and I don't mean to hurt you."

She had, though. For if she'd felt the distance, so had he, though he knew something she didn't. He knew what caused it. "There's one place our marriage has always been good," he said.

Color stained her cheeks and she lowered her head, making him smile a little. Oh, yes, when they were in each others' arms, any differences they might have melted away. "Yes." She looked up, her eyes troubled. "But it's not enough."

"What would you have me do, Kate? I cannot be a useless fribble, like so many others in the *ton*."

"I know, nor do I wish you to be. I simply wish we were closer."

"We could start by taking down that ridiculous bolster between us."

"No."

"Just like that? No?"

"Not yet, at least."

"Then when, Kate?"

"I don't know." Again she looked at him. "I've no more answers than you do. I simply know things have got to change, else I can't go on."

"You'd leave me?" he asked, quietly.

"Oh, no. It wouldn't be good for your career, would it?" she said, bitterly.

"I'm not thinking of my career. 'Tis you I want. I always have."

Her eyes met his again, and this time their gaze held. "Our parents arranged our marriage."

"So they did, but 'tis not why I married you. You know that."

"Yes." She searched his face. "But I've always felt that distance from you, Robert. I cannot help it. 'Tis there."

"You've not helped, Kate, immersing yourself in our children's care."

"Immersing myself!" She stared at him. "If I did not, who would? And let me remind you that I'm often busy doing things to help your work!"

"I know, and I'm grateful."

"Then—"

"Kate, I've felt the distance, too. Yes, I have," he said, as she made a noise of startled surprise. "I don't wish it any more than you do."

"Then—"

"I cannot seem to help it. Pray don't blame my career. This has nothing to do with that."

"Then what?"

" 'Tis something in me. I've tried, Kate. I have."

She looked down at their hands. "When I was *enceinte* with Georgina, you could not have been more solicitous of me," she said, apparently at random.

"You were carrying my child. Of course I was."

" 'Twas somewhat different with William, and with Pamela, I barely saw you."

"But I was by your side when both were born," he said quietly.

"I needed you, Robert, more than you could know. My mother was no help. She simply told me I was doing my duty."

"Duty!" He snorted. "That damned word."

"Robert!" She stared at him. "You so rarely talk in such a way."

"I care not. Duty has ruled my life, Kate. My duty to my title, to my estate, to my work. My duty to marry well. My duty to my family."

"Is that all we are to you? A duty?"

It was his turn to gaze down at their linked hands. "No. But it feels so at times."

"As what I do for you does."

Again they looked at each other, and he let out his breath. "So what do we do?"

"I don't know." She shrugged helplessly. "I do know I need this time away."

"Without me?"

She didn't answer right away. "No. I'm glad you came, though I wasn't at first."

He let out his breath again. "Then I'll stay."

She stared at him. "You will?"

"Yes." For he'd felt the distance between them as keenly as she had. He'd wanted their marriage to work from the beginning, oh, he'd wanted it. Somehow, though, there'd always been a lack. It had begun, he thought now, with their courtship. *No.* He pursed his lips. They never really had had a courtship. Instead, both had dutifully followed their parents' dictates, only shyly and wordlessly acknowledging anything more by looks, by touches. Perhaps that was part of the problem. He needed to court his wife.

He grinned, and though he saw the look of surprise on Katherine's face, his sudden good mood continued. For he was a man who liked always to have a clear path in life, and he thought he'd found one. He was, he thought, going to court, and win back, his wife.

In the days following, Katherine sometimes wondered if she had a new husband, so different was Robert in his behavior. There didn't seem to be much to do in Thame, and yet always they found something to keep themselves amused. There was the town itself to explore, from the old houses lining the streets, their gardens in glorious bloom, to the small square church, indeed filled, as the maid Michael had informed them, with monuments to dead people. The sight of them made Katherine giggle, though she knew it was disrespectful. Robert didn't join in, but his eyes gleamed with humor. "The chapel at Trent has tombs of my ancestors," he reminded her, referring to his country estate as they emerged into a cool, cloudy day and he took her arm.

"This is different, somehow. The names are so very obscure."

"Ah, but the monuments themselves are fine," he argued. "Quite an attraction, I am certain."

She gazed at him suspiciously as they walked along, and then relaxed into a smile. "You're bamming me."

"Now, madam, would I do that?"

"Yes," she said, though how she knew that about him, she could not precisely say. He seemed rarely to laugh or jest. "Though I think this is a grave subject for you to laugh at."

He let out a laugh. "A grave subject? Indeed."

"You know what I meant," she said, squeezing his arm. "I'd no idea you have a sense of humor."

He looked down at her, a slight frown wrinkling his forehead. "I do know how to laugh, Katherine."

"Do you? I rarely hear you do so."

He pursed his lips and raised his forehead, staring somewhere into the distance. "I suppose because I rarely deal with humorous issues."

"What is your work about? You never do tell me."

"Why do you not come to the House of Lords to hear for yourself?"

"I have the children to consider."

"Ah, the children. Of course. They're more important than a mere husband."

"No, they're more important than politics." She looked away. "It has been such a wonderful afternoon," she said in a small voice, as they neared the inn. "Let's not spoil it."

"It seems we cannot talk but that we enter into a quarrel."

"I know." She sighed. "I will promise to try not to take offense, if you will."

"I will," he said, his face surprisingly serious. She eyed him, wondering what he was thinking, but he had rarely shared his thoughts with her. He rarely, in fact, shared much of anything. She wondered if she could change that.

"What is your work about?" she asked again. "Please. I really want to know, and I cannot very well go to Parliament now."

His look was searching. "Will you, in future?"

"Yes, if I'm not busy with the children."

"Katherine, if you are so involved with them, 'tis by your own choice," he said. "As I recall, I encouraged you to hire a nurse and a governess to see to them."

"And so I did. I believe, however, and I thought you felt the same, that children need their parents far more than they need any servant. Servants can't love them as we do." She paused. "As I do."

"I do love them, Kate."

"Do you? Then why have you not attended any balls or routs or such with Georgina and me this Season?"

"I was there for her presentation at Court, and certainly at her come-out ball," he said dryly. "And, yes, I noticed she looked lovely each time."

"I wish they'd all received more of your looks." He started when she reached up to briefly run her hand through his thick, wavy hair. "Straight hair is well and good in a boy, but for a girl 'tis quite a trial. Poor Georgina." She smiled. "She has such trouble keeping her coiffure neat."

"And yet she always looks beautiful." He gazed down at her. "Like you," he repeated.

"Compliments, Robert? Unusual of you."

"Can I not tell my wife that she is beautiful?"

"You rarely do."

"More fool I. Look at you, Katherine," he said, as though they stood before a mirror. "There's not a strand of gray in your hair, and your figure is that of a girl's. As for your face." He touched a finger to her nose. "I love this little nose. Have I ever told you that?"

She gazed at him, transfixed. "N-no."

"And the freckles you hate so much. And your green eyes." His gaze traveled to her hair, which had been as much of a trial to her as Georgina's was to her. Yet it did shine, and she had to admit the fashionable cut devised for her by the hairdresser, which left the hair itself long but kept tendrils to curl about her face with the aid of curling tongs, was flattering. Robert wasn't dealing in Spanish coin. He wasn't the type.

At the thought, something within her relaxed, though she wasn't sure why. "I can't believe you feel this way. Why have you not said something before?"

"I have." He cocked one eyebrow at her. "But I won't mention just where in the street."

Color rose in her cheeks again as she realized what he meant. Their bed, where there never was any separation between them, where they both seemed to feel the promise of their marriage fulfilled. "Oh."

His grin widened. "Perhaps we can continue that part of our discussion later?"

She started to speak, hesitated, and then drew in a breath. "I need time, Robert," she murmured. "I told you that before."

"Time." He frowned at her. "How much more?"

"I don't know." She wished she did. For if she had expected to feel happy away from her family for a time, she knew now that she had been wrong. Her place had been with them too completely, for too long, for that expectation to come true. Her place was with Robert.

She sighed, and Robert looked down at her. "What is it?"

"Nothing."

"No?" He continued to study her. "That sounded quite heartfelt."

" 'Tis nothing we haven't discussed before. This morning, as it happens."

"Oh?" He opened the door to the inn, where they would have luncheon, to let her precede him inside.

"No." She knew men felt differently about these matters than women did; she knew they rarely spent much time with their families or, for that matter, with their wives. Foolish of her to want more.

"Katherine, I try," he said, his voice low, making her turn and look at him as she stood, one foot on the first stair. His face was somber; the expression in his eyes unexpectedly tender. Their gazes held for a long time, and then she turned away.

"I shall get ready for luncheon," she said, not wishing to continue this topic where anyone, not just the innkeeper or his wife or their servants, could hear.

"Katherine—"

"Could we not talk later?"

He took time to answer, making her look at him. Poised at the bottom of the stairs, he now appeared thoughtful, making her wonder what was going through his mind. "I've the time, if you do."

So much for the solitary hours she had imagined, she thought wryly. Yet she was glad Robert had come after her. *Contrary,* she thought, annoyed at herself. It was no wonder Robert so often didn't understand her needs, if she didn't understand them herself. "Very well," she said, and continued up to their room.

Some time later, she returned back down and headed for the private parlor. Surprisingly enough, Robert had never come upstairs; she wondered what he had been doing. "Oh, ma'am," a voice said, and she looked back to see the maid, Michael.

"Yes, Michael?" she said.

"Beggin' your pardon, ma'am, but his lordship—I mean, Mr. Hawthorne—said as how you were to meet him outside."

"Michael, why did you call him 'lordship' just now?"

"I don't rightly know, ma'am," she said, looking puzzled. "Just a certain way he has, I suppose."

Katherine allowed herself a slight smile. "True. Very well. Where exactly is he?"

"Outside, in his gig, ma'am."

She frowned slightly. In his gig? "Thank you," she said, and went out.

The sun had come out since their morning ramble, and under it the limestone houses across the street glowed. Above, the sky arched a deep blue, with nary a cloud to be seen; just before her, in the inn yard, stood Robert by his tilbury, a groom holding the horse's head. "Robert?"

He smiled. "I thought we'd have a picnic luncheon today."

It was impossible not to return that smile. "That sounds the very thing! Whatever made you think of it?"

"Mm, this and that," he said, handing her into the gig. "Mind your step."

"I will." She glanced behind her at the large straw hamper, bundled into the gig with what looked like a thick rug. "Did Mrs. Tanner put this together?"

"Yes." He took up the reins and set them into motion with an expert flick of his wrist. Robert might not be a member of the Four-in-Hand club, but at driving, as at so much else, he was still competent. "Where are we going?"

"Mrs. Tanner suggested a spot by the river Thame. 'Tis just outside of town."

"I know. We crossed it coming in."

He chanced a glance away from his driving. "And how did you find riding in a public coach?"

She grimaced. "Not at all the adventure I thought it would be."

"Adventure?" This time his glance was startled and longer. "You, too?"

"Yes." She returned the look, as surprised as he was. "Goodness. I suppose we both felt the need for it."

"Yes." He frowned slightly. "Though I didn't know it until I was off. And I found, like you, that 'tis not very comfortable."

"I know. Your poor back, Robert. Is it better?"

"Tolerable. But I shall never drive so hard again."

"I doubt you'll have need to."

"Oh?" His eyebrow was raised again. "Then shall I hope that you won't attempt such a mad start again?"

"We-ell." She grinned. "I didn't say that."

"Baggage," he said, but mildly, making the word sound like an endearment.

"Your Grace," she replied impudently, and this time he was the one to smile. She wished she could lay her head on his shoulder, so in charity with him did she feel, but there were too people going about their business on the street. All stared at them curiously, if covertly. "I'm surprised the vicar hasn't invited us to tea."

"Thank God he hasn't."

"Why, Robert. That sounds supremely undutiful of you. I would also think the squire would wish to meet you," she went on. "Michael called you 'my lordship' just now."

"Did she?" He glanced at her again. "But none of them know the truth."

"No." Her good mood of a moment ago was fading. "Including the fact that we really are married."

Somewhat to her surprise Robert reached for her hand and gave it a reassuring squeeze, before releasing it to attend to his driving. "I rather enjoy that."

"Robert! You yourself said we need worry about the scandal."

"But admit it, Kate." His eyes sparkled. "Don't you enjoy being someone other than you usually are? No pressures of children to raise, or dinners to arrange."

The children, her one worry; her one guilt. "What if the children need me? I did leave Georgina in an awful mess. A girl making her come-out must needs have her mother."

"And the mother must needs have some rest."

"What of you?" she said, warmed by his unexpected words. So he did understand, more than she'd thought. "I thought you'd miss your work."

He looked thoughtful. "No, not so much as I expected."

They were rumbling over a bridge outside of town now. "You never did tell me exactly what concerns you most."

Robert was expertly tooling the gig off the road. "You

must have some idea, simply from listening at dinner parties."

"I've hardly the chance to attend to anyone save the people near me." Katherine clutched the side of the gig as it bounced along the uneven ground. "You know that."

"No. Here, hold these." He tossed the reins to Katherine and swung down to the ground, quite as youthful as the boy she had once fallen in love with, and far more exuberant in his movements. "All right. Let me have them."

"What a lovely place," Katherine said, looking around at the glade of shady trees and the quiet river. The Thame was broad here, its banks sloping steeply down to the water's edge. "Oh, look at the violets."

Robert turned from setting the horse to graze. "Beautiful," he said, holding his hands up to help her from the gig, and she had the absurd notion that he was speaking of her, not of the carpet of flowers nearby. And when she did step down, he grasped her at her waist, rather than taking her outstretched hand, to swing her down to the ground before him. Acutely aware of his touch, Katherine looked up at him, her lips slightly parted. This was the closest they had been since her flight. Since before, actually. One couldn't count the nights they had spent at the inn, with the bolster between them. Now that she thought about it, that was a ridiculous object. Yet she wasn't sure she was ready to remove it. Robert, she reflected, was showing her far more patience than she had realized.

He chose that moment to step away from her, after what seemed like a very long time. It left her bereft, still feeling the warmth where his hands had rested. "I'll get the basket and the rug, shall I?"

"Yes." She turned away, as brisk as he. "Where shall we sit?"

"Under that tree, I'd think." He indicated a place under an old, wide beech tree, its leaves rustling in the soft breeze. Together they spread the thick blanket, and then turned to the large straw hamper. "Mrs. Tanner must have thought she was feeding an army," Robert commented, watching

Katherine produce cold chicken, a salad, sliced strawberries, and a flagon which, upon investigation, contained lemonade.

"She's a remarkably good cook. I believe we're fortunate in our choice of inn."

"I believe you were fortunate in your place of refuge."

Katherine, engaged in filling a plate for him, looked up quickly at that. "Refuge? Is that how you think I view this?"

"I don't know." He took the plate from her. "I hadn't thought of it before, but now I do it stands to reason. You needed someplace to go, did you not?"

Forehead raised thoughtfully, Katherine nodded. If she had been fleeing from all that oppressed her, she had needed a safe haven. Thame, as unlikely as it seemed, provided it for her, all the more so because Robert had found her here.

She looked up. "This is how I once thought it would be."

"How you thought what would be?"

"Our marriage."

Sprawled on the blanket in a pose most uncharacteristic of him, Robert looked up. "Why do you say that?"

"The two of us talking, Robert. Not about your career and what you need me to do, not about the children, but about us. Or about silly things. Or about—oh, anything. Never mind." She bent her head to her own plate, aware her face must be flaming. "Forgive my speaking such fustian."

"What you're saying," he said, slowly, "is that our marriage is unlike that."

She kept her attention on her food. "Yes."

"I see." Plate still poised, he seemed to consider that. "So we are not close."

That made her look up. "Do you think we are?"

"I thought we rubbed along tolerably."

"We do. I simply wanted . . ."

"What?"

"More."

"Katherine, I'm not certain I'm capable of more."

That hurt. "Oh."

" 'Tis not to do with you," he said, hastily. " 'Tis me."

"So you've said, but how?"

He gazed off toward the river. "You've said so yourself, Kate. You've always felt a distance from me. But, look you, do you think I wished matters to be as they are? To have a typical *ton* marriage?"

"I don't know! Robert, I rarely know what you want!"

"Well, I didn't. That first time I saw you." He smiled over at her. "Do you remember?"

Oh, yes, she remembered. " 'Twas at my come-out."

"Yes. I'd no idea, you know, that our parents had already arranged matters between us. All I knew was that when I saw you, in your white dress with your hair piled high—I knew I'd never seen such a beautiful girl. Or one who seemed to know exactly what she wished."

"Is that how I appeared to you?" she said, surprised. "But I was quaking inside. I felt so conspicuous in that dress—it was only recently the fashion, you know, to wear slim dresses rather than panniers, and not to powder one's hair—and I was so nervous about what would happen. Mama and Father expected me to marry well, but I knew I couldn't marry someone I disliked. I just couldn't."

"Surely they didn't ask it of you."

"We-ll." She looked down at her hand. "Lord Grafton did ask for permission to pay me his addresses."

"Grafton!" Robert looked startled. "But he must have been twenty years older than you."

"Something like. In any event, it never came to that. I saw you," she said, simply.

"And we danced."

"Twice." She smiled. "My mother was not best pleased with that, no matter what she and my father had planned."

"The supper dance, as I recall." He smiled. "I felt so lucky, to be able to exchange above half-a-dozen words with you."

"And I with you." She looked at him. "We were chaperoned so, wherever we went. If you drove me in the park, if we went walking or riding—always there was someone there."

" 'Tis the way of things, Kate. You chaperon Georgina."

"Yes, of course."

"And your court was always flocking about you."

"My court." She dismissed that thought with a wave of her hand. "A few silly boys who sent me flowers and bad poetry."

"I was jealous of all of them—"

"Were you?"

"—of any smiles you gave them, any time you gave them, any attention."

"But none of them mattered."

"How could I know that? You hid your feelings well, too." His face was serious. "You still do, Katherine."

"Oh? I thought I was rather transparent."

"I'd no idea you were unhappy until you left."

"Well, neither did I," she said, frankly. "As I said—'twas the note."

"What is it about that damned note that bothered you so?"

She huffed out her breath. "Don't you see? There was no thought in it as to what I might have planned, what I had to do. No thought as to what's involved in planning such a dinner. I know I told you that morning how busy I'd be with Georgina, yet it seemed you hadn't listened. And it wasn't the first time." She was serious, too. "I resented it, Robert. I still do."

"Yet you never said a word to me."

"I didn't think I had to."

"Katherine, I cannot read your mind!"

"No, but you must have seen how I disliked arranging such things at the last moment. It wasn't the first time." She frowned. "I cannot remember when I last laughed for no reason, or when I thought about other things besides my responsibilities." She paused. "I cannot remember when we started drifting apart."

"We haven't," he protested.

"Oh, Robert! Of course we have. 'Tis no one's fault. 'Tis simply that you have been busy with politics, and I with the children."

Robert concentrated very hard on cutting a piece of chicken. "Katherine, no one forced you to do so much for the children."

"No one forced—Robert, someone had to do it!"

"I would have helped," he said, quietly.

"Oh, would you."

"Yes. If I'd felt I would be allowed."

"What do you mean?"

"You shut me out, Katherine." He looked her full in the eyes. "All of them turn to you rather than to me."

"Because I'm there—"

"First Georgina, then William—do you know how strange that feels, having your son turn away?—and then Pamela. All of them. I sometimes feel they're your children, rather than ours."

"William is not like you, Robert. You know that. He hasn't the political mind you do. Or a scholarly one, for that matter."

"And yet I had no idea he was having trouble in school until you told me this week. I didn't know Pamela has been in the sullens—"

"More than the sullens, I think."

"—either. Yes, I know, had I paid them more mind and left my work, mayhap I would have, but I doubt it. You kept it from me, Katherine. If you have worries to deal with, and if you're tired from helping me, you brought it all on yourself."

"I did not," she said in a low voice. She was so angry she wanted to strangle him. "I was doing what was expected of me."

"Had you asked me for help, though—"

"Would you have given it?" she challenged him. "Or would you have been too busy with your career to have time for us?"

"I hardly think that's fair."

"It's happened, Robert. There have been times when I needed you, but you had an important bill in Parliament, or some such thing. And lord knows, politics is more important than anything."

"If that is so, then all I can do is apologize and promise that I will try to do better in the future. You must stop being a martyr, trying to do everything yourself. Ask me, Katherine. I'll do my best."

Tense silence fell between them. It mattered not that the mid-afternoon sun, slanting through the trees, was bright and warm, or that the river looked enticingly cool. They sat there, not eating, not speaking, simply looking away from each other.

"I don't want matters to be like this," Katherine said after a few minutes had passed. "Maybe I have caused some of my own unhappiness. I don't know. What I do know is that I want our marriage to be better."

"So do I." He held out his hand to her. "Shall we try?"

Katherine looked down at his hand, large and square and solid, even if all his labor was done indoors with a pen. He could make her so angry! Yet she did very much want things to change.

Looking up, she saw Robert's eyes for the first time. They looked vulnerable, uncertain, and they caught her as nothing else could. "Yes." She reached out her hand and his fingers closed around it, capable, comforting. "Let's try."

And that night, Hadrian's Wall was breached.

Robert was already at breakfast when Katherine floated into the private parlor the following morning. "I've no idea how you eat that so early in the day," she said by way of greeting, eyeing his beefsteak and ale.

Robert had risen at her entrance. "And good morning to you, too," he said, pulling her close for a long, deep, and thoroughly satisfying kiss.

"Good morning." She looked up at him, and that seemed to set him off again. Only after a suitable interval had passed did he release her, a little crumpled, a little mussed. "You've set my cap askew," she complained, as she sat across from him.

Robert eyed the offending article of clothing thoughtfully, and then, before she could prevent him, reached over and untied the strings to pull it off her head. "There."

"Robert, I need that."

"Why?"

"Because—must I explain? I'm nearly middle-aged. Don't laugh at me!"

"Middle-aged? The way you behaved yesterday?"

"Oh, spare my blushes," she muttered, but her hands were to her cheeks. She had behaved like a girl, laughing, caring not for the responsibilities she had left behind. But then, that was partly why she had left home, was it not? It seemed like a silly thing to do, now. Freedom was where she found it. Last night she had found it in her husband's arms.

There was a soft knock on the door, and then Michael came in, apologizing softly as she handed a note to Robert. Katherine frowned as he broke the wafer. "Who could that be from—oh." The warm feeling of being cherished, started last night, began to dissipate. "Your secretary."

Robert was frowning over the square of vellum, so dirty that it was obvious it had seen hard use. "Mm.

"Oh, Robert." She watched him tuck the note away, his face shuttered. "Is it bad news?"

"No, but I have to go back."

"To London? Now? Oh, Robert, not now!"

"I'm afraid I've no choice." He rose and held out his hand. "Come with me."

She looked at him. Oh, she was tempted. Were she to go with him, though, nothing would change. Last night had, after all, been only a start. "I can't."

He paused impatiently at the door. "You'd prefer to stay here, after yesterday?"

"No, I don't prefer it. But I so fear we'll lose what we've found. If I return now, everything will be the same. All this will have been for nothing."

"I've told you I'll try to change."

"I know, and I believed you."

"Believed?" he cut in.

"Look at you. You receive a letter about some political crisis, I imagine, and our own problems are forgotten. How can I expect it won't happen in the future?"

He opened his mouth to speak, closed it again, and then took a deep breath. "Of course it will happen. I'm only human. But, Kate." His eyes were grave. "I promised I'd try. 'Tis all I can do." He held his hand out again. "Come with me."

She wanted to. Oh, she wanted to. During these past days with Robert, even when they'd been quarreling, she had felt more alive than she had in many a year. Yet what she'd said to him was true. If she returned now, all her hard-won gains would be lost. He needed still to know how serious she was. He wouldn't, if she went back. "I can't," she repeated, simply.

"Life's not perfect, Katherine," he said, impatiently. "Even were we to stay here another week, completely happy, things would change once we got home."

She looked away. He was right, unfortunately. Nothing *would* change. She would be simply a wife, a mother, a hostess again. Katherine the woman would be forgotten. "I'm sorry, Robert," she said, truly regretful. "I can't."

"Damn it." He slammed the door closed, a rare display of temper for him. "What is it that you want?"

"Respect," she shot back.

"You have that. Does anyone treat you ill? Speak to you in a manner less than you deserve?"

She made an impatient gesture with her hand. "I don't mean that! I mean from you and the children."

"Kate." He braced his hands on the edge of the table and leaned toward her, making her edge back. "Do you think you don't have that now?"

She returned his look without flinching. "I know I don't."

He put his hand to the back of his neck and took a turn about the room. "For God's sake," he said, and it was a measure of his irritation that he used any sort of an oath. "I swear I've no idea of how to reach you."

" 'Tis not what I want, Robert."

"But you'll stay anyway. Is that what you were about to say?"

"No. I was going to say I want our lives to be as they were yesterday, like last night! Oh, you needn't tell me they won't always be," she said, as he opened his mouth to speak. "But, Robert. Think. Can you remember any other time when we were like that with each other? So open, so close?"

"I know there were moments we came close," he said, slowly. "Especially in the beginning."

Unable to bear the tenderness in his expression, she looked away. If she didn't, she would give in. And then what would she have gained? "They'll not be like that at all if I go with you now."

"Kate—"

" 'Tis not you alone, Robert. 'Tis the children, too. You say I've absorbed myself in them, and you're right. And children are self-centered creatures. Unfortunately," her lips twisted, "I fear I've encouraged that."

"And I, madam?" he said, quietly.

"Oh, Robert." Tiredly she ran her wrist across her brow. "Soon you'd be taking me for granted again, as well. Oh, I know you wouldn't mean to, of course, but you'd become involved in your work. And then nothing else would matter."

"Do you truly believe you and our children don't matter to me?"

"No, of course not. But you cannot deny you've put your career ahead of us."

"Because you were always there to see to things. You stood between me and the children, Kate."

"No, Robert," she said, quietly. "You've done that by yourself."

He snorted and turned to the door, stopping only when he reached there. "You won't come with me, then?"

"No. I won't."

"I see." For long, long moments he stared at her, his gaze unfathomable, and then, stepping into the hall, was gone.

Robert's tilbury stood ready in the inn yard, his baggage already loaded, a groom tending to the horse as it danced and strained against the bridle, impatient to be off on this cloudy spring morning. From her window above, Katherine watched as Robert came out, his many-caped greatcoat swirling about him and his hat set firmly upon his head. In the few hours since the note had arrived, they'd hardly spoken to each other, unless they'd had to. Hadrian's Wall had not been rebuilt, but in a very real way, it was back in place between them.

Look up, Katherine commanded silently, suddenly filled with panic at his imminent, inexorable departure. Look up and see her, so she could at least wave to him. He didn't, though. Instead he climbed into the tilbury, leaving her with no choice. Gathering up her skirts, she set off at an undignified run down the inn's uneven stairs, stumbling once or twice and not caring. At last she burst out into the inn yard, only to find it empty of the one person who mattered. Down the road, dust swirling behind the tilbury, drove Robert at a spanking pace, leaving her.

An absurd lump formed in Katherine's throat. But this was what she wanted, wasn't it? Time to herself, to relax, to find some peace again, before returning home and hoping that her disappearance had had the desired effect. Of course, all that had been before Robert had arrived. Never had she felt so alive as she had these past days. Even while they argued, she'd felt a current between them that was new, a connection that gave her hope for the future. And last night . . . She put her hands to her cheeks. She had never before behaved as she had last night. Had he taken a disgust of her, perhaps? No, she decided, going in, her shoulders in a decided slump. It hadn't seemed so this morning. It was that damned note, she thought, the unaccustomed oath giving her an odd measure of satisfaction. One look at it and he needs must dash back to London. Nothing had changed.

Climbing the stairs heavily, she at last reached her room. She was aware of Mrs. Tanner and Michael whispering below, and knew full well what they were discussing. Her. She had come here alone, apparently fallen in with Robert, and now, just as apparently, had been deserted. Depressing thought. But then, that was what had happened all her married life, was it not? Robert had promised her he'd try to change, but at the first sign that he was needed, off he went. Her flight had been for naught.

She leaned her head against the window, longing for just a glimpse of Robert, knowing he was gone. The trouble was, she could no longer stay here. Oh, her shot was paid, Robert had seen to that, and what the servants had made of *that,* she didn't know. It was simply that Thame was no longer a refuge. She could find things to do, she supposed; she could read, or ramble about the town and meet people, if not the squire or Miss Wykeham of Thame Park. Or, she thought, entertaining the thought for the first time, she could simply leave. True, she'd no idea of how her defection had changed things at home, but that didn't matter. Penitent or not, her children would likely fall back into their old ways, anyway. So would Robert. The difference now was that she wouldn't allow them to act in such a way. If she could keep them off-balance, she just might receive what she'd wanted.

There was no doubt about it, Katherine thought with sudden briskness. She would have to return home. Oh, not right away, she thought. Not on tonight's stage, much as she longed to, much as she wished to be with Robert again. To do so would appear to be capitulation. No, it would have to be tomorrow night. Today and tomorrow would be lonely, of course, and tonight—ah, tonight. She turned away from the window, and faced the bed, now neatly made up. Tonight would be unbearably empty, without Robert, without the closeness they had found. Yet, if she did go home now she would soon find herself mired in the same mindless routine, and that, she couldn't bear. Suffering for just a little while longer would be worth it, if it brought about true change.

Tomorrow night, then, she thought, nodding decisively and feeling an upswelling of anticipation. Tomorrow night she was going home.

All agog, the inn's servants, along with Mr. and Mrs. Tanner, crowded at the windows of the inn, looking out at the yard. There, pulled by a fine team of horses, four all told, and all matching, stood a magnificent, shiny carriage with, of all things, a ducal crest on the door! A duke! The George had never before had the honor of welcoming such an august personage. Why he had chosen here, Mr. Tanner thought, when the Crown was considered by some to be superior, was a mystery. No matter his reasons, he could only bring credit to their establishment.

A footman came around to open the carriage door and let down the step, making Mr. Tanner scurry out to greet his new guest. Behind him crowded his wife and his staff, along with those who had been drinking a pint in the tap-room, making him grimace with embarrassment. The duke would think they were all a bunch of rustics.

Just as he reached the inn yard, from the carriage stepped a young woman, attired in a pale blue muslin dress that even he could tell was modish, with a spencer to match and a modest chip straw bonnet perched upon her shiny auburn curls. Mrs. Tanner drew in her breath. "Such an ensemble," she murmured. "They must be fine folk, Mr. Tanner."

"O' course they are," he said, irritably, annoyed at having his dignity disturbed at this important moment. If a duke approved his inn, it would soon be all the crack, as he'd heard the London men said.

The young woman was looking about her with an apparent air of boredom, though he had noticed that she had looked up, just once, at something on the building behind him, anxiety in her eyes. He didn't have time to ponder that, however, for behind her came another female, this one considerably younger. By her side stood a woman who looked by her clothes to be her governess, straightening the girl's pinafore and pigtails. And now—this must be the heir, he thought, looking at the very young man who climbed out. His attire was a bit more outlandish than his sisters'; his coat of green merino, while undoubtedly well cut, was nipped in at the waist, and under it he wore a waistcoat rather startlingly striped in red and yellow. Fortunately his pantaloons were a biscuit color, and boots shone like a mirror.

At last, a man stood poised in the carriage doorway for a moment, looking up as his eldest daughter had done, before stepping into the sunlight. He was a rather ordinary looking man, not above average height and with hair that could simply be described as brown, and he was attired in clothes that, if more modest than his son's, were as well made. He was also startlingly familiar.

"Mr. Hawthorne! I mean, your Grace," Mr. Tanner stammered, and bowed.

"How are you, sir?" the duke said, holding out his hand. Mr. Tanner looked at it in awe. Finally, he took it, feeling as if he'd entered some bizarre dream.

"But how can you be a duke if your name is Hawthorne?" Michael, the maidservant, blurted out, making Mr. Tanner roll his eyes in dismay.

The duke smiled at her, too. " 'Tis the family name. But, pardon me. I have not introduced myself. I am Trent."

The Duke of Trent. Even Mr. Tanner had heard of him, and of his great speeches in Parliament. " 'Tis an honor, sir. Your Grace."

"Thank you."

"What brings you to my inn, your Grace? Do you need rooms?"

"The duchess is here, or she was. I do hope she hasn't left?"

Mr. Tanner stared at him in blank incomprehension, and behind him he heard his wife draw in her breath again. "Mrs. Hawthorne?" she said. "Yes, your Grace. She's in the parlor. Poor thing did something to her knee, and she has her foot propped on a pillow."

The duke stopped in mid-stride. "She's hurt?" he said.

"Yes, this morning. She was in the graveyard looking at the old stones, and she tripped on some sort of a hole. Well, the ground is very uneven, your Grace. But the doctor assured her it isn't serious."

"That's comforting," he muttered, striding toward the inn again. "Has she dined?"

"No, your Grace."

"Then have us all sent dinner, please."

"Of course, your Grace. Michael?"

"Yes, Mrs. Tanner?"

"Come with me," she commanded, and Michael followed, Mr. Tanner came in last, shaking his head. Such goings on they had never seen at the George before; mayhap they never would again.

So much for plans, Katherine thought with a sigh, looking down at her foot. 'Twas only a twisted knee, but she was, according to the local doctor, to stay off it for at least a week. A week! The time stretched before her, bleak and empty. It may have been what she had wanted, but not like this. Not when she had made the decision to go home. If only she had not decided to explore that wretched graveyard. She'd needed something to do, though, and that had seemed a harmless enough diversion. What she hadn't bargained on was that the ground would be so uneven, or that she would take so bad a fall. Luckily the vicar, just coming out of the church, had seen her. So, while anyone who happened to be nearby stopped and watched, she had been brought back to the inn. And here, it seemed, she was destined to remain. Oh, she'd written a letter to Robert, to be sent on this evening's stage, telling him of what had happened, but she had little confidence it would help. He'd be too busy, of course. Likely he'd send his secretary for her instead, she thought with unaccustomed bitterness.

The door to the parlor, where she would be ensconced until the evening, opened, and she looked up. 'Twas early for dinner, and yet too late for luncheon. Perhaps it was someone come to keep her company. At this point, she would welcome any diversion.

She didn't expect what happened next. First Georgina came in, followed closely by William and Pamela, with Robert, of all people, bringing up the rear. It was so unexpected a sight that for a moment she simply stared. Then Pamela hurtled across the room to cling to her neck, and it suddenly all became very real. "Pammie!" she exclaimed, her arms going up reflexively. "What in the world—"

"Careful of your mother," Robert said sharply. "Mr. Tanner told us you were hurt."

"Oh, Robert." She held out her hand to him. Her face practically hurt from smiling, but she couldn't seem to stop. Of all things to happen! Could this possibly be Robert's doing?

"What was the note about?" she asked him.

"Well." For the first time since her escapade had begun, he looked abashed. "I'd written to the children to ask them to do certain things, and it seemed they weren't doing as I wished."

"I wrote a letter, Mama," Pamela volunteered. "Father's secretary mailed it for me."

"I don't understand." Katherine looked up at Robert. "What things?"

"We didn't mean to make life difficult for you," William burst out. "It's just that—well, you always see to things."

"Oh, William." She reached her other hand out to him. " 'Tis only what I should do."

"But Father helped us to see that we were being selfish." Georgina's eyes were downcast. "We truly didn't realize it."

"But a girl's come-out is important."

She looked up shyly. "It wouldn't be any fun without you there, Mama."

Goodness! "Even though I impose rules and strictures upon you?"

"Even then. So," she took a deep breath, "I've asked cousin Harriet to come live with us. If you don't mind," Georgina added hastily.

"Harriet! But why on earth—"

"Since her brother married she hasn't felt she has a home," Robert put in quietly, and she turned to him.

"Then that was your idea?"

"No. Georgina's."

"I know you've things to see to, Mama, and so I wrote to her. She needs a home, and I need someone to accompany me to the modiste's for fittings or to Hookham's, or such. I think we'll suit each other's needs admirably."

"Goodness," Katherine said faintly, impressed and stunned by this new, adult Georgina, who actually considered other peoples' feelings, other peoples' lives.

William cleared his throat. "And I've engaged a tutor. At least, Father's secretary has."

"A scholarly young man, but one with a sense of humor," Robert put in.

"And you should see him drive, Mama! I do believe his cattle would be bang up to the mark, if he had any."

"My goodness," Katherine said again. "I am impressed by both of you, and proud of you. Come here." Since Pamela was comfortably ensconced on her lap, she was able to catch both of them about the neck in a quick hug. William quickly struggled free, his face cherry red, but not before returning the embrace. "You could not have given me a better present."

"And, Mama?" Pamela looked up, her eyes troubled.

"What, poppet?"

"I know you were upset when I broke the shepherdess."

"Oh, Pammie." She hugged her daughter again. " 'Twas only a thing. It shouldn't have bothered me so."

"But I know it was worth something, and so," she, too, took a deep breath, "I bought you this, from my pin money."

Katherine took the figurine Pamela held out to her. Though it, too, was a shepherdess, it was a clear imitation of the one that had broken. Katherine had to bite back a smile. In her own way, Pamela had tried to make amends. One day she would tell her daughter that her most important contribution to this reunion had been writing to her father.

" 'Tis lovely, Pamela," she said, knowing the child expected some reaction. "I shall place it just where the other one was."

Pamela's face broke into a smile. "Then you like it?"

"I will always treasure it," Katherine promised. "Is this what's been bothering you?"

"No." Pamela looked up at her. "Actually, it's—"

"No, Pamela!" Georgina burst in, and at the same time, "Pammie, if you dare," William began, making them both stop speaking at once.

"What?" Katherine looked from one to the other. "What is so terrible?"

"I was afraid I made you go away," Pamela said in a low voice.

For a moment, Katherine wasn't sure she'd heard properly. "Goodness! Why?"

"Because when I broke the other statue you said you were tired of us all."

"I did?" She stared blankly ahead, trying to remember. "Goodness, I did! Oh, Pammie." She hugged her again. "I didn't mean that. I must have been tired that day. Not that that's an excuse." She drew back. "I truly didn't mean it."

"It felt like you did."

"I am so sorry." Oh, the damage a parent could do, without even being aware of it, she thought, looking up at her other children. "I'm sorry about everything."

That started a firestorm of protest, about who had done

what, and how much worse each transgression was. Only Robert was quiet, leaning against the wall of the parlor with his arms crossed and one knee bent, his foot casually braced against the wall. Looking up, Katherine met his gaze, and then had to look away, lest she start laughing. It would be disastrous, when her children were so in earnest; when they had gone to such lengths, not only to please her, but to make a genuine effort to mend their ways. 'Twas only fair that she meet them halfway.

"We'll never behave so again," Georgina said. "So please don't run away again, Mama."

"I think we can safely say that I won't," Katherine assured her.

"Well," Robert said, and she looked up at him. "We shall dine, and then I believe we should start for home."

"At this late hour? Robert," she gestured him to her, and he bent down, "I believe we owe the Tanners something."

His face was serious. "Have they treated you well, since I've been gone?"

"Oh, yes, even though for all they knew we weren't married. They're truly kind people. And," she smiled, "if we stay, we may just bring the inn into style."

That made him laugh. "Very well, then. I'll see about engaging rooms for the children. Only for tonight, though, Kate. You belong at home."

"But home is with you," she whispered.

An odd look crossed his face, and he swallowed, hard. "William." His voice sounded strained. "Since you are nearly grown, pray ask Mr. Tanner if there are any rooms available."

"Yes, Father," William said, and left the room with such alacrity that Katherine had to hold back her laughter again.

Georgina had been looking at her father's face. "I believe I'll go, too, should he need any help. Pamela?"

"What?" Pamela said.

"Come with me."

"Why? I can't do anything."

"Never mind. Do just come along."

Pamela looked up at Katherine uncertainly. "Mama?"

"I rely on you, Pamela," Katherine said gravely. "You know what sad scatterbrains your brother and sister can be."

Pamela scrambled down. "I shall see that all is well, Mama," she promised, and scurried from the room, leaving Katherine and Robert alone.

"Well," Robert said again, looking expectant and, at the same time, insecure. She wondered just what exactly his contribution was to be to the changes that would apparently take place in their lives. Oh, not that she expected things to be perfect; not that she expected her family never to lapse into their old ways, but at least they finally knew that she was a person, and not merely a wife and mother. "Shall we?"

"Robert, I cannot walk," she said. "In fact, I'm to stay off my feet for a week."

His expression came close to a leer. "That can be arranged."

"Robert!" She stared at him. "I'll have you know I'm an old married woman, and a mother."

"Never old," he said, and scooped her up in his arms.

"Robert!" she squeaked. "What in the world—oh, do please think of your back!"

"You're supposed to stay off that leg, are you not?" He smiled down at her, held close to him. "And," he whispered into her ear, "this is far more romantic."

"Robert," she said yet again, but in a quite different tone of voice as she leaned her head against his shoulder. Now she knew what his contribution was to this effort: not only seeing to it that the children attempted to gain some measure of independence from her, but to be a better husband, as well. She rather liked that last idea.

"After all," he went on, his voice still pitched low, "there is more to life than a career."

She nestled closer. "So there is."

"So, no more Hadrian's Wall?"

Now she laughed. "No, no more Hadrian's Wall."

"Good," he said, and proceeded to carry his runaway duchess up to their room.

More Zebra Regency Romances